OVERDOSE IN PARADISE

PARADISE SERIES

BOOK 16

DEBORAH BROWN

This book is a work of fiction. Names, characters, places and incidents are either the product of the author's imagination or used fictitiously. Any resemblance to actual persons, living or dead, or to actual events or locales is entirely coincidental. The author has represented and warranted full ownership and/or legal right to publish all materials in this book.

This book may not be reproduced, transmitted, or stored in whole or in part by any means, including graphic, electronic, or mechanical without the express written permission of the author except in the case of brief quotations embodied in critical articles and reviews.

OVERDOSE IN PARADISE

Chapter One

Opening the door of the Hummer, I set my feet on solid ground and breathed out a big sigh of relief. I gave myself a casual once-over, making sure all my body parts were in the same place they were when I left home.

Heading south on the Overseas Highway through the Florida Keys, Fab had maneuvered the Hummer in and out of traffic like a woman possessed, leaving Tarpon Cove city limits in the dust, headed towards Marathon. It was a beautiful, clear day, the sun flickering off the water, and I barely had a second to enjoy it as we raced by.

Smoothing down my skirt, I grabbed a sheet of paper from my purse and started across the gravel patch at the far end of the parking lot. "It's too bad you couldn't park any farther away from the entrance," I grouched. "Especially with all the *paved* empty spaces."

Surprised not to get an answer, I turned and saw my best friend and the subject of my ire leaning against the front bumper. "Could you walk any slower?" I tapped my watch. "The line is getting shorter." I tossed a glance over my shoulder at the dozen or so people filing slowly inside the building. "They're going to lock the doors."

"I don't like this place." Fab crossed her arms, a militant look on her face. "I'll wait out here."

Sure she will. How many times have I heard that before? "This is the visitor center, not the jail, and it's not our first trip here for inmate visitation."

The county had spared no expense, bringing in a prefab building and dumping it on a piece of empty land across from the jail, then filling it with row after row of uncomfortable chairs and installing monitors for that up-close-and-personal experience with friends, relatives, or fellow criminals. Anyone with an outstanding warrant had better stay in their car and out of sight as they ran checks.

Fab continued to glare.

"Great idea," I called her bluff. "Don't expect a recap when I get back in the car." I turned, hurried across the gravel — thankful I had on flats — and hustled up the steps.

I was the last to go inside, and the deputy was about to close the door when Fab yelled, "Wait for me." The deputy took one last glance outside while Fab hurried inside.

"Madison Westin and Fabiana Merceau to visit Dr. Stan Ardzruniannos." I shoved my ID across the countertop to the deputy.

Fab handed over her ID.

"Can you spell that?" He half-laughed.

Knowing that I'd most likely be asked that question and they wouldn't accept Stan's preferred nickname, Dr. A, I'd memorized it. Shades of prepping for a school spelling test.

"Last row against the wall."

The two of us passed through the metal detectors and went in the direction the deputy had pointed.

It didn't take long to locate Dr. A, whose face showed on the monitor outside his unit. He nodded, his dark-brown eyes locked on mine. I sat, lifting the receiver off the wall. Instead of grabbing a chair, Fab continued down the aisle, checking out each station.

"I'm not sure how many visitors you've had, but just remember these visits are recorded." This was the last place a prisoner should be talking about their case, with every word used against them. I smiled at the haggard-looking man, his black hair a disheveled mess, a first in all the years I'd known him. I plucked the piece of paper I'd brought in off my lap, a print-out from the local newspaper's website, and held it up to show the headline: *Local Doctor Arrested in Overdose Death*. "You fared better in your mugshot than most."

Dr. A's girlfriend, Nicolette Anais, had been found dead of a massive cocaine overdose in the living room of his beach house. Upon finding her, he had tried to resuscitate her before calling

911. The article included a picture of the dark-haired beauty, a former fashion model, it said.

The first news accounts had cited the discovery of a large quantity of drugs as the reason for the arrest. The exact amount and kind had not been disclosed.

"I'm innocent." Dr. A held up his right hand. "I want you to know I don't do drugs, sell them, or anything else." He sighed. "Thank you for agreeing to help. You're my only visitor thus far. I'd offer you something to drink, but this place lacks amenities."

"You don't have to convince me of your innocence. I've known you and your godfather since I moved here, and neither of you are..." I grabbed my throat and made a strangling noise.

He laughed. "I needed that. There have been zero laughs since the cops showed up at the hospital. I had just come out of surgery and they handcuffed me and walked me out in front of my colleagues. Now that was humiliating."

It surprised me that he hadn't been arrested at the scene, when the cops arrived at his house and the coroner pronounced the woman dead, but had instead been allowed to go back to work.

"They probably chose to do it that way so you'd be less likely to cut and run." I smiled at the man, who appeared to be the victim of a run-through-a-wringer and hadn't bounced back. "I hear they offer educational classes in this place — crocheting, knitting... You should sign up to keep your mind off...well, everything."

"See these?" He held up his hands, wiggling his fingers. "They've been groomed for surgery, not knitting." He narrowed his eyes. "How do you know such classes are offered?"

My cheeks heated up. "I hear stuff."

"Where did Fab go?" He craned his head.

I scanned both sides of the aisle. "She's down at the other end, visiting with another inmate." I shook my head, wondering what she was up to—she had a soft spot for those incarcerated who were expecting a visitor that didn't show. "When's your bail hearing?"

"Already had the first one; it was automatically denied." Anger filled his face. "It didn't help when my lawyer went into cardiac arrest."

"That headline made the next edition. You should get points for jumping into action to keep him breathing until the paramedics got there."

"Thank goodness he lived." He grimaced.

"You get a new lawyer?" I was almost afraid to ask, unsure how good a lawyer one could hire from behind bars. "Is the new guy trying to set up another bond hearing?"

"Samuel Beaton, Attorney at Law. Doc hired him. He's a friend of his who's on the verge of retirement but was a big deal back when he had a full-time practice. Doc thought he'd be better than a public defender." He huffed out a long sigh. "I spoke to the guy once, and after a short consultation, I entered a plea via video feed."

It would be mean to ask, *Who?* "I've never heard of him."

He rubbed the bridge of his nose. "I don't want to be a dick, but the man is old. Not to be ageist, but is he up on the law? I know doctors that have been around a long time and tune out the latest techniques — the know-it-all syndrome." His frustration seeped through the screen.

"I'm not here because I think it's fun to flirt with men behind bars. I want to help."

"Up until I got arrested, I'd have thought my so-called friends would be lining up to offer help. It appears you're my only one. I didn't expect you to show up. Have I said thank you?" I nodded. "I don't know why they arrested me, except that — "

I shook my head at whatever he was about to say. "I'm here. Call it payback for all the times I called and you showed with no questions asked."

"You can't imagine how frustrating it is to be in control of every facet of my life one minute, and the next, control nothing. I follow orders, no questions asked. Not doing so would downgrade my accommodations, and they're already rock bottom as far as I'm concerned." His frustration was building with every word. "I know your connections are far-reaching, so I'm asking you to get me an attorney that can get me the hell out of here."

"One first-class attorney coming up. One that will go to work and hopefully keep you from languishing behind bars. One who'll keep you in the loop; none of this wait and wonder stuff."

"Sounds like you've got someone in mind," he said hopefully.

"Ruthie Grace, counselor extraordinaire." Her slogan. "I'll get her on the phone before we clear the parking lot, and if she doesn't answer, I'll stop by her office and make so much noise, she'll open the door just to shut me up." He shook his head in amusement. "I don't suppose you have a bondsman on standby?" He frowned. "No worries there, either. It's Fab's connection, with a 'no screw-you' rate for friends. So you're telling me that your lawyer's planning to go into the hearing unprepared to post bond for your release?"

"I don't suppose it matters, since the prosecuting attorney's opposing bail regardless of the restrictions." He slapped his hand on the ledge. "Instead of telling Doc how completely ineffectual I find the man, I backed off. I chalked it up to my own ignorance, since I don't know my way around a courtroom; thought maybe this is the way the process works. If I had a do-over, you'd be my first call."

Fab showed up, nudging me with her hip to move over and share the chair. She reached up and turned the receiver so she could hear.

"How's life?" Fab winked at Dr. A.

"Just about as bad as you can imagine."

"You look good in blue."

"I'll never wear this color again." Dr. A's nose wrinkled as he stared down at his prison uniform. "I've got matching shoes."

"Use your sense of humor to keep yourself sane in here," I said.

"Where did you to disappear to?" Dr. A asked Fab.

"Tank, a roomie of yours, was waiting on his no-show girlfriend, soon to be ex when he gets out. Good citizen that I am, I seated myself in front of his monitor and chatted with him." She lifted a brow, as though daring me to challenge her story. "Poor Tank, he's here on a misunderstanding. The cops need to clear up who started the fight, who owned the weapons. I talked to him about putting his bulk to work doing something that won't get him arrested, and how his first step needs to be disassociating himself from people with criminal tendencies and ones that don't care about dusting it up with the law. I suggested that he think about turning his talents to legitimate bodyguarding—he'd be intimidating and, in most cases, wouldn't need a weapon."

"You're always telling me that you don't have people skills, and here you're making friends in the joint." I smiled lamely.

"We're all misunderstood in here." Dr. A

frowned. "Tank's the biggest guy here—several hundred pounds of muscle—and no one looks cross-eyed at him. He's even a favorite with the guards."

"Do you have money in your commissary account?" The light overhead flashed, signaling two minutes left.

"It's embarrassing to have to ask, but would you front me a few bucks? That way, I can get a package of cookies or something to disguise the taste of the crappy food. Doc will reimburse you."

"That won't be necessary. I like the idea of you owing me." I hurried to get some reassurance in before the phone shut off. "Don't worry. I'm determined that you get a stellar attorney, and I'll use my connections to make it happen."

Dr. A stood when the phone went dead. We waved through the glass.

"This place is depressing," I said. "I'd forgotten how much."

"Hurry up." Fab jerked my sleeve. "We don't want to get caught in the crowd and have to rub shoulders on our way out."

I practically had to run to keep up with her.

Chapter Two

Fab had worked out her aggression on the road coming down, and the return trip stopped short of making me want to puke. I flicked my finger at an exit sign. "I want to stop by Ruthie Grace's office. I decided against a phone call and thought I'd surprise her. Fingers crossed, that'll make it harder for her to turn down my request to meet with Dr. A."

"I hate to point this out to you, but being such a good friend…"

"I'll bet," I mumbled.

"You're not on the lawyer's favorites list." Fab careened off the highway.

"That's not news. As many times as we've offered our services, she's consistently turned us down. My ace in the hole is Mother. They're friends, and don't think I won't exploit that angle."

"Maybe Brad can put in a good word."

"Don't you dare tell Ruthie that Emerson is dating my brother. She's sized him up and found him wanting. Defending someone against murder charges will do that."

"I like the daughter better. Too bad we can't use her."

Emerson Grace, whose specialty was family law, was definitely a family favorite after she expedited my brother's case, getting him permanent custody of his daughter and accelerating Mila's transition out of a foster home.

Fab pulled up in front of Ruthie's office, which was located at one end of a strip mall of offices, her daughter's office at the other end.

"First time I've seen the blinds open." I pointed. "If she has a client, I'll wait."

Fab and I got out. I was disappointed to find the door locked. I'd left my lockpick in my purse...not that I'd use it. It wouldn't surprise me if, in addition to not finding it amusing, she had me incarcerated.

While I knocked, Fab pressed her face to the window. "Just so happens Ms. Grace is seated behind her desk." She groaned. "She looked up and, after making eye contact, went back to reading the stack of papers in front of her. So she knows we're here."

I knocked again, knowing it wouldn't do any good with the stubborn woman.

"A dollar...no, make it ten, that I can get Ms. Snootsy to open the door." Fab held out her hand.

I smacked it away. "I'll pay up when she invites us in."

Fab ran back to the car and climbed in the back, getting out with a megaphone in hand. I covered my face and laughed.

"Ruthie Grace," Fab bellowed, "open up." A guy on the sidewalk turned, shook his head, stepped into the street, and stuck out his thumb.

The door flew open. Ruthie, anger etched across her face, stood barefoot in the doorway. "You've got two seconds before I have you arrested for a noise violation."

"Can we come inside?" Fab asked via the megaphone.

"No."

Before she could slam the door, I put my hand up, stopping it midway. "Just hear me out. I've got a client for you. High profile. And he can pay."

"Have him call me and we'll discuss his case."

"He's in jail, and I'm willing to bet that you don't accept collect calls. I'm here because he's a longtime friend and deserves the best representation."

Ruthie motioned me inside. "I'll write the information down, and if I'm interested, I'll go for a visit. Does this person have a lawyer?"

I followed her in, and Fab closed the door, standing guard.

"Samuel Beaton."

"Never heard of him," Ruthie stated flatly.

The door flew open, Fab barely managing to jump out of the way and not get hit. Emerson crossed the threshold, out of breath. "My assistant informed me there was a ruckus going on down here, and I didn't want to miss a minute."

Ruthie and her daughter couldn't be more different style-wise—Ruthie a throwback to the sixties with her loose flowing hair and caftan, some annoying scent burning in the pot behind her desk, Emerson the height of fashion in a suit, killer heels, and conservative bun.

"It's just these two in need of an attorney for one of their criminal friends," Ruthie grouched.

Fab stepped up to the desk. "I've had enough of you and your surliness. I don't care that you're one of the best lawyers around."

"Ignore her bad attitude," Emerson instructed. "She gave up sugar cold turkey. I told her to wean herself off, but did she listen? As you can see, she did not." She motioned to Fab and me. "Step down to my office. I can get a criminal attorney on the phone. A good one."

"Sit the hell down." Ruthie's hand slammed down on her desktop. She winced. "You're making my headache worse." We filled the chairs in front of her desk. "Who's the client?"

"Dr. Stan Ardzruniannos, aka Dr. A. Made headlines when his girlfriend OD'd in his house."

"He's a cutie," Emerson gushed. "Did he provide the drugs? The news makes him out to be a drug-dealing scumhole."

"Never ask the guilt or innocence question." Ruthie used her courtroom voice. "I'll go by the jail tomorrow and talk to the man."

"Don't you need to make an appointment?" Fab asked.

The esteemed counselor actually snorted.

"If, for whatever reason, you decide not to take the case, would you please call me?" I took my business card out of my pocket, shoving it across the desk.

"Mother, you should call either way. On your drive back to the office would be a good time," Emerson told her mom and got a frown in return. "Don't worry." She patted my arm. "I'll make a note on my calendar to remind her."

I stood. "Thank you for your time."

"Out of curiosity, how long would you have stood out there and made spectacles of yourselves?" Ruthie asked.

I looked at Fab.

"As long as it took." Fab smiled.

Emerson stood. "I'll show them out."

"Don't get too friendly. They're both trouble." Spoken like a mom.

"Come on, bad girl." I looped my arm through Fab's, and we laughed. There was more truth to that assessment than most people knew. Soon after we got outside, Emerson's assistant came out of her office and held up five fingers.

"I've got a conference call coming in," Emerson explained. "If you ever need a referral to another lawyer, give me a call. I'll set you up with someone with a good track record."

"You're the best," I said to her retreating back, and she waved. "She's the only woman I know other than you that can run in heels and not end up face down."

"Just another of my talents." Fab gunned the Hummer out of the driveway. At the signal, she held her hand out. "Pay up."

I reached down and grabbed my wallet. "Here's what I owe, plus a tip because that performance was outstanding." I put a twenty in her open palm.

"I've got a surprise for you later."

"I don't like surprises, and you know it."

"You can damn well get over it before Didier and I arrive early to pick you and Creole up for dinner at Brad's."

I leaned my head against the window. "Family business meeting." I sighed. "Last I heard, no one could agree on the agenda. Brad demanded, in his snooty authoritarian voice, that my talking points be submitted in writing."

Fab laughed. "And? You'd never let him get away with that."

"I wrote them down all right. On a sticky note pad and told him he could keep the rest."

"You want anything before I take you home?"

I shook my head. "You mean Creole's? I know I sound whiney, but it's an adjustment when one's house burns down." I sighed again. "Sorry for the pity party. After all, you and Didier lost everything too."

Fab and I had been roommates since the day she showed up, bags in hand, and moved into the house I had inherited from my Aunt Elizabeth. Then, one sunny afternoon six months ago, a deranged man with revenge on his mind decided it was a good day to torch the place with me in it.

"What I hate the most is having to drive over to drink morning coffee with you."

"And I thought I was the sentimental one." I winked. "When is your monstrosity of a house going to be ready? First morning after you move in, it's coffee on the beach."

When she and Didier got married, Fab had had her eye on a house at the other end of the street from where Creole lived. She'd mentioned it to her father, and he bought the whole block, except Creole's house, as a wedding gift. The two other houses that were part of the deal now stood empty. That's one way to pick your neighbors.

"We've just gotten our occupancy permit, and I emailed the contractor with a list of repairs that need to be addressed. Didier was surprised at how active a role I took in the renovations. I didn't abuse the free reign by leaving him out and instead ran every detail by him so that we could agree on it."

"Married life," I cooed. "Housing is another item on the list of things Creole and I need to discuss. We really do need more space. I don't want to give up entertaining the family, and we don't have the room to fit everyone at his house."

"Why isn't getting married at the top of that list?"

"Yours, Mrs. Didier, was so outrageously over-the-top beautiful, who can compete? I know it's not a competition," I said in response to her frown, then sighed. "Do you promise not to tell anyone what I'm about to share?"

Fab locked her lips with her fingers. "Would you like to seal it by comingling our blood?"

"Eww. You're weird."

"Takes one to know one."

I leaned back against the seat and laughed. When I caught my breath, I said, "Creole and I are in agreement on eloping."

Fab gasped. "O-M-G. Not only will your mother flip out, but so will I. I'm *not* being excluded from the big day." She sniffed and wiped the corner of her eye.

I stared and asked incredulously, "Are you crying?"

"Would you drop this idiotic idea if I did?" she roared.

Guess not. I rubbed my ears. "When we decide for sure, I'll let you know." I didn't see any reason to upset her with, *We'll do it on our own timeframe.* After all, I had thus far ignored everyone else's version of, *Hurry up already.*

Chapter Three

Fab turned off the highway and wound around through a bank of trees onto a dead-end street that ran along the water to where we lived. She stopped in front of the security gates, bypassing the security panel by hitting a button inside the car, then drove through the gates and waited for them to close before continuing down the road.

When I'd heard about the over-the-top gift of property, I suggested security fencing. The day after they closed on the property, a fencing company showed up and began the installation of ten-foot-tall spiked wrought iron. Caspian had informed his daughter that once the project was complete, trees would be planted to provide more privacy, and he was as good as his word.

"I was hoping Creole would be home." I pouted at seeing that the only car parked in the front of the beach house was Fab's Porsche. "I'd hoped we'd have time to do...stuff."

Fab rolled her eyes. "Sounds romantic."

I got out, expecting her to do the same, but instead, she waved and backed out, leaving me with her overpriced ride. We needed to have a reminder talk about the Hummer belonging to me and that she could at least ask.

Creole had found the beach house through a business acquaintance looking for a fast sale. He'd renovated the interior himself, ripping out the walls and turning it into one large space. He'd also added wood security fencing. I closed the fence behind me and went inside, dumping my bag on a stool under the kitchen island.

The view from anywhere in the house was gorgeous. Creole had installed sliding pocket doors along the far wall that opened onto the patio/pool area, which had steps leading to the beach below, making the space seem larger. The bathroom had a six-foot-tall picture window, so I could relax in the bathtub and enjoy watching the water breaking on the shore.

Sliding onto a stool, I'd pulled out a legal pad and was on the phone to my Information Consultant, GC, who preferred the moniker over his real name, Alexander Mark, when Creole strode through the door, broad-shouldered, with cobalt eyes and bristles of dark hair sticking up that I knew were soft to the touch. We immediately locked eyes, and I sat up a little straighter, leaning forward and blowing him a kiss. My two cats, Jazz and Snow, meowed and intercepted him, hoping for treats.

"Any information you can dig up on Nicolette Anais would be helpful," I said to GC, referring to Dr. A's deceased girlfriend. I'd gone back to read the subsequent news accounts and found nothing remotely interesting.

"How involved are you in this case?" GC asked.

Creole brushed a kiss across my cheek and went to feed the cats, succumbing to their incessant meowing.

"Dr. A is a friend, and if I can be of any help, I'd like to."

"Keep in mind this case has to do with drugs, and depending on the amount, you don't want to inadvertently end up tangling with a dealer," GC said gruffly.

"Your concern for my well-being is new. Does this mean we're friends?"

GC laughed. "You're a hard woman to shake, and that friend of yours is even worse."

Fab would be amused by his assessment of her. "Oh good. Friends, then." I wasn't sure whether he heard, as he'd hung up. Another person that didn't bother with "good-bye."

Creole slid a manila envelope across the island, dragging a stool over to sit next to me.

"Paperwork? Great."

"It's an offer on your tentative bar space."

Soon after I met the original owner of a valuable parcel of real estate down by the docks, he decided that he wanted to rebuild the area and couldn't do it himself. So I introduced him to Fab's husband, Didier, and they formed a partnership. I also used my connections to expedite the construction paperwork. In return, I got to choose a space to do with what I wished and decided on an upscale bar.

"The design process was the best part," I said. "My enthusiasm for the rest has waned, and I don't know what I would do without you seeing to the endless minutia." I closed my eyes. "Maybe I should opt out, but it would feel like a failure." I pushed the envelope away. "I'm not interested."

"Open. It," he growled.

"This from some friend of yours?" I ripped off the corner and tore it open. "I'm telling you now, N-O!"

Shaking his head, he grabbed the envelope out of my hands, pulling out a professionally packaged proposal. "Listen to me. Who knows what goes on in that overactive brain of yours better than me; often even better than you do? What you need to admit to yourself is that you enjoy being a fixer—of people's problems—much more than being a hands-on restaurant/bar owner."

"But—"

He put his finger to my lips. "It's still my turn."

I tried to bite it, but he moved too fast.

"You've got a lot on your plate, and even you have to admit that if you want this space to succeed, it needs someone with ambition and drive. I'm thinking you threw out the idea of another bar to be shocking, knowing that your family wishes you'd sell the one you already own."

I made a faux shocked face.

"I got approached by a local man who wants to turn the space into an ice cream bar, which would be a good fit for that area. A better location for your bar idea would be on the piece of property that Brad is in talks to acquire." Creole held up his finger. "But if having the bar at the docks is what you really want, then I'm going to make it happen."

"I'm not cut out to be a restaurant entrepreneur, since that would have to be my prime focus. Call me crazy, but I love the ice cream idea, and more so if the store carries my favorite flavor." I smiled sadly. "It just feels…"

"It's okay to change your mind," he said adamantly. "Check out the amount he's offering for you to do just that, and you might see it as a savvy business decision. Page two."

Reaching out, I flicked over the pages, running my finger down the page and scanning for the amount. My eyebrows shot up as I continued reading to the last page. "I should get my CPA to look this over before I sign."

"Didier and I were running project numbers with Whit and ran the idea by him. He sat down, read the offer, and gave it a thumbs up. He wasn't happy with the bar/restaurant idea, as he says they're money pits. He said, 'Whisper *real estate* in her ear. A better bet.'"

I'd inherited Ernest Whitman, my aunt's CPA, when she died, and I'd never regretted continuing to use the same professionals she had. Pen in hand, I signed on the dotted line. "You know, that run-down dump of a motel on the main drag a few blocks from The Cottages is for sale." I laughed at his disgruntled look.

He reached out a hand and curved it around my jaw. His fingers reached behind my ear, and the warmth that flowed from them made me forget what we'd been talking about. His arms slipped around me, and his lips brushed mine. "Life will always be an adventure." He stood and scooped me into his arms.

Chapter Four

"You better hurry it up." Creole sat back on the couch, watching me with amusement as I alternately held each of the only two dresses I owned up in front of me and studied them in the mirror. "Fab and Didier will be here any minute. Knowing her, she'll pull up out front and lay on the horn."

Once again, I disappeared into the closet. "This isn't as easy as picking a pair of pants and a shirt."

"Babe." He grimaced. "Totally forgot. The dress bag in the closet is a surprise from Fab…or so Didier said when he dropped it off."

I unzipped the bag and pulled out a full black cotton skirt and backless short-sleeve shirt, very casual by Fab standards. I loved them. In the bottom of the bag was a pair of black flat slides.

Holding the outfit in front of me, I turned to Creole and got a nod.

"Why's she shopping for you?" he asked.

"She's been complaining that I lack enthusiasm for rebuilding my wardrobe after the fire, so she went out and bought up half of one of her favorite stores. I chose a couple of things and took the rest back."

"Thought maybe you weren't buying anything because we need another closet. There's no room to enlarge, but what do you think about adding a second story?"

I scanned the room, as though looking at it for the first time. "Put in a staircase." I pointed to the corner. "Two bedrooms and ensuites upstairs. We could use the space down here as a large living room, and in addition, there'd be room for an oblong dining table that we could use on nights we can't sit outside. Do you think we could get county approval?"

"Maybe. The other option would be to find another beach hideaway."

"If that's your plan, you're going to be the one to break the news to Fab that you're ixnaying her compound idea."

Once the papers were signed on the various properties, Fab had decided family members should move into the empty houses—one big happy family, all living on the same block. So far, there had been no enthusiastic takers.

I stepped into the skirt, pulled the top over my head, and twirled around.

Creole whistled.

"Do you know anything about the surprise Fab and Didier are planning to spring on us? I'm assuming Didier knows about it, since they're still enjoying marital bliss and, according to her, sharing *everything*."

A banging at the door prevented him from answering. Creole stood and stomped through the kitchen. Before opening the door, he said, "As a housewarming present, I'm going to kick the hell out of their front door."

"On the bright side, she only picked the gate lock, stopping short of coming all the way inside." I swallowed a laugh, knowing that Fab was annoyed with Creole for not letting her upgrade his security system.

Creole threw the door open. No Fab or Didier, but the gate stood open. My Hummer was parked in the road, window down, Didier sitting inside with an apologetic look on his face.

"Five minutes. If you honk one time, we're not going and we're blaming you," Creole yelled, loud enough for the neighbors to hear, if we had any. He shut the door with a resounding bang, a smile on his face. "That was fun."

"I'm ready." I slid into my sandals.

"Have a seat." He sat back down on the couch, reaching out and tugging me onto his lap. "We're staying in here for the next four and half minutes. To pass the time, we'll make out."

"I hope you set a timer." I leaned in for a kiss. Eventually, I said in between kisses, "Fab's been good for two or three minutes; we should give her a break."

Creole set me on my feet, turned, and knelt down. "Hop on."

"I love these piggyback rides." I hopped up,

Creole's arms gripped my legs, and we headed out the door and through the fence.

"That looked fun," Fab said after we got in the back.

"It was." I brushed Creole's lips with mine.

Didier—just one name, like a rock star—turned in his seat. "I want to apologize." His blue eyes sparked in annoyance. "Fab led me to believe that she'd just be ringing the doorbell, not barging into your house."

The French duo made a stunning couple even when they were shooting sparks at one another.

"She stopped short of opening the door," Creole said with an amused huff.

Didier wrapped his hand in Fab's long brown hair. "Try driving the speed limit."

Creole and I looked at one another and exchanged a silent laugh.

I leaned over and whispered, "Five bucks says she can't do it."

"Do I have 'stupid' tattooed on my forehead?"

I ran my finger over his skin and shook my head.

"Where are we going?" Creole asked when Fab had bypassed the turn to get back to the highway.

"I told Madison that we were picking you guys up early because we have a surprise," Fab said.

"I thought it was my new outfit, which I love. It's so me. Thank you."

Fab hit the gate opener clipped to the rearview mirror, and the gates to her house rolled back. She drove in and parked in front of three sets of arched double glass doors, each covered with an intricate wrought iron pattern, which opened into the entry.

"Now that the house is finished," Didier said, clearly pleased, "we wanted the two of you to be the first to get a tour."

"We're going to have a big housewarming party once we get it furnished." Fab glowed.

Fab had been adamant that I couldn't see the renovations in progress. I didn't bother to remind her that the house had just undergone a complete transformation, courtesy of the previous owners, and I found it hard to believe that it needed any additional work.

"Pretty spectacular entrance." Creole whistled. "Like how the u-shaped driveway turned out. One thing I miss with mine is having a garage."

Didier pulled some keys out of his pocket and hit a button, and the garage doors went up, his Mercedes looking lonely in the overly large space. Fab's Porsche was, of course, still in Creole's driveway, where she'd left it that morning when co-opting my Hummer. Not a speck of dirt to be seen, and it would probably stay that way, knowing Fab and Didier.

When I saw the floor plans, my first question had been, "Who's going to clean this place?" Fab looked at me like I was nuts and never answered.

Didier ushered us to the front door, guiding us inside the u-shaped house and into the living room, an open space that looked out through French doors to the pool area, which overlooked the beach.

"You do know that all the furniture you ordered will have to be placed to take advantage of this amazing view?" I said to Fab.

"There isn't a room in this house that doesn't have a view of either the pool or the pool and the beach. I can't believe the previous owners were content with windows. I had them torn out and replaced with doors, so we don't have to walk through the house to get outside."

"Your house belongs on the cover of a design magazine." I smiled at her.

Didier stared contentedly at all the open space. "When it's your house, and you know you're going to make it your home, it makes dealing with the construction process that much more fun."

He motioned for us to follow and started the tour, veering to the right into the stainless-and-marble kitchen, which had a fireplace, an island that could seat eight, and dining room space. Then down the long hallway ending in front of a set of double doors that opened into the master suite, which took up the entire left side of the house, with its own private patio and a view of the pool and beach.

Creole leaned down and whispered, "This one

room is the same square footage as the entire second floor I was thinking about adding."

Fab took the lead, doubling back to the other side of the house, where we connected to another hallway that led to four more rooms. "Guest bedrooms." She waved dismissively as we passed. She continued to the end, coming to a stop in front of an oversized louvered door with a white bow on the handle. With her back to the door, Fab turned and grabbed my hand.

"This is my surprise. I really want you to like it. Okay?" She eyed me nervously.

I knew she was expecting an affirmative answer, but face it, the woman was sneaky personified. I looked at Creole, who winked and half-laughed, *I'll follow your lead* written on his face.

"Maybe," stumbled out. "I guess. What did you say? Oh yeah, okay."

"You're impossible." Fab placed my hand on the handle. "It's unlocked."

I pushed open the door and took a step forward, standing in a small entry, and glanced around at the biggest bedroom I'd seen after the master bedroom. You could call up twenty-five of your closest friends, have them each bring a chair, and they could sit wherever they wanted. I opened another door, which led to an enormous ensuite with a sunken tub, a skylight overhead, and a walk-in shower with enough room for all those friends to crowd inside. The bedroom also had its own enclosed private patio, which was almost identical to the master's, and a second room that could be used as a...sitting room? Office? I wasn't sure what the builder had in mind.

My eyes zeroed in on the largest bed I'd ever seen, dressed in white with an enormous pile of pillows running the width. "What size?" I asked.

"Double king size," Fab said.

Twelve feet wide, I calculated in my head. I'd never seen such a huge bed before. I refused to allow myself to ask a few practical questions, and instead, casually sat on the edge, not wanting to mess anything up, then jumped up, smoothing the duvet cover.

"You planning on having the neighborhood in for a sleepover?" Creole asked. He, like me, scanned every corner of the room, drinking in the view. "Oh, that's right, you don't have neighbors. Except for us."

He and Didier laughed.

I rolled my eyes at them both and walked around one of the thick white throw rugs. "Love everything you've done so far. You have a talent for decorating. I need to get you a large conch shell to christen the room."

Fab tugged on my hand and pulled me back down on the bed.

"Would you mind if I jumped up and down?" I asked. "Test it out."

"We'll do that. But after you..." Whatever she

was about to say, she stopped. "This is my surprise." She waved her arm around. "Didier and I took two bedrooms and turned them into a suite for you and Creole. The cats could have the run of the entire house."

I wasn't often shocked, but had to remind myself to keep my mouth closed.

Fab hurried on. "The reason that there's only a bed is because I thought you'd want to choose the rest of the pieces for yourself."

"You want—"

Fab cut me off. "This room is bigger than Creole's entire house. Think of all the space the two of you would have. The best part is, we'd be living in separate wings but under the same roof. Hello, morning coffee together. We know the living arrangement works because we've been doing it for years."

"And you know people find it weird," I reminded her. "Adult couples don't live together unless they're doing something..." I scissored my fingers.

Didier and Creole wolfed out a laugh.

Fab slapped my hands down. "Stop that. It's juvenile. We..." She circled her finger. "...don't give a damn what other people think."

"You got the last part right." I smiled weakly. "We're non-conformists. This is so...extravagant. Over the top. I don't know what to say."

"Just say that you're moving in. The first morning and every morning after—well, maybe not every one—we'll celebrate with coffee in the kitchen. I'll even stock that cheap stuff you love. And I won't complain if you commandeer the island for your work space."

Didier sat behind Fab and put his arms around her. "You need to give Madison and Creole time to think over your proposal."

"I don't want to." Fab sulked.

I squeezed Fab's hand. "Creole and I need to talk about it in private."

"That better not mean no."

Didier tightened his hold.

"Come stay and try it out," Fab whined a little. "It'll be like a vacation."

I willed Creole to come sit next to me, and he did.

"I was also thinking," Fab added, "that when the two of you move in here, we can turn Creole's place into a guest house."

I leaned sideways against Creole's chest.

"I agree with Madison that you two did an excellent job on the entire place," Creole said. "You on board with this?" he asked Didier in a tone that suggested he didn't believe Didier would agree.

"Absolutely." Didier laughed. "I do have my own selfish motives. If you two move in, I won't have to build an overhead walkway to your house. I had to put my foot down on Fab's first choice of a tunnel."

I shuddered at the thought of traipsing around

underground. I'd never use it. Creole snorted, shaking his head. I'd lay odds that he was thinking the same thing.

"You sure know how to spring an over-the-top surprise, but I shouldn't have expected anything less." I leaned over and hugged Fab. "You leave me speechless," I whispered in her ear.

"The only word I want to hear from you is yes."

"You two have all the time you need to discuss our proposition," Didier said, returning Fab's scowl. "We've got to get out of here so we won't be late for dinner." He tapped his watch.

I lingered to be last out the door and took the bow off the handle, wrapping it around my wrist.

Chapter Five

Fab and I raised our eyebrows as we passed GC's door on the way to Brad's. GC owned one of the two penthouses in the building and Brad the other. No one else in our acquaintance knew that Alexander Mark and GC were one and the same and our go-to guy for information, and it needed to stay that way.

Mila answered the door in a princess dress and crown, Brad standing behind her. Father and daughter had similar features, with big brown eyes, her light-brown hair getting more sun-bleached every day, just like her father's. "Come in." She waved at us enthusiastically. It was great to hear her speaking, since it had taken so long.

Fab bent down, handing her the wand she'd forgotten to get when she bought the rest of the outfit. "The perfect accessory."

Mila stared in awe and threw her arms around Fab's neck. Fab lifted her into her arms and walked into the living room.

All the men in the room belonged to the over-six-foot club, and Brad was no exception. I stood on tiptoe, and still Brad had to lean down so I could kiss his cheek. "You been staying out of trouble, bro?"

He chuckled. "I thought about jaywalking the other day and changed my mind."

My brother and I had been close our entire lives, but after he was the prime suspect in his ex-girlfriend's murder, we grew closer than ever. During that ordeal, I discovered that he had a daughter who'd been left by her mother to languish in a foster home, and Brad and I had worked together to bring Mila home.

Brad had since hired a therapist to bring his daughter out of her shell. Now, she spoke sparingly but wasn't silent for long, as she reacted with bright animation, and the sweet sound of her laughter filled the penthouse.

He hooked his arm around my shoulders and followed the others into the combined living room/dining room, the sliding doors open to the patio and a view of the water.

The table was set, which meant that Mother had arrived early, probably with sacks of food. Mother did her cooking off a to-go menu.

In her sixties with a blond bob, she stood next to her burly, dark-haired husband, Jimmy Spoon, who was younger by ten years. Both were dressed to the nines in tropical attire, and a quick glance told me that Mother had been shopping again.

Spoon took drink orders. He'd already brought out an array of beers for the guys to argue about, comparing the taste and other factors beer lovers deemed important. He arched an eyebrow at me.

"I'll have a margarita, Fab a martini." I smiled sweetly.

"A full-bodied Cabernet or a Chardonnay?"

I wrinkled my nose. "Red and I'll wait for dinner."

The front door slammed. "Time to party." Liam blew like a wild wind into the room. He lifted Mila out of Fab's arms and waltzed her around the room, laying a big kiss on her cheek that had her giggling and kissing him back.

"Does the university know that you've wandered off?" I asked.

"It's not a prison." He snorted without looking away from Mila. "Your aunt thinks she's so funny." He rubbed noses with her and she laughed.

Liam had been adopted into the family when his mother dated Brad, and when she left for her big break in Hollywood, he stayed to finish school, only making quick trips to the west coast. He could easily pass for Brad's son, as they shared many of the same features.

The doorbell rang. Brad answered and came back with six large pizza boxes and one small one and set them on the table. A true Westin, Mila clapped her hands in delight at seeing one of her favorite foods. Mother came out of the kitchen, a gigantic salad bowl in hand.

"Grab a plate and choose your topping," Mother directed.

I sidled up to Creole. "Grab me a slice of grilled shrimp." I looked over the boxes. "Make it two. If I can't eat it all, I'll take it home."

He grinned down at me. There wasn't anyone in the family that didn't enjoy leftovers.

There was a loud banging on the door. Brad opened it, and dark-haired, blue-eyed Caspian Dumont, Fab's papa, crossed the threshold. "My plane got in late. Had to fly around a weather disturbance," he thundered.

Caspian had become an automatic member of the family when Fab introduced him to us right before her marriage. He fit right in, often regarding the rest of us with undisguised amusement.

"How did you get in the building?" Brad demanded.

"My daughter," he blew her a kiss as she flew across the room, hugging him, "gifted me with a lockpick and showed me how to use it. She claims I'm her star pupil." He winked at Mother, who blushed.

So Caspian had unseated Mother, grabbing her title.

Everyone heard Spoon growl. Mother did her best to get in trouble, and he worked overtime to make sure she didn't.

Caspian bent down in front of Mila, who put her hands on his cheeks and kissed one and then the other. "*Bonsoir*, baby Mila."

Mila beamed back at him. "Bonesy."

Mother handed him a plate.

After everyone was seated, Spoon raised his beer bottle. "To family."

"We might as well talk business over dinner. That way, we're not sitting here all night," Brad suggested with a touch of attitude.

Didier banged his fork on the side of his beer bottle. "Meeting called to order." He grinned. "First on the agenda: Caspian, the rest of us took a vote, and you're welcome into the group as long as it's understood that you don't contribute a dime more than anyone else."

Caspian reached over and patted Fab's arm. "I'll be a silent partner. You and Didier can vote for me when I'm not here. I only want to be included because of my daughter."

Fab leaned over and kissed his cheek. She'd been raised by her stepfather and didn't get to know Caspian until college. He'd recently bought a home in the Keys to be close to his daughter when he jetted into town—his own island, to be exact, twenty-six acres far enough off-shore that it required a helicopter or boat ride to visit.

"Paradise Real Estate, Inc. is official," Didier said. "We did this once before, then broke up to go off on our own. I think it will work this time, and in addition, each of us brings a different set of skills to the team."

"We need a project," Spoon said.

Creole spoke up. "I say we get our ideas together. Call another meeting to discuss them or send by email. Brad, Didier, and I can investigate the options, run the numbers, and bring them to a vote. How are talks going to acquire the vacant land opposite the Boardwalk area?" he asked Brad.

The land was owned by Brad's ex-partner, who'd had plans to build his own kingdom. When he wasn't able to acquire all the land, he'd opted to move to Chicago and take over family interests there instead. *Good riddance!*

"I submitted an offer; 'take it or leave it' implied. I don't expect a speedy response," Brad updated us.

"Not to be Madison-downer, but..." I ignored the groans. "This sounds like it entails a lot of paperwork, and I'll be doing mine and Fab's unless she gets an assistant. The very one I've been harping on for a while. We could share this paragon."

Fab glared at me. "I suggest, in the meantime, that we use Mac."

"Absolutely not. She'll quit on me for sure," I said.

Mac Lane managed the ten-unit beach cottage property that I'd inherited from my aunt. It was a full-time job corralling the tenants into some semblance of normalcy, which was rarely achieved.

"You two are so high-maintenance, you'll be lucky if the paragon stays a week," Liam said with a big smile.

Caspian laughed. "I'm liking these family dinners."

"Just wait, it's not over," I whispered loudly to him. "A fight hasn't broken out yet." The Westins were known for having a brawl or two, mostly started by me.

That had everyone laughing.

"It's agreed that we're all in?" Didier raised his hand, and Mila raised hers. The rest of us nodded. "The grand opening party for Tarpon Boardwalk has been scheduled, and we're in the middle of putting together a big advertising campaign. I expect all of you to attend."

"I have a bit of news about my space," I said. "It is no more. I signed over my interest to an ice cream bar." It was news to everyone except Didier, who'd directed the lawyer to draw up new contracts.

"It's a great idea." Creole's tone defied anyone to argue. "If Madison decides to go ahead with her other idea, there will be plenty of opportunities as we begin to expand."

Mother's hand shot in the air. "I vote for a cigar bar. And who better than me to recommend a selection of hand-rolled cigars? I can introduce you to the family-run store in Miami where I get mine."

That got a couple of laughs, but everyone

knew she was serious.

"Even Mother is getting into the entrepreneurial spirit." I beamed at her.

"I wouldn't mind getting in on that idea." Caspian grinned at Spoon's glare.

"You know what would make me really happy?" Mother asked, an innocent look on her face. "A certain couple announcing a wedding date."

I patted Creole's leg under the table, telegraphing that he could answer the question for the umpteenth time.

"You'll be the first to know." He pasted on a smile.

Didier and Brad grinned at him.

Fab banged her hand on the table. "No eloping," she came closing to yelling.

I shook my head slightly as a reminder not to go any further and spill that Creole and I had talked about doing just that.

"Madison wouldn't do that," Mother assured everyone.

Caspian smirked at me, guessing that I'd at least thought about it.

"Any other *business* issues?" Didier asked. Not getting a response, he held up his bottle. "To a thriving partnership."

After we all drank, Liam looked at Brad. "You still got the same girlfriend?" he asked, putting Brad in the hot seat. All eyes zeroed in on him, waiting for the answer.

"One of these days..." Brad shook his finger at Liam. "You're going to get a girlfriend, and you're going to hate payback."

"I like Emerson," Mother said.

"Me too." I tipped my glass in Brad's direction.

"You get a background check done?" Spoon asked.

"The one to ask is Madison. So, did you?" Fab flashed me a narrow-eyed smile.

"I'm happy to announce that the report on Ms. Emerson Grace came back clean as a whistle. No mental health issues anywhere in the family." I'd asked GC to run the additional check, since my brother had a track record of choosing unstable women.

"Good heavens! If her mother finds out..." Mother sighed. "She'll flip.

"Emerson knows," Brad said. "I can't have a relationship with her and be sneaking around. To my surprise, she laughed and said she wished she had a sister like you. I felt I needed to warn her that sometimes you're a big pain."

That had everyone laughing.

"I gave Emerson a copy of the report," I said. "A couple of days later, she sent back a note saying, 'I'm disappointed. It was rather boring.'"

Mila, who'd been sitting quietly between me and Brad, concentrating on dissecting her pizza, stood up on her booster seat and held out her arms to me. I picked her up, plopped her in my lap, and cleaned pizza sauce off her face.

"Doesn't Mila have a bedtime?" Mother tapped her watch.

The table got quiet.

"She does," Brad grumbled. "But not on the nights when we have guests. I didn't like being sent to bed as a child—I always figured I was missing out on something—and I'm not doing it to my daughter." He stared at Mother.

Brad and I had hated being sent away from the action. Oftentimes, we'd done our best to eavesdrop and were disappointed to find the adults a yawn.

"You know I'm here for parenting advice," Mother said in a soft tone.

"I do. Actually, Emerson helped me to realize that, like all parents, I'll make mistakes and that Mila and I will get through them."

Spoon put his arm around Mother and squeezed, and whatever she had on the tip of her tongue, she left unsaid.

"This seems like as good time as any…" Caspian laughed devilishly. "Do you, my dear, have any new cases that you haven't shared?" His dark stare had his daughter in the crosshairs.

Sizing up the silent interaction between father and daughter, I knew he was onto the fact that Fab shared only what she wanted to, in a lot of cases, leaving out pertinent details. I scrutinized her closely, waiting for her response, and she appeared speechless for a moment.

Didier smiled. It was okay with him that his father-in-law had put his wife off her guard with his question.

"It's been quiet," Fab said. "I'm using Toady on the riskier jobs. Right now, he's off retrieving a boat for a client whose high school-age son decided to throw a party onboard without asking. Then got the bright idea to move it down to Lauderdale and keep it hidden for his friends to use. As though no one would notice." She shook her head.

"Toe!" Mila clapped.

Brad rolled his eyes. "I stopped by to see Didier at his office and that old rodent was sitting there. He takes one look at Mila and lets out some ear-splitting noise that I was sure would have her in tears. Lucky for him that didn't happen, or he'd be d-e-a-d. To my horror, she wanted down to go play with her new friend, egging him on for more sound effects, to which he obliged her."

Brad had met Toady when he bought a house out in Alligator Alley, where the war veteran was his neighbor. Now the man looked after the property for Brad, discouraging two-legged trespassers with a shotgun.

"He's over six feet, so rodent isn't quite accurate," I said.

Brad snorted. "In some ways, Mila's too much like you, warming up to the oddest people."

"One thing about Toe," I said. "Mila is safe in

his presence. Anyone bothers her, and they'll find their arm ripped off and shoved up their — "

"Madison Westin," Mother gasped.

"Sorry," I said, somewhat apologetically.

Creole leaned over and whispered, "Try to behave. Save your antics for when we get home." His eyes twinkled.

I reached over and grabbed a spoon, putting it in Mila's hand. My hand wrapped around hers, we banged the spoon on the table. "Where's dessert?"

Chapter Six

"Where are you going?" Fab demanded, appearing in Creole's living room via the patio doors. She sized up my work outfit of jean skirt and top.

I squealed and jumped. "Doorbell. Knock. Something before you barge in."

"I'll keep that in mind for next time." Fab dumped her bag on the couch and sat primly, her brow arched in a *well?*

"I've got to check on The Cottages. I thought about calling you, but you hate going there."

Fab made a face. "Haven't I always gone along? Mostly anyway. Why should today be different?"

"Calm down. I planned to drive up to the manse and lay on the horn. Happy now?" I stared down at the three pairs of shoes I had lined up.

"Tennis shoes." She pointed. "I've got a job and need you for backup."

I groaned. "If I'm scaling a building or running, I'm changing into sweats. I'm not marring my legs with scrapes and scratches."

"I'll explain in the car." Fab picked up my bag

and hers and headed to the door.

I locked up and followed her, sliding into the passenger side of the Hummer. "You never mentioned a new case at dinner."

"It's not that big of a deal. My client wants me to check out his current security system and make recommendations."

"Hmm…" I tapped my cheek, more to annoy her than indicate any deep thought going on. "Sounds a little too up-and-up for one of your clients." I fished my ringing phone out of my pocket. Looking at the screen, I groaned, "This can't be good." An automated voice asked if I'd accept a collect call from the jail. I pressed 1 and the speaker button. "Good morning."

"For some people," Dr. A growled. "That lawyer you sent over just left, after calling me an arrogant SOB and telling me she had a busy day. What the…"

I tugged on Fab's shirt. *Coffee,* I mouthed. "I take it that you two didn't hit it off." I squeezed my eyes shut. *Stay calm,* I talked myself down, *this isn't your first rodeo with high-maintenance personalities.*

"I've got a proposition for you and it pays good. I'm hiring you to find me a first-class criminal defense attorney and do it today. Get his/her ass down to this jail with a plan to get me out of here." He calmed down, barely. "I'd do it myself, but I'm short on resources. I'd call Doc, but the last thing he needs is for his blood pressure to go through the roof. Besides, I trust you."

I only knew one other attorney that fit Dr. A's description, and I was certain he wouldn't take my calls. "I...uh...will get on it for you."

"Another thing: I'm going to hound the hell out of you, now that I know you'll take my calls."

"I can't promise overnight results, but I can promise that I'll get on it and find you a lawyer."

"You mind if I call later for an update?"

"Call anytime, and if I run out of things to say, I'll pass you off to Fab."

"That should be fun." He half-laughed, and the call ended.

"I'll take a shot of tequila in my coffee."

Fab scrunched up her nose and turned into the drive-thru lane.

I craned my neck to look back over the seat. "Go back and park in front. GC's here and he's just the man I need to talk to. I'm thinking you should call one of your shyster connections and have them on standby to get the good doc out on bail while I work on finding him a lawyer."

"Don't go all uppity on me." Fab swung around the back side of the building. "Every one of my so-called shyster connections, you *also* have on speed dial. You make the call."

"Not all of them." I almost laughed at my own whiny tone.

Fab pulled up and parked in front of GC's table. He looked up and I waved. He continued to stare without a sign of recognition.

"Let's hurry before he gets up and disappears." I jumped out of the SUV, crossed the sidewalk, pulled out a chair, and sat down, Fab next to me. "Happy you didn't make a run for it. Now I don't have to ask my friend here to nick you in the butt."

"Leave your ugly disguise at home?" Fab asked.

The last time we ran into him here, he had on an oversized, worn-out men's shirt meant to disguise his well-honed abs, a hat slung low over his mop of brown hair, and sunglasses covering the rest of his face.

GC snorted. "Against my better judgment, I'm going to ask. What do you want?" He flagged down a server. "Coffee's on me. Let's make this quick. I'm meeting someone."

I ordered for both of us.

"Female? Run a background check yet?" Fab teased.

"Time's ticking. Unless you thought it would be fun to annoy me. It worked. You can go now."

"If I didn't know you, I'd be offended by your surly rudeness." I smiled.

The man smirked.

"On that fancy phone of yours…" I pointed to where it lay on the table in front of him. "…does there happen to be contact information for a criminal lawyer, one you'd want representing you if necessary?"

"As a matter of fact… I do know one. Just relocated here and is opening an office, but he's not interested in defending criminals anymore."

"Then why bring him up?" Fab snapped.

"How about I pony up cash? Name your amount. Then could you come up with a name? Say in the next five minutes?" I returned his glare.

"Must be something in the air," Fab said. "Everyone's grumpy these days."

I smiled at the server as he delivered our coffees, ready to pick up my cup and leave, since it didn't appear that GC's attitude would lighten up anytime soon.

"Damn. Of course, he'd be early," GC mumbled, then raised his voice to say, "Would you mind leaving now? I'll call you later."

"Just a few more minutes to see what you're hiding. Then we'll leave." Fab unleashed "creepy girl smile" on him.

"I'm Alex and your brother's neighbor," GC stated flatly. "Don't you damn forget."

"Hey, bro." The man who appeared at the table was GC's twin but at least ten years older. He pulled up a chair. "Introduce me." His voice was deep and dark and he smiled wolfishly, checking the two of us out; his eyes going back to Fab.

I reached out and held up her left hand, displaying the diamond that could put out both his eyes.

He chuckled. "Another good one gets away."

"Be happy. She's way more high-maintenance than your usual," GC said. "The one you're ogling is Fab and the redhead is Madison."

GC's bookend was an easy six feet, shoulders wider than his brother's, with tousled brown hair and dark-brown eyes with laugh lines. He was dressed in the standard beach uniform of shorts and a short-sleeved shirt.

"Since you're...related?" I asked. He nodded. "You're aware of *Alex's* limited social skills. I assume you have a name?"

He held out his hand, which Fab intercepted and shook. "Lucas Mark."

I held out my knuckles, which he bumped without hesitation.

"You wouldn't by chance be a criminal lawyer, would you?" Fab asked.

GC growled.

Lucas laughed and said, "Yes." He looked at his brother, his expression saying, *What?*

"Good deduction." I beamed at Fab.

"This has been fun," GC said, conveying otherwise. "Don't let us hold you up. I'm certain you have somewhere else to be."

I stood and motioned to Fab. "I was hoping you could help. Guess not. I'll find my own criminal lawyer by the end of the day." I engaged in a stare-down with GC, not expecting him to be the first to look away.

"You can be a real asshole," Lucas told his

brother. "Maybe I can be of help to these two ladies."

"Trust me. You don't want to get involved." GC waved. "See you around."

"I get it." Fab looked down her nose at GC. "It's your nice way of saying your bro is short on skills."

I managed to pull off walking back to the car as if I didn't have a care in the world.

Fab slid behind the wheel.

"That ended badly." I adjusted my seat into a reclining position. "What time is your appointment?"

"Whenever we get there. Mr. Mott is out of town right now."

"Cottages and then Mr. Mott. When we're done, we can go get tacos and tequila shots."

Chapter Seven

Fab backed into Mac's driveway and parked. Conveniently, Mac lived right across the street from The Cottages. Not only was it a short walk to work, but she could keep an eye on the property at all hours.

"Mac's got a connection with our old lawyer. I'm going to see if I can get her to act as a go-between...if she still has a relationship with that office." My phone rang, and a number I didn't recognize popped up. I answered. "If you're selling something, I'm not interested."

"That's not professional," Fab said, motioning for me to hit the speaker button.

When have I ever forgotten to let her listen in? Only when I talk to Creole.

"Lucas Mark. What's the job?"

"How did you get my number?"

"Baby bro isn't as crafty as he thinks. Left his phone on the table when he went to the men's room, and I, even craftier, scrolled through his contacts and found your number."

"Just so we're agreed that when he finds out, and odds are high that he will, I wasn't the one to track you down and hound you until you caved. Got it?"

He snorted a laugh. "Deal."

"I've got a friend sitting in jail for an overdose death that he didn't supply the drugs for. Can you get him another bail hearing? I've got a bondsman on standby." Next call would be to Fab's friend to put him on notice that his services would be needed. He'd never let us down in the past. "That would give me additional time to compile a list of lawyers, so he can choose who he wants."

"I can do that. But just know that it will depend on the facts of the case."

"You have time for a jail visit tomorrow? I've got a connection that can get me on the visitor list."

"Text me with the details, and I'll meet you there."

"If you can make this happen, I'll owe you one, in addition to whatever you charge."

"Not a word of this to Alex. This will be our secret for now."

My neck hairs warned me there'd be trouble in the future. "He's going to find out, so be prepared. And he's not going to buy, 'Oh, I forgot to tell you.'"

Lucas roared with laughter. "See you tomorrow."

Disconnecting, I said, "Remind me to do an internet search on Lucas Mark and see what turns up. I'd rather have a more in-depth background check, but I can hardly ask GC to investigate his own brother." I opened the door and, instead of getting out, leaned my head against the seat and made a couple of calls, including calling in a favor to secure a jail visit.

"What if Lucas can't come through and you're wasting time?" Fab asked.

"A hunch! I'm thinking Lucas was the one GC was about to recommend before he changed his mind. What does your inner Fab think?"

"Who?" She got out and slammed the door.

I watched her cross the street, her shoulders shaking.

I inherited the ten-unit beachfront property from my aunt. Since I took over, I'd updated each of the units, inside and out. It used to be a place that criminals called home, but after learning the same lessons over and over, I'd weeded them out. They occasionally snuck back in, but I'd honed my felon radar and sent them packing, whether they wanted to go or not.

"You're not as funny as you think," I yelled after Fab and moved out of the driveway to let Kevin Cory, our resident sheriff's deputy, breeze by in his squad car.

Kevin parked at the far end, in front of his cottage, got out and waved, then started in my direction.

Mac had come out of the office, her multi-colored gauze tent dress flowing behind her.

She'd been headed in our direction but changed course when Kevin's car pulled in and went to intercept him. She sliced her neck with her finger, the gesture clearly meant solely for the deputy's eyes.

Kevin ignored her and yelled, "Did you get Joseph out of jail?"

It couldn't be my tenant Joseph, as no one had called me. But what other Joseph was there? Fab came to a halt close enough to hear everything Kevin had to say, a slight smile on her face.

Mac planted herself in front of Kevin, arms akimbo. "I can explain."

At the sight of her pink-and-white, black-clawed animal slippers, I did a double take and returned my attention to the conversation. "Are you telling me that Joseph is in jail and no one called me?" What started in a reasonable tone of voice ended in a yell. "I suppose *you* arrested him?" I stalked toward Kevin, and Fab grabbed my arm.

"If you hit him, you'll go to jail," she reminded me.

Kevin put his hands in the air. "I didn't have any choice. Joseph picked a fight, which he lost, and the other guy pressed charges. Didn't know until a few minutes ago that he was transferred from the hospital to the jail this morning."

"The hospital!" I shrieked.

"If I have to get my hearing checked, you're paying the bill," Fab griped.

Mac stepped forward, waving her arms in a dramatic fashion. "I didn't call because it was late and he wasn't going to be released from the hospital right away anyway. I figured a call could wait until I knew the amount for bail."

"Take a deep breath." Fab patted me on the back.

"Fight?" I zeroed in on Kevin. "He's an old man with terminal cancer."

"Don't bitch me out for doing my job. And while you're at it, save your threats to kick my butt to the curb. Not happening." He stomped away, then stopped and turned. "*You* break it to the wife." He laughed all the way back to his cottage.

"Wife?" I asked Mac. "Tell me Joseph didn't find someone to marry him. What about Svetlana?" Mac started to say something, but I wasn't listening. I headed for the office, feeling the need to sit down for this story. "Plan on starting from the beginning." Since I was first in the door, I took Fab's spot on the couch, stretched out, and shoved a pillow under my head.

Fab shoved my feet over and sat on the other end.

"Snacks?" Mac asked.

"Water," I croaked, holding out my hand.

"You need aspirin?" Mac asked, handing me the bottle.

"I don't have a headache...yet."

Mac fluffed out her dress, sitting behind her desk with her animal slippers resting across the corner. "Joseph was out walking Svetlana, aka the wife." Anyone eavesdropping would think Svet was a dog; it wouldn't occur to them that she was Joseph's blow-up blond rubber companion. "I happened to be out on my porch when Ronnie Butthead showed up, looking for a fight. He got in Joseph's face. Not sure what he said, but Joseph threw the first punch and Ronnie finished it, beating the snot out of him. Then the skinny little bastard stood over him, foot on his chest, and called the cops."

"And you sat and watched?" Fab asked in disdain. "I know you carry. You could've ended it with one shot."

Mac leaned forward. "You can't just shoot willy-nilly in a residential area." She ended with a huff.

"Ladies, please," I said.

Mac sat up, tugging on her dress. "I hotfooted it across the street at the first punch, but the fight didn't last long. Butthead is younger and in much better shape. Worried that Joseph might have a heart attack, I kicked Butthead's foot off his chest."

"And Joseph ends up in the hospital." I let out a long sigh. "What about Butthead?"

"Not a scratch." Mac shook her head. "You know, I moved a table in front of the living room window so I could play games on my laptop and keep an eye on the property. When I saw Butthead coming up the street, I had a bad feeling and went outside. Good thing I did. Although, as it turned out, I wasn't much help."

"You were there for Joseph," I said. "Who knows what Butthead — is that his real name? — what he would have done." I squirmed at the thought.

"His last name starts with a B, and that's all I remember," Mac said. "Another thing, I got the fight, from start to finish, on my security camera. That came in handy." She nodded at Fab.

"What happened to Svetlana?" Fab asked.

"I took care of my girl." Mac beamed. "Took Svet and her stroller home and got her situated in her favorite chair. I honestly didn't think the cops would arrest Joseph, since Ronnie's in his twenties and what he did was overkill, or I'd have paid him off."

"You pay off one person, word will spread like wildfire and it'll be fight night every night," I said. "This means Joseph needs a lawyer, since he'll have to appear in court. He hasn't been arrested in a while, but still, he has a rather long misdemeanor rap sheet; drunk in public and the like."

"Get me Butthead's address," Fab ordered. "He's going to drop the charges. We know he likes beating up old men — let's see him take on a woman."

"I'll go as backup," I offered. "In case it gets

messy and you need help with clean up."

Fab grinned.

"Whatever the bail is, put it on the credit card. That way, we get the money back when the case is settled." I took a deep breath, hoping I wouldn't kick myself for asking. "Anything else going on that I should know about? Miss January?" Another original tenant, who came with the property and, like Joseph, had terminal health problems she thumbed her nose at.

Mac dropped her feet from where she had them propped on the corner of the desk. "I have to go check on her. She was outside a little while ago, wandering aimlessly."

Someone screamed, and it sounded close.

The three of us flew out the door.

"We split up and each go in a separate direction," I said.

Before any of us could take a step, "help" drifted across the driveway. Then again. "Help."

Fab drew her Walther and ran toward the pitiful-sounding voice. She peered around the corner by the pool, then edged slowly down the walkway and peeked inside the open doors to where the dumpster sat. A moment later, she re-holstered her gun and jumped over the side of the dumpster.

Mac and I skidded up behind her.

"I fell," Miss January moaned, her head poking up over the top of the dumpster. Fab had helped her to her feet.

How did the woman get in there in the first place?

"You two get over here and grab an arm," Fab said.

"I want a raise," Mac said, hands on her hips.

"We need to talk," I said, which caught her interest.

"Pay attention. I'll hoist her up." Fab turned Miss January's face to her. "What are you doing in here?"

"I threw away the wrong bag. It has my vodka in it." She sniffed, her eyes filling with tears.

The woman had a standing order to have a fifth delivered every day.

"You start crying and I'll leave you in here. Ready?" Without waiting for a response, she pushed Miss January parallel to the side and lifted one of her legs over the top. "Don't let go of her." She jumped up behind the woman, wrapping her arms around her middle and flipping the other leg over the side.

Mac pushed me out of the way, lifted Miss January into her arms, and set her on the ground. "You are *never* to climb in the trash again."

"But..." Miss January stuttered.

"No buts and no boozy stories." Mac shook her finger at her. "You do it again, and you'll have to wait for the trash man."

Curiosity and all, I peeked in the dumpster and saw that there was less than a foot of trash, so pickup had been recent. I couldn't imagine how she managed to get inside. I shuddered and closed the lid.

Mac looped her arm in Miss January's, leading her back to her cottage, lecturing all the way and ordering her to take a shower.

"Super girl." I smiled at Fab. "You're so amazing."

"Darn good thing I have a change of clothing in the SUV or you'd be buying me a new outfit." Fab sniffed her clothing. "Do I smell bad?"

"Not from here." I laughed. "And I'm not coming any closer." Meeting Mac in the center of the driveway, I asked, "What if Miss January gets out again?"

"I woke up the boyfriend and gave him an earful. He sleeps in boxers that are way too small." She beamed from ear-to ear.

"If you weren't the best manager ever, I'd fire you for that," I said.

Mac preened. "Do you want a call when I spring Joseph from the pen?"

"He needs a lawyer, and not Ms. Grace. We need two attorneys on speed dial—a criminal one who has a track record of getting his or her clients acquitted and one who'll take odd clients that need occasional representation. Maybe one close to retirement that doesn't have a reputation to worry about. I'm open to suggestions."

"What is it you wanted to talk to me about?" Mac asked.

"I'm pitching you a new job. I'm thinking we should go back to the office."

Mac squinted at me with one eye closed. "Here's fine."

"Would you like to become an assistant for Fab and me? Instead of managing The Cottages, you'd be helping out on our other business interests."

"Am I fired if I don't take the job?" She stared intently.

"Of course not."

"No thanks, then. Thanks for thinking of me." Her big smile was one of relief.

"Macster," Captain, Miss January's boyfriend, hollered from his doorstep. "Need your help on...something."

"Miss January is probably stuck in the bathtub again. I bought her a shower bench; she needs to use it." Mac twisted up her dress and hustled across the driveway.

"I hope if we have another job applicant, that person doesn't look quite so relieved to get away from us," I said.

"Don't take it personally." Fab attempted to pat my head, and I scooted away. "Think of it as divine providence—you'd never be able to replace Mac here. A second circus ringleader would be hard to find."

"You're right. Don't get used to hearing that all the time."

"This has been fun, but we've got another appointment. Race you to the car." Fab broke into a run.

Run! I rolled my eyes and deliberately slowed my pace.

Chapter Eight

"I'm not going to even ask where we're going. I'm guessing a private island in Miami. Would be nice if you could get uber-rich clients in the Keys."

"I'll drive double the speed limit and it won't seem so long." Fab smiled.

"I've yet to make good on my threat to barf on you, but if you manage to exceed a hundred, today will be the day." I mimicked a cat horking up a furball. "Just pull over; I'll walk."

"Calm down, Drama Queen."

"I want a crown and wand, like Mila." I princess-waved.

"Not happening." Fab hit the gas. "Since the morning has been weird enough, I've decided that this job will be in and out as quick as possible."

"I like it when you put your foot down. We'll see how that works out." I smirked. "I think it's weird that your client hired someone else to install his security system, then you to check it out. Why not you from the jump?"

"I was annoyed to be second choice but managed not to bite his head off. There's a slim possibility I'll learn something I didn't know."

My phone beeped. Creole's old partner, Help, had come through, arranging for me and Lucas Mark to visit Dr. A tomorrow. I texted, "Owe you," and immediately got back, "I'm keeping track." Then I texted Lucas the address of the jail and the time to meet.

"You're getting off at the wrong exit," I said.

Fab sniffed. "Like that would ever happen. The client's mansion is in Coconut Grove."

I stared out the window as she zipped through the streets. The Grove was located in the middle of Miami, yet completely separate, and seemed a world apart. We drove through the upscale area, past sidewalk cafes and plenty of shopping, as we headed toward the bay.

The client's house sat at the end of a circular driveway protected by a set of ornate gates. Fab pulled up to the security panel, pushing a button.

After a minute with no response, I said, "Isn't it odd that no one's answering? A house this size must have staff."

"Maybe Mr. Mott told them not to answer."

"Do you have a code?"

Instead of answering, Fab backed up and repositioned the SUV so she could get out.

Of course, she doesn't.

I jumped out of the car and hustled to her side. "Slow down. Call me the cautious one, but I don't like that you'll have to break in, which is a crime, to do this job. At least check out the perimeter first." I pulled out my phone.

"Who are you calling?" Fab asked suspiciously.

"I'm going to videotape this adventure. You can narrate as you check out the property and give it to your client."

I followed her, scoping out the quiet street of waterfront properties.

Fab climbed through the bushes and walked along the outside wall to one end, then headed back in the opposite direction. She came to a halt as two security patrol cars pulled up, blocking the Hummer. A uniformed man got out of each car, guns drawn.

"Hands in the air," one ordered.

My hands shot into the air.

"What do you have in your hand?" he asked.

"My phone."

"Drop it."

I kept my hands up and let the phone drop to the grass. "My friend is in the bushes; please don't shoot her."

"You, in the bushes," the same man ordered, "back out, hands on your head."

Fab followed his directions.

"Both of you turn around, hands behind your back."

The other guard approached and cuffed us.

"What's the charge?" Fab asked.

Before he could answer, two police cars came to a stop in front of the house.

"Breaking and entering, burglary." He joined the officers, who were out of the car and stalking up the driveway.

When I get my phone call, it will be to Creole. He'll bail us out, and if he can't, since it's a local jail, he can at least arrange perks.

"Over here." One of the officers motioned, separating Fab and I, putting two feet of distance between us. "What are you doing here?"

"I have a gun in my back waistband and a license to carry in the car." I looked over at Fab, and she was also being relieved of her gun. I told him about Fab and her client, and from the sneer on his face, he didn't believe me. "I taped our walk along the front of the house." I pointed to my phone. "We didn't enter the property."

"That remains to be seen."

"Wouldn't a call to Mr. Mott clear everything up?" I asked.

"Thanks for the suggestion. Have a seat. Don't go anywhere."

I eased down on the grass, managing not to fall and at the same time swallow my grumbling about their having no evidence. Getting comfortable with my hands behind my back wasn't going to happen.

The officer questioning Fab had moved to the SUV. He and another officer searched it, came out with our IDs in hand, and went back to his car. While he ran a check, two more officers arrived and entered the property. It surprised me that they were able to just push the gate open to gain access.

A white minivan pulled up, and the driver got out, bag in hand. I assumed he was a crime scene technician.

Fab and I watched and waited.

My arms ached beyond belief by the time that, what seemed like hours later, the officer came back and helped me to my feet. "You're not under arrest at this time."

"If you need to talk to either of us later, Chief Harder of the Miami Police Department can guarantee our cooperation." I hadn't used our connection to Creole's old boss in a long time, and it would cost me a favor, but it was well worth it.

He whistled. "Good person to know…if he'll actually vouch for you."

"The chief has known the two of us long enough to know that neither of us are criminals and we had nothing to do with whatever happened here." There was a time the chief had thought otherwise, but now wasn't the time to mention that. "We were on a legit job for a client of hers." I tossed a glance in Fab's direction.

"Thank you for your cooperation."

As if we had a choice. I smiled but wasn't certain it looked sincere. I didn't run to the SUV, but almost, and wasn't happy to find it tossed. I got in, straddling the contents of my purse on the floor, and shoved everything back inside.

Fab had to clean her seat off before she could get in.

"What happened?" I asked. "I didn't get any info out of the cop questioning me."

"Mr. Mott's house was broken into and ransacked. It's clear the thieves made off with everything they could get their hands on, including taking the artwork off the walls." Fab climbed behind the wheel. "They're going to request an inventory from Mott."

"Did they make contact with him? Is that why we got released so quickly?"

"I'd say it has more to do with lack of evidence, since according to Mott's office, he's out of town. News to me, and I talked to him yesterday." She tapped her foot impatiently, waiting for the patrol cars to move so she could back out.

"It's surprising that he'd leave his house empty."

"Call me paranoid..." Fab gripped the wheel like a woman possessed but managed to drive just under the speed limit back to the main street through the Grove.

"Not usually."

"This feels like a setup." Fab checked her rearview mirror for the umpteenth time. "I've got plenty of questions, and I'm going to get answers."

"Mott have a grudge against you? It doesn't make any sense to set you up for arrest."

"It wouldn't be the first time." Fab grumbled something incoherent. "I'm not going to have it get around that I'm a thief!"

I'd never known her to steal anything. Retrieving property and returning it to the rightful owner was actually a specialty of hers.

I leaned my head back against the window. "Since it's illegal to drink and drive, maybe we could hustle home—and not tempt fate by speeding, considering the day we've had—and get our drunk on."

"We haven't had time to stock the bar."

"That's easily remedied. When we get back to the Cove, detour through the drive-thru liquor store. I'll order food to be delivered and we can party it up in that new kitchen of yours."

"Who's going to call the guys?" Fab shot me a you-do-it look. "You know they require timely updates."

"Little FYI for you: in a desperate moment, I dropped the Chief connection, and if the officer followed up, then Creole probably already knows. To cover our backsides..." I retrieved my phone from the cup holder and texted, "Dreadful day. You want more details, meet us in Fab's kitchen for dinner."

Chapter Nine

Fab had barely gotten past the Welcome to Tarpon Cove sign when my phone rang.

"Don't answer it," Fab groaned.

An image of my tiki bar popped up. "It's Jake's. I can't ignore it. Yes," I said in a not-in-the-mood tone.

"Hey Bossaroo, it's Kelpie," she said in a chirpy tone.

Fab shook her head.

The long silence on the phone annoyed me. "Are you waiting for me to ask what's up?"

"It's not all bad. It might seem like it at first..." she said, not sounding as confident as when I answered.

I cleared my throat in an attempt to say, *Get to the point,* without having to use the words.

"Don't get all excited. Once you hear the entire story, you'll see the potential for a happy ending."

"What already?" Fab roared.

"You could've told me there was an eavesdropper on the line." Her tone had turned sulky.

"If you don't get to the point in the next ten seconds…"

"We had a fight. Okay? But it was in the parking lot." She was definitely disappointed. "One of those girl-on-girl deals. One got the snot beaten out of her. Apparently, they're both engaged to the same guy, and it came out during the slugfest that he hasn't divorced his wife yet. And…" she said in a ta-da fashion, "it was over quickly."

Why my bar? "Is Snot Girl okay?"

Fab covered her mouth and laughed, much to her disgust, I was certain.

"Did I mention there were three girls? Two were sisters, and they left Snot Girl unconscious." Kelpie snorted a laugh. "That's a good one. Where was I? Oh yeah."

Fab rolled her eyes.

"Pretty certain it was the kick to the face that did SG in. It was good they didn't drag her out into the middle of the driveway; she might've gotten run over by a car, the way people drive." Kelpie sighed. "My tips would go through the roof if that happened. If she was to get smooshed, that is."

Fab turned her head and made a stupid noise. Rendered a bit speechless, I squeezed my eyes shut.

"They left her by the planter. Are you ready for the happy ending?" Not waiting for a response, she said, "By the time the ambulance got here, SG was coming around."

"Is this where you tell me, 'The End'?"

"How can you get better than SG alive and refusing a ride to the hospital?" Then Kelpie lowered her voice and added, "This next part isn't happy and the reason for my call. The cops are still here, and if you make an appearance, it might speed them along. A few of the customers went on the run when they heard the sirens — sneaking out the back; one even jumped over the side of the deck. The cops hanging around is bad for the bottom line."

"That's the price you pay when you go out in public with a warrant hanging over your head," I said unsympathetically.

"Almost forgot. Not really, just saved it for last. I left off where the happy ending took a detour." Kelpie sniffed. "SG rode off on her bicycle but didn't get far — she ran into the side of a truck. More good news: she knew the driver. He pitched her and her bike in the truck bed and off they went."

I groaned at that image and hoped that wherever SG ended up, it was in one piece. "I'm on my way," I said and hung up. I peeked over at Fab. "You can drop me off, and Creole can come get me."

"Is it going to take all night?"

"Let's hope not."

"Then we'll put in a to-go order for a Mexican sampler platter and take it with us."

I licked my lips. "That was yum the last time we did that. We can also get whatever liquor we want, and that saves another stop."

Fab flew into the parking lot of the short block I owned. Junker's, an old gas station turned antique store, sat on one side, Fab's lighthouse on the other. I'd tried several times to get the straight story from her about how it had appeared out of nowhere and got zip. It had been there a while and never gotten towed off, and I took that as a good sign. And the current tenant, who leased it as office space, had yet to attract the cops. Also good. A pink-and-lime roach coach, Twinkie Princesses, was parked parallel to the curb. I ignored the fact that it sat there like a colorful eyesore, never opening, and just cashed the rent checks. Two cop cars partially blocked the front door of Jake's, but otherwise, there wasn't another person in sight. To those who suggested I sell, I politely pointed out that under my ownership, Jake's had been named one of the best dive bars in the Keys...several times.

Fab zipped around the back and parked next to the kitchen door. We both jumped out. On the way in, I waved to Cook, who sat in his office, haggling with a vendor. One of his sons was at the grill. We made our way down the hallway and stopped at the end of the bar.

"Margarita, rocks." I pounded my hand on the countertop. "Make it a pitcher. I'm not driving."

"Triple martini, don't slack on the olives," Fab

ordered. "I'll go talk to Doodad about the liquor. You deal with Kevin."

Kelpie twirled around. I blinked a double-take, waiting for her two large friends to pop out of the too-small hot-pink tankini bathing suit top she'd paired with a very short full skirt and glittering tights she'd cut off mid-thigh.

Kelpie stared over my shoulder.

I turned. "Hello, officer," I said with so much sweetness that Kevin's eyebrows went up.

"I take it you know what went down here and that's why you're here?"

"I got the happy-ending version."

He frowned, clearly trying to think what that might be.

"You're not going to blame Jake's, are you? We can't control what happens in the parking lot."

"You could hire a guard," Kevin snapped.

"Please..." I rolled my eyes, which annoyed him and delighted me. "Okay...said guard jumps into the middle of a chick fight and what do you get? Two in the hospital. Besides, we don't have enough fights, inside or out, to justify scaring the you-know out of our select clientele by having someone patrol the lot all gunned up."

"See what happens when I try to be helpful? Just wait until the injured party sues."

"Bring it on," I snapped back at him. "Snot Girl started the fight." He appeared confused, and I didn't bother to enlighten him. "Besides, that's what Sparky's for, and before you ask, he's my insurance agent. Once he gets ahold of it, I'm certain that's the last I'll hear of any claim."

"You're hilarious." His tone conveyed *clearly not*.

"Boss," Kelpie called, setting down a margarita.

I picked it up and sucked down about half, motioning for a refill. "Coke?" I asked Kevin. "Send your partner over for a cold something. On the house."

"Bribing me?"

"To do what? I'll think about it if you come up with a good suggestion." I ignored Kevin while he tried to think of a way to arrest me for being annoying.

I finished off the rest of my margarita and picked up the pitcher. "We'll be out on the deck," I told Kelpie. "We're not to be disturbed unless it's another emergency, and a fight doesn't qualify. I have a one-a-day limit."

"Got it." Kelpie air-boxed.

Before anyone could ask anything else, I headed out to the deck, not waiting for Fab, who'd stopped to talk to Cook when he came out of his domain for some special concoction he ordered from Kelpie. I removed the Keep Out sign we kept hung on the back of the door, placed it on the front, and closed the door. I was done dealing with people and wanted the deck to myself.

A few minutes later, the door opened and Fab slipped through. She eyed me stretched out on the bench, back to the wall, and set her martini on the table so she could push two chairs together.

"It's your fault we need a ride home," Fab grouched. "My martini had been sitting there a while, and I couldn't have it go stale, so I downed it and ordered another. Now that I'm here and somewhat comfortable, I say we tie one on and toast to a bad day."

"With just a little bit of restraint, we could have been jumping on that beautiful bed you bought. The one the size of a football field."

"And..." Fab rolled her hand in a circle.

"We call the guys or a cab. I vote for walking home via the beach."

"Hey, that wasn't on the list. Besties and all, so I'm not going to tick off all the reasons your idea sucks."

I picked up the pitcher, toasted her with it, and drank from the side.

"Doodad is here, holed up in that hole of an office. We'll bribe him to take us home." Fab fished out her phone and called inside, ordering another drink.

"Let's go shopping."

"No, thanks. I've been drunk-shopping with you before, and you're obnoxious."

Turning my head, I gave her a full-on pouty face.

The door blew open and Kelpie skipped in, delivering Fab's drink. "Food, anyone?"

"Got that covered," Fab told her and winked at me.

"It's all quiet inside. The cops blew the joint. Now I'm waiting on my regular crowd to return."

I gave Kelpie a thumbs up.

Fab held up her glass. "To not getting arrested."

I held up the pitcher.

"You have a glass, you know."

I closed my eyes and ignored her suggestion.

The door opened. "The sign says Keep Out," I said without opening my eyes.

"Yeah!" Fab giggled.

"Look what we found," Creole said to Didier. "Looks like the party started without us, and we didn't even get an invite!"

"What's going on, *cherie*?" Didier asked.

I glanced up and said to Fab, "He means you."

"I'm with her." Fab giggled.

Didier growled.

"How was your day?" Creole asked. He moved my feet and sat down, putting them in his lap.

"Arrested. Handcuffed. Fights. Hospital." I slurped from the side of the pitcher. "Probably missing something."

"What she said," Fab said.

"How did you find us?" I asked.

"When I got home and found neither you nor dinner, I called to place an order with Cook," Didier said. "I texted you, but apparently you didn't read it."

Creole took up the story. "Cook said, 'Girls here, out on deck with door closed. That spells trouble. You better get over here pronto. If you don't, you remember Cook warned you.'" Creole tried to ease the pitcher out of my hands and I jerked it back, upending the rest in my lap.

"Ohhh…" I watched as the liquid soaked into my skirt.

"Hand me that napkin holder," Creole said to Didier.

"No." I brushed his hand away. "I'm going to wear my margarita like a badge of honor."

"You're going home," Creole said sternly.

"Noo," I whined.

"I'm staying," Fab whined along with me, her lips curling in amusement.

"Oh no, you're not."

Fab grinned at Didier in response.

Creole scooped me into his arms and carried me out of the bar. I craned my head around his shoulder and saw that Didier had Fab slung over his shoulder.

Chapter Ten

Fab opened the console and tossed me the aspirin bottle as she sped down the Overseas Highway, wanting to arrive at the jail before Lucas Mark.

I groaned, pressing my forehead against the window. "Hangovers are the worst. Instead of going home and doing some research, I convinced myself to have one more drink." I guzzled the last of my coffee, taking off the lid to make sure I got it all.

"Are you licking the inside of the cup?" Fab asked in disgust. "Stop that. You can have what's left of mine."

I made a strangled noise. "I don't like the vegan bean, soy, no-sugar whipped cream that they dare to call coffee."

"How long is this meeting going to take?" Fab careened off onto the exit ramp.

"You don't have to move from behind the wheel." I wanted to stomp my foot to annoy her, but that would take too much energy. "We need a lawyer, a star lawyer, for death penalty and life-in-jail cases. We had that kind of lawyer until his grandmother did the diddly dance with Crum. But even Cruz balked at representing my tenants. He only did it once, and it cost me sixteen favors. I'm over doing favors; I'd rather pay."

"Maybe Emerson will take your 'spitting on the sidewalk' cases and such." Fab laughed to herself.

"My brother would kill me if I asked. She did offer to refer me to an attorney if I needed one. The problem is that my tenants don't show well, and even a public defender would be put off by their abrasive attitudes."

Fab rubbed her forehead. "I feel a premonition coming on."

"Now that's the kind of stupidity I would pull. Sorry for the interruption," I said in response to her glare. "I'm going to hang on every word. I'm ready."

"If you get me Butthead's address like I asked, Joseph won't need a lawyer. Problem taken care of."

"You're on." I beamed at her.

"And in the meantime, you need to get some new contacts on your speed dial." Fab pulled into the parking lot of the visitation center and, once again, parked in the hinterlands.

I threw my hand out, running my finger in a circle and clearing my throat. Now it hurt, and I had to restrain myself from rubbing it. "All those empty spaces, and we have to park back here. Again."

Fab made a shooing motion. "Hurry up or the

deputy is going to lock the door."

I got out and followed Fab across the lot. Once again, we brought up the end of the line. This time, after clearing security, we were directed to a middle row.

"Try not to get us thrown out of here and our privileges revoked." I knew that Fab would at least check out the rest of the row, now that she'd given Dr. A a brief wave.

I scooted around the chairs and people standing in the aisle and dragged the only chair left over next to Lucas.

"I see you two have met," I said into the phone. "Just know you're not stuck with legal eagle here. If you want, you can just use him to get you out of here. I didn't make any promises."

"Hold on." Lucas put a hand up. "Give me the courtesy of listening to my pitch as to why I'm the best lawyer to see this case through from beginning to end. You'd be my first client here in the Keys, but I come with a long list of impeccable references. And not a single client on death row."

"That's comforting." I leaned back in my chair and crossed my arms, doing my best not to roll my eyes. "Keep it concise; we've got limited socialization time here."

Dr. A laughed.

As it turned out, Lucas Mark had graduated from Yale, summa cum laude, moved to New York, and earned a position in a prestigious law firm. "You may remember this case…" He'd gotten an acquittal for a politician accused of offing his wife. Another for a doctor accused of killing his girlfriend. One of his clients, he got off with an insanity defense, which he noted that juries were loath to go along with. "I have a ninety-five percent win record, and those that I lost didn't get the death penalty."

"You're hired," Dr. A said.

"Your lawyer of record will need to sign off on your case, and the sooner the better. Is that going to be a problem?"

"Since Samuel and my godfather are friends, there won't be a problem. I'm fairly certain that he'll be relieved."

I moved closer to the phone. "If you need me to set up a meeting to get the hand-off dealt with, I can make that happen today at Jake's. I'll entice the men with food and liquor."

"You're the best." Dr. A smiled and waved as his focus centered on something behind me.

Fab had shown up.

I scooted over to share my chair with her. "I'm a tad annoyed that this guy," I cast a glance at Lucas, "couldn't highlight his credentials sooner, but it's worked out, and that's one less worry."

"I'll get Beaton's signature today," Lucas told his client. "And talk to the Prosecuting Attorney to see if we can get another bond hearing scheduled. On my way out, I'll reserve the conference room for tomorrow so we can meet and go over your case."

"Here's a down payment to get things started." I reached in my pocket, pulled out a twenty, and handed it to Lucas.

Lucas teasingly held it up to the light for inspection, then shoved it in his shirt pocket.

"I requested a background check on Nicolette," I said. "And the police report was delivered this morning." Dr. A showed no reaction, which surprised me, since I hadn't forewarned him I was planning to do that. "I'll make sure Lucas gets a copy today." I hurried to answer what was sure to be asked: "I haven't read it."

Fab nudged the receiver out of Lucas's hand. "You mind if we toss your place? We don't need a key."

Dr. A's eyebrows went up; I couldn't see around Fab for Lucas's reaction. "Don't make a mess."

"If I find anything interesting, do I get to keep it?" Fab and Dr. A engaged in a staredown.

He nodded. "Help yourself."

I was a little annoyed that they had some kind of secret code going that I had no clue how to decipher.

"You'll never know I went through your drawers." Fab winked. "We'll also be checking out any previous addresses for Nicolette." She glanced at me, and I nodded. She handed the phone back to Lucas.

"Anything you need, let us know." Fab unleashed creepy-girl smile on Lucas, who did a double take.

The two-minute warning light blinked.

"Anything you need, call," I said to Dr. A, then stood, wanting to give him time with his lawyer.

On the way out, I said to Fab, "Meet anyone interesting today?"

"Everyone's visitor showed up."

"Let's hang around. I have a few questions for Lucas Mark." I went on to give her a rundown of the conversation she'd missed.

Fab scoped out the parking lot. "We can sit in the car, since I'm willing to bet that the Mercedes parked a couple down from us belongs to Lucas." She pointed. "People with nice cars leave space around them unless there's VIP parking."

It didn't take long for Lucas to come strolling across the parking lot, a scowl on his face. I suspected it was because we were leaning against the hood of his car. "Waiting for me, ladies?" He'd gotten over his irritation quickly and exuded charm.

"Do you have an office?" I asked.

He seemed surprised. "I'll be working out of my home until I find a place. I rented a waterfront condo on the outskirts of town."

"You want to type in the address so I can deliver the report?" I handed him my phone.

"Do you have a card?" Lucas asked when he

finished. "The doctor tells me that you have connections in all strata of society."

"Yes, I'm well acquainted with lowlifes, if that's what you're hinting at."

"I wasn't. But good to know."

Fab walked over to the car, retrieved her card, and came back, putting it in his open hand.

"PI!" He pocketed the card. "Another good connection."

"We have stipulations that need to be agreed on before you even ask us to do a job," I said.

We do? Fab mouthed.

I ignored her. "Nothing illegal. Grey-area jobs to be negotiated. And no 'tudiness if we tell you 'Heck no.'"

"Agreed. I would like to know what my brother's got against the two of you. He had a fit when I showed interest in the case."

"You'll have to ask him," I sidestepped. "Maybe it has to do with neighbor relations, since he lives next door to my brother. Or maybe it's just his prickly personality."

Lucas laughed. "He does have that." He pulled his phone out. "How do I get in touch with Doc Rivers?"

I scrolled through my phone, found Doc's number, and hit the call button.

"What?" Doc answered, his surly tone coming through loud and clear.

"I'm here at the jail. Just finished visiting the other good doc," I said. "Found him a new lawyer. No offense to Mr. Beaton, but this one is better. His name is Lucas Mark, and he needs your help on a couple of matters."

"Name the time and place."

"You got time now?" I asked. Both men said yes simultaneously. "Where are you?"

"Where do you suppose I am?" Doc snorted. "You know this is poker day."

"I'm sending him over and will call to have Doodad clear the deck so you can have privacy."

"You're a sweet girl."

"Aww. Tell Mother she needs to be reminded of that."

Doc laughed. "You tell the lawyer not to drag his feet; I'm waiting on him."

"Yes, sir." We both hung up. I texted Lucas the address of Jake's. "Don't dawdle. Doc Rivers is a crusty fellow, but you can't have a better friend."

"I'd like to get my hands on the police report ASAP." Lucas hit his key fob, opening the car door. "You'll need to call first; it's a security building."

"No problem, we'll leave the package at your doorstep," Fab told him. "Upscale address, prissy security building...probably so your neighbors don't steal."

He glared down his nose at Fab, and she returned the look. "It's been interesting."

"You'll be hearing from us." I smiled.

"When you go to Stan's place, videotape it and make sure I get a copy."

I saluted. "FYI: No one calls Dr. A Stan."

Fab grabbed my arm as we walked away. "Maybe hit him up for some lawyering for Joseph."

"I'm embarrassed to say I gave brief thought to the idea but didn't have the nerve to ask a Yale-educated lawyer to besmirch his record with a street brawl case."

"There's that."

We laughed.

Chapter Eleven

The next morning, I sat nursing my second cup of coffee, feeling better than the day before. Fab and I had split up after the jail visit and gone back to our respective homes, and I'd indulged in a nap, waking up with my head no longer in danger of falling off my shoulders.

Over coffee, I read the police report, and as Fab had requested, copied down the address of the deceased. I got up and pulled the copier out of the cupboard to make a copy for Lucas. Once finished, I clipped Didier's card to the top after writing on the back, "Call re: office space."

I grabbed up the envelope and headed out the door to deliver it myself. Fab wasn't the only one who knew how to pick a lock. In fact, thanks to her, most everyone in the family knew how.

Lucas's condo was no more than a five-minute drive away. He lived in a multi-story condo building with a view of the water from every unit. It surprised me that there were no security gates. I parked in front, and was about to pull out my lockpick when an older woman came out the main door and held it open for me. "Here you go, honey."

I didn't bother to knock, instead propping the envelope against his apartment door. I waited until I was back in the SUV to text him about the delivery. "Give him a taste of how clever we can be," I said to myself and laughed.

I was pulling into Creole's driveway when my phone rang and Fab's face popped up.

"Busy day today," she said as soon as I answered. "Dress business-like; we're going to surprise Mr. Mott at his office."

"I thought he was out of town."

"Funny thing, he's not and never has been, according to my source," Fab growled. "Since he won't take my calls, I'm having to resort to making a personal call."

"Give me a half-hour." I hung up and raced inside the house and into the shower.

When I finished in the bathroom and came out, it turned out I'd miscalculated the time it would take Fab to arrive. She was early and rooting around in the closet. Apparently, just because I'd dressed myself for many years before meeting her didn't mean I could do so now.

Oh well. I mentally shrugged.

Fab glanced over her shoulder. "You really need some more clothes." She came out with an above-the-knee black dress that she'd bought for me and a pair of black heels that I assumed were bought on the same shopping foray.

"I've decided to try out being a minimalist." I grabbed the clothes from her and went back in the bathroom to finish dressing.

"I picked out another outfit for you to change into when we're done," Fab yelled through the door. "After dealing with Mott, we're going to go do some breaking and entering."

I came out, and she gave me a head-to-toe once-over and nodded her approval. I reached in my bedside drawer and pulled out my Glock. "Do you think this goes with my outfit?"

"You know what I always say." Fab shook her finger at me.

"Never leave home without a firearm," we said together.

"Let's hit the road," Fab said. "We've got time for coffee."

I grabbed my purse and tote bag and followed her out the door.

Fab flew north up the highway and through most of the lights. Thankfully, all were green and traffic was light. Mr. Mott was yet another CEO with an office on Ocean Boulevard overlooking the white sands of Miami Beach. Fab had no choice but to pull into the underground parking, which had her grumbling. It didn't fit into her quick getaway blueprint.

"What's my role?" I asked as we headed to the elevator.

"Don't let me leave without a nice big check."

"In the future, before accepting a job, get an agreement to be paid in cash, and no crypto-currency, thank you. There's not a shoe store in town that will take the latter, which is a good reason for us not taking it."

"You're crazy." She jerked me into the elevator by the arm, jabbing a button.

"At least, admit it's in a good way."

"I'll think on it." She smirked.

We got off the elevator and saw the reception desk not more than a couple feet away. Fab approached, pulling money out of her jacket pocket. "Taylor?"

The woman nodded and smiled. "Can I help you?"

Fab reached out and put the cash in the woman's hand, along with her parking ticket. "Thank you for all your help. Is Mr. Mott in?"

The nerve. I stood there with a stupid smile on my face, trying not to laugh.

"Yes, but he's not seeing anyone." Her eyes were as big as saucers. "I don't want to lose my job." She validated Fab's ticket and handed it back.

"Where's his office?"

"Down the hall to the end, make a right; it's the last one. You won't get past Mr. Mott's assistant, who has the adjoining office."

The elevator doors opened, and a delivery guy rolled out a cart with an assortment of boxes.

"If asked, you not only don't know anything, you never even saw us." Fab motioned to me, and we headed down the hall.

Turning the corner, we saw Mr. Mott's office

door standing open. Fab walked in like she owned the joint while I closed the door behind us.

Mott looked up, and his pudgy face paled considerably. "I didn't realize we had an appointment."

"You know damn well we don't." Fab seated herself in front of his desk. "I'd like to hear why you really hired me, and don't insult me with the story you used when you first called, since we both know that your security system was installed by a company with impeccable credentials."

I stood by the door, looking around the chrome-and-glass office. Paintings lined the walls; the biggest one an oil painting of himself. Mr. Mott wasn't much for personal items except for the enormous silver humidor sitting in the center of a side table.

The man shifted uncomfortably in his chair. "I'd heard rumors of a lawsuit against that company and couldn't take a chance that they'd do shoddy work. It appears they did."

"What a crock," Fab snapped. "I'll tell you what I know. The so-called robbers..." She paused. "They had easy access. It's as if they walked in right past the security gates and locked doors, hauled your worldly goods out, and packed them with care in the back of a van. The thieves were in no hurry. The system didn't trip until we arrived. Funny thing: that was *one hour* later, and security claimed it had just gone off."

"What are you getting at?" Mott demanded, not pulling off angry but instead looking scared. "You'd better not be suggesting that I had anything to do with robbing my own house."

"That's exactly what I'm suggesting." Fab eyed him like a cockroach she was about to squash under her heel. "In light of your liquidity issues, it's not a stretch — your insurance claim will bring in millions. I assume this is your first attempt at insurance fraud — that you're not good at it, even factoring in that you have to start somewhere. Adjusters aren't stupid. If I can smell a scam, then they sure as heck can. Better get your jail perks lined up."

"Get out of my office or I'm calling security," Mott spit, wiping his mouth.

"Go ahead, call the police. I'm sure they'll be interested in hearing what I have to say about the so-called robbery at your manse."

"What do you want?"

"Payment, for one thing." Fab held his attention with her burning glare. "Three times the negotiated amount in reimbursement for the time my partner and I spent sitting handcuffed on your stinkin' grass."

"That's blackmail."

"Actually, it isn't. It's your choice, and if you decide the fee is exorbitant, I'll send a collector." Fab made a strangling noise that sent his eyebrows up to his hairline. "Once our business is concluded, it's understood that we don't know each other. In fact, we never met."

Mott opened a side drawer and pulled out his checkbook, filling out a check and handing it to Fab. "Now get out."

Fab stood and lifted the hem of her silk blouse, tucking it behind her Walther. Mott's eyes bugged.

"I don't appreciate your setting me up as a suspect." Fab leaned forward. "You're lucky. I planned to come here and blow your brains out and watch your blood dribble down the glass behind you. Say 'thank you' to my friend." She motioned over her shoulder. "She's the one who talked me down."

"Thank you," Mott squeaked, not making eye contact.

I opened the door, Fab flounced through, and I turned back to Mott. "Don't do anything stupid, like stopping payment on the check, because you really won't like what will happen." I smiled sweetly and closed the door.

We passed the reception desk without so much as a pause.

When the elevator doors closed, I asked, "Where did you get the info? Judging by Mott's reaction, you were spot on."

"Unleashed Toady. He paid off one of the housemaids, who'd been ordered to take a few days off but stayed behind because she had no place to go. He's also the one who made a connection with Taylor, and lucky us, she can be bribed."

I squirmed. "Toady says he's a babe magnet; do you suppose it's true?" I conjured up an image of the man, who had the skin of an old reptile, in his jeans and wife-beater and shuddered.

"I don't ask how Toady gets his info. I just appreciate that he gets it fast and it's accurate. I did have to talk him down from strangling Mott."

"That's because you're the girl of his dreams and he'd do anything to protect you. If you'd been hauled off to jail, bye-bye Mr. Mott; he'd disappear without a trace."

"Toady stopped all the romance talk once Didier and I got married. He even congratulated the two of us."

The parking attendant brought the SUV around and ogled Fab as she slid behind the wheel.

"In the spirit of keeping one another informed..." she said as she drove out of the underground garage.

I didn't want to ask.

"Toady got an interesting call from Brick, who had a job offer, but Toady had to agree to tell no one before he got to hear the details."

"Toady needs to watch his back." I turned my attention to the waves crashing on the sand.

Brick Famosa was Fab's oldest client and a pain in the…

"An auto hauler full of classic cars went missing on its way to auction," Fab related, excitement in her voice. "Brick wants it found and doesn't want the cops involved."

"That crosses off insurance fraud." Her tone had me worried that she'd want in on the recovery. "That still leaves someone stupid enough to steal from Brick, and my guess is he knows who did it and why. No cops could mean another felony—perhaps, they were stolen to begin with—meaning whatever method works to get it back is acceptable." Brick's jobs never failed to give me a headache. "Assure me that you're not getting involved."

"Brick's finally gotten the message that I'm no longer working for him."

Her non-answer bothered me. Apparently, it showed, because after a moment, she continued.

"If I did accept another Brick job, Didier would divorce me, and I'm not letting that happen. But if Brick continues to go directly to Toady, I'll miss out on the opportunity to bill the man double."

"We need to bring in some new clients."

Fab gave me the "you grew a second head" stare. "I'm not interested in rounding up stolen bicycles."

I clasped my hands to my chest. "You wound me."

Fab pulled over in front of a two-story apartment building and parked.

"This is...?" I'd wondered why she was winding around neighborhood streets instead of taking the direct route back to the turnpike.

"Nicolette's place," she said in a tone suggesting that I should already know the answer.

"We're here to search the place, I assume? Does this have anything to do with the secret code you were exchanging with the good doc?"

"It would be interesting to know who Nicolette Anais was. If the drugs didn't belong to Dr. A, then they had to be hers. If so, I'm not sure how we prove that she bought her own drugs, but it's worth a try."

"Quiet neighborhood." I craned my head around. "Are we using our special key?" Code for lockpick.

"That's Plan B."

Now that surprised me, and I hoped that Plan A was legal, since I wasn't sitting this one out in the car. As I got out, I noticed Fab pocketing some cash and her PI badge. "First, we look for a maintenance office. Last resort, we talk to the manager," she said.

"And if neither cooperate?"

"Then we'll be coming back at night."

"In case you haven't noticed, it's not as easy to sneak out at night now that the guys keep regularish hours," I reminded her. "The window of opportunity to do as we please and update them later has closed. And don't think that you can come up with some yarn about the job being legal and then spring it on them at the last minute. Keep in mind how much you hate going without sex, and you know that's what Didier will do." I scissored my fingers.

"How come you don't complain about such issues with Creole?"

I harrumphed. "Because I'm not the sneak-around chick. Look in the rearview mirror; that would be her."

Fab turned towards her reflection in the mirror and waved.

I laughed. "Okay, we've used up our allotted time talking about sex."

We got out and cut across the sidewalk and over to the entrance to the building.

Fab stopped at the mailbox, but none of the slots were marked. The first apartment had a "manager" plaque on the door, which Fab marched right on past. "We'll walk to the end and see what we can find. Checking out the upstairs is a waste of time."

The manager's door opened, and I caught a glimpse of an older woman peering out at us. I hurried to catch up to Fab, who'd bolted up the walkway. "If it turns out that you don't need to chat with the manager, I suggest that we go out the back and around the block to get to the car."

"There's nothing down here." Fab doubled

back, and when she got to the manager's door, the woman was standing behind the screen. "I'm here to ask a few questions about Nicolette Anais." She held up her badge, then gestured at me. "New trainee," she said dismissively.

Trainee now! No fun for me. I smiled at the woman.

"The police have already been here," she said. "I told them Ms. Anais kept to herself and I didn't know anything. Don't want to get involved in any murder case."

"Have you re-rented her apartment?"

The woman shook her head. "The owner has to get a court order releasing the place."

"How about you let me look around her place?" Fab pulled cash out of her pocket. "Answer a couple of questions, and then you can pretend I was never here if you like. It saves me getting a warrant."

The woman's eyes glittered at the sight of the money. "Let me get my keys." She was back in a second. "This won't take long, will it?"

"I'll be quick." Fab handed her the money, which disappeared into the pocket of the woman's housedress.

I followed them back down the sidewalk. It surprised me that Nicolette had rented a unit on the alley, but then, it would have offered a quick getaway if she'd needed one.

Fab walked inside, snapping on a pair of gloves.

"What did you think of Nicolette?" I asked the manager, wanting to distract her attention from Fab. It worked, as she turned in my direction.

"I still don't want to get involved." She hesitated only slightly. "The truth is, Ms. Anais wasn't around much. She certainly didn't sleep here, not that I ever saw. More of an expensive place to collect her mail. She usually parked a block over and walked, even when there was an open space on this street. I know because I followed her once. Husband tells me I'm damn nosey, and I guess he's right."

"Did the cops remove anything?" I asked.

"Not a single thing. Although, the fingerprint guy was here for over an hour."

"Any visitors?"

The woman shook her head.

"How often did Nicolette come by?"

"Every few days. She'd check her mail, go into her apartment for an hour or so, and leave."

"Interesting woman."

"More like sneaky little thing." The woman harrumphed. "I told my husband she was up to something, but he told me to stop looking for trouble since she paid her rent on time. One thing we do agree on—we're happy she didn't get murdered on the property. I'd be the one stuck with the cleanup." She shuddered.

Now probably wasn't the time to mention that I knew a great crime scene cleaner if she ever needed one.

Fab took one last look around and arched her brow at me. I nodded, letting her know I was finished asking questions. The reality was the woman was eager to talk, despite her fear of getting in the middle of the case. I'd also noticed that, like us, she hadn't introduced herself.

"Thank you," I said, and we both waved as we left. "Did you find anything?"

"Not a single thing," Fab said as we walked back to the SUV. "She didn't live there. Not one personal item. Ugly rental furniture." She turned up her nose.

"The manager said that Nicolette never stayed long. Didn't occur to me that she'd never moved in. Hope you got your snooping on tape?"

"Who do you think you're talking to?"

I laughed at her faux outrage. "What was I thinking? Of course, you did." After I got in the SUV, I informed her, "I want to stop and check on Joseph, since he's out of the hospital. But first, hit up a convenience store so I can pick him up some food."

Fab gasped.

"I'm not talking a hot dog that's been twirling on a stick all day but Ding-Dongs, Twinkies, etc. Where else do you buy those kinds of treats?" I convulsed in laughter.

Chapter Twelve

"Nice house." I scoped out Dr. A's two-story beach house on stilts as Fab parked in the driveway. "Before we get out... For the second time today, why are we here? It's one thing to help Dr. A find an attorney and another to search his house."

"I just threw it out there, expecting him to give me an emphatic 'not my house' response. When he didn't object, how could I pass up the opportunity to take a look around?"

"Yes, how?" I shook my head. "Wait until he finds out everything that entails."

"Are you certain of your friend's innocence? You only know what was reported on the internet, and you haven't had the opportunity to ask him directly, which I wouldn't recommend anyway." Fab reached over the backseat and retrieved the duffels where we kept an extra set of clothing. Having experience changing in the car, we swapped for jeans and t-shirts in record time.

"He was emphatic during our visit that he's not involved in drugs. As long as I've lived in the

Cove, Dr. A has had a stellar reputation, with no hint of criminal activity." I shoved my phone in my pocket, sliding my feet into tennis shoes. "One of the reports that GC sent over included the drug test results of all of the employees in his office, including Dr. A himself. They were routinely tested, and the tests always came back negative. At the very worst, he may have purchased the drugs for her, and maybe it's as simple as a little recreational use gone out of control. But he denied that also."

"A kilo?" Fab questioned, the amount found in a briefcase on the scene, according to the police report. "That's not recreational. I believe he's looking at big-time jail for the quantity alone. And if he *is* dealing, then why agree to let us search his home?"

"After reading through the reports GC sent over, I have a few questions. No way can the prosecutor make a murder case unless it can be proved that the good doc supplied the drugs. Especially since she was already dead by the time Dr. A got home and attempting to resuscitate her had no effect. When he left the hospital and when the call came in are both documented."

Fab shoved some tools into her back pockets, hanging onto her lockpick, and we got out of the car. I stood in the driveway and surveyed the quiet neighborhood while Fab walked the property line, opening the mailbox. It was empty.

"I'm assuming the reason he got arrested was because the briefcase found near the body belonged to him and happened to be full of drugs and an unregistered gun," I said. "Which is pretty damning."

"How do the investigators know that it was his briefcase?" Fab mused. "His name on it? There was no mention of whether his fingerprints were found on it anywhere."

"Since we don't have a good reason for snooping, I feel it's important to remind you that we're not here to be totally invasive. In our last phone chat, Dr. A told me that Nicolette used one of the guest bedrooms for her clothes and shoes and such."

"To answer your original question, we're here to learn more about the girlfriend." Fab tossed me a pair of gloves.

I caught them and snapped them on. "Inquiring minds would also like to know where the drugs were purchased. They didn't come from Tommy the dime dealer. Too bad the toxicology reports on Nicolette haven't come back yet. Wouldn't you think, if she were a user, that Dr. A would notice the signs?"

"Love, or wall-banging sex, has a tendency to make people overlook pesky bad habits. In the beginning anyway." Fab picked the lock and opened the door, and we scooted under the yellow police tape.

"The cops did a thorough job," I said over

Fab's shoulder as we stood in the living room. It was evident that every inch had been searched, as cupboard doors and drawers stood open. "The report included a photograph of the coffee table where she'd snorted the coke, and what was left was minimal."

I followed her down the hallway to the bedrooms, which were in the same messy condition. Not a single piece of furniture had been spared. "This is probably a waste of time. Like you said, it was probably over-indulgence. I don't see how Dr. A can prove he didn't provide the drugs. Even if we locate the dealer and he admits Nicolette bought the drugs from him, he's not going to incriminate himself in court."

"That could turn ugly. The quantity, as you said, doesn't suggest the corner dealer." For once, Fab didn't appear eager to go looking for trouble. Not of that caliber, anyway. "There's more to Nicolette than meets the eye, as evidenced by her address of record, which she's had for months and used for hour-long visits once a week. That's a lot of moolah for a mail drop." Fab toed her way through the pile of clothes blocking the door of the walk-in closet. "If there's anything to find, I'll find it. Nicolette wouldn't be the first person to hide things so even the cops can't find them."

It annoyed me that I didn't know how to ferret out secret hideaways and, therefore, was currently zero help. The guest bedroom had been sparsely furnished, and to my untrained eye, it appeared that the cops had searched every inch. Even the mattress and box spring had been tipped against the wall.

"I'm going to need a chair so I can look inside the register." Fab called, pointing at the grill high on the wall. She dropped to her knees, producing a pen flashlight.

I located a stepladder in the kitchen and carried it back to the bedroom. Then I poked my head inside the walk-in closet, which looked like a bomb of women's clothes and shoes had gone off in it, the garments exploding into the air and landing in a haphazard fashion.

Fab crawled around the perimeter of the enormous closet, pulling out the drawers in the built-in organizer and knocking on the bottoms. She opened the side doors, stuck her head in, and searched there, too.

"Since I'm certain you have a screwdriver in that back pocket of yours, hand it over, and I'll climb up and check out the vents." I personally didn't think it was that great of a hiding space. Too much work to get to, for one thing.

"Hold on." Fab, who always came prepared, whipped out an army knife. "Look what I found." She pried off one of the baseboards on the organizer and then another, lowering herself flat to the floor and continuing until she'd removed all of the trim. She stuck her hand in and slid out a long metal storage box, and then another, before continuing her trek around the enclosed area.

I was officially impressed.

Finally, Fab sat up and inspected all sides of the two boxes. "Damn, they're locked," she said, clearly disappointed.

"Since when has that ever stopped you?"

"Oh, I'll get them open, just not with my lockpick. They've got combo locks, so I'll need a different tool." She stood and set them on top of the organizer. Reaching over, she grabbed the stepladder, snapping it open and centering it under the register. "Pull off the front of that vacuum cleaner." She pointed to the corner, where a brand new upright sat, instruction booklet hanging off the side.

Flipping it around, I unsnapped the cover over the bag. My jaw dropped at the sight of the large manila envelope that had been shoved inside in place of a bag. Undoing the clasp, I saw that it contained a sheaf of papers and a small notebook. "I'm impressed that you knew this trick. Hidden paperwork in a vacuum…should make for interesting reading." I held up the envelope. "Miss Nicolette is getting more interesting by the minute."

Fab stared down from her perch, then went back to unscrewing the grate, which she handed to me, then pocketed her tool, trading it for her flashlight. She shone the beam straight down the long passage. "Nothing in here." She turned the light onto a smaller passageway off to one side. "Wait. There's a fire safe in here that I can't reach. Wonder how Nicolette did it…unless she had chimp arms?"

I tried not to laugh, saying a silent thank you that my knuckles didn't drag the ground. Turning back to the task at hand, I said, "Don't move." I disappeared into the closet and came back out with a rod that had caught my eye. I'd wondered what the heck it was.

"A garment hook!" Fab said.

"Now I know what it's used for." I handed it to Fab. Peeking back inside the closet, I noted that all the clothing rods were easily accessible. Clever woman!

After several attempts, Fab hooked the box and reeled it over to her. Handing down the rod, she said, "Ready? I'm going to pass this down to you. It's heavy." She tipped it on its side, hanging onto one end.

I reached up and grabbed the handle, hefting it down and setting it on the floor. I retrieved the other two boxes from the organizer and set all three together.

"While I check the rest of the rooms, you go over the room one last time; maybe more hidden treasures will turn up."

I'd given the small pile of jewelry on the island in the closet a cursory glance when I passed it the first time, but nothing had caught my interest. I turned in a circle, surveying the room, and noticed Nicolette's designer purse upended on the floor at the foot of the bed, lying on top of what appeared to be the contents. Hunching down, I picked up her wallet and checked the pockets, including the slots for credit cards. Same with her makeup bag, which didn't yield anything either. Turning to the purse itself, I unzipped one side pocket, then another — barely noticeable unless your own purse had similar pockets — and discovered a set of keys.

Standing, I twirled the keys, disappointed that there weren't any lockbox keys. Heading to the front door, I tried two of the four keys that could possibly fit the lock and neither worked. That left two mailbox-type keys.

I went in search of Fab, who had moved into Dr. A's bedroom. The door stood open, showing that it had been thoroughly searched and was in the same chaotic shape as Nicolette's, personal belongings strewn on the floor. It was hard to visualize what the room had looked like before.

"Do you suppose Nicolette hid anything in here?" I asked.

"Doubt it. My guess is that she hid everything in *her* closet. All it would take was the doc coming home early and finding her with her backside hanging out of an air vent. Even I couldn't come up with a lame excuse for that."

"Cleaning?"

"As Didier would say, 'Try again.'"

"What do you suppose the woman was hiding

to go to the lengths that she did? Why not a safe deposit box at the bank?"

"Good questions. Wonder if Dr. A knows the answers."

I wandered back down the hall and lingered in the doorway of Nicolette's room, lost in thought, wondering where this case was going to lead, as Fab went room to room for one last check.

She came back and entered the bedroom, hands on her hips, scanning it as though seeing it for the first time. "Fake tree in the corner." She pointed. There was a price tag hanging off a branch, and it had been tipped over, showing that, miraculously, no soil spilled out.

Long ago, I'd ixnayed houseplants, except for the tropical ones that had sat in my garden window. I'd once bought a small tree that came with a fly nest in the soil; when they hatched, it was unending flies for several days until source of the problem was discovered. I turned up my nose at the long-ago memory.

"Decoration only." She kicked the pot. "Or another creative hiding place." She bent down, grabbing the trunk and giving it a good shake. "Hmm...you hold the other end, and I'll pull this one."

The tree dislodged from the pot and...nothing. No interesting find that would answer the mounting questions. All we got was a wad of burlap wrapped around...?

Fab slit the fabric and exposed two large

mayonnaise jars. Yanking one out and letting the tree topple to the floor, she unscrewed the lid.

"Careful. Mayo stains don't come out of clothing."

She stuck her finger in the jar, running it around the inside, and the glove came back out clean. "Paint." She pulled out an enormous wad of bills, which she handed to me before unscrewing the lid of the other jar and finding a similar stash.

"Hundreds." I fingered the stack of bills and reached for a jar, peering inside. Sure enough, Nicolette had painted the sides so that no one would suspect it contained anything other than mayo, if not for where we found it.

"Mine too." Fab handed me her jar. "This chick was into something."

"Do you have a mental checklist of every possible hiding place running around in that crafty mind of yours?"

"I used to keep a list; I'll email it to you. There will be a test." Fab shook her finger at me.

I let out a long sigh, wishing we hadn't come here, but that cat had cleared the block. "What are we going to do with what we found?"

"We're taking everything with us. There's a possibility we'll find answers in one of the boxes. Since you're the professional one, you keep an inventory, and when Dr. A gets released, we'll return everything."

"I'm as anxious as you are to get a look at the

contents, but I think it's none of our business and we should put them back. Not to mention that it could be evidence in a murder, and if we remove it, it can't be proved that it was ever here or that it belonged to Nicolette."

"Or it might be safer to take it with us and hope that whatever is inside will prove Dr. A's innocence. Plus, there's a real possibility that there's a third party wanting their product back."

"Maybe. It is theft."

"Dr. A gave me permission to take what I wanted," Fab huffed.

"Not exactly." Maybe because he had no idea how good Fab was at finding things people didn't want found. "What if these boxes belong to Dr. A and not Nicolette?"

Fab's frown was the only sign she heard me as she examined the boxes. "I haven't replaced my tools since the fire. This is just the kick I need to trick out my workspace in the garage at the office. In the meantime…"

Trying again, since she'd ignored my last question, I said, "Does Didier know that you're planning that space at the office?" Throwing out her husband's name might slow her down and make her realize this wasn't a good idea.

"Of course, he does." Fab blushed. "He caught me sketching out a few ideas that included a list of tools and gave me a few good suggestions. I'm happy I didn't attempt my first 'surprise,' presenting it as a done deal and something I did for the two of us."

"Pretty soon, you'll be no-more-sneak-around Fab. Will I even recognize you?" I laughed at her glare.

"There's one person we know has every tool known to man, and that's Spoon. We can swing by the garage, but I'm certain he'll suggest that we not get in so deep." Oh yeah, too late. "If he's not there, I'll pick the lock and say you did it."

"Except that he'll check the security footage. Busted. My guess is that he's going to harp on us minding our own business and suggest that we go get a coffee. So you better have an answer ready."

"If the cops had found this cash, they'd have confiscated it and Dr. A would have to prove where every penny came from." Fab shoved the money back into the jars and screwed on the lids. She handed me the long boxes and placed the envelope on top. "Let's get the heck out of here." She picked up the fire safe and jars. "We're not leaving anything behind, are we?" She spun around, giving the room one last check. "I'll call Toady to get someone over here to repair the baseboards in case the police come back. They see the damage, it'll raise red flags." She'd shoved the trim boards back in place, but they leaned precariously and, with a nudge, would easily fall over.

"Next time Dr. A calls, I'm going to ask if he wants me to get someone to clean up the place.

At least, get the stuff off the floor and the clothing rehung. It would suck to come home to such a mess."

"Before you do that, get an okay from Lucas. We don't want to get anyone in trouble."

Except ourselves. Removing evidence?

We slid under the tape and back to the SUV, storing the boxes behind the front seats. I tossed a couple of cloth shopping bags on top so they wouldn't be noticeable to someone peeking in the window.

"There's more to this case than an overindulgence in drugs." Fab slid behind the wheel and was quiet as she merged back into traffic on the main highway through town. "The apartment was a ruse, and aside from the clothing, there wasn't a single personal item belonging to Nicolette at Dr. A's house. At a quick glance, it appears as though she and Dr. A lived together, but did they? Or was it another temporary address for her? A place to change clothes? Collect mail? Did she have yet another address?"

"Nothing would surprise me at this point. I'm waiting for a 'what next?'" I pulled the keyring from my pocket and gave her a rundown on the keys. "How do we go about finding out if there's another residence?" I examined the keys again, as though they'd give me the answer.

Fab took a shortcut well known to locals, which wound around down to the docks, and headed over to the far end. She pulled into the driveway of JS Auto Body and parked in front of the barbed wire-topped gates, which were chained and locked. No cars were parked in front.

As soon as the car doors closed, dogs started barking and jumping on the ten-foot chain-link fence with a green cover to block the view of the inside.

"How many?" I asked.

"Sounds like two."

"Wonder when Spoon got them. We can't get in safely. I'm assuming the dogs are here to keep people from gaining access by jumping the fence or picking the lock, so that leaves the front door, which you and I both know will sound alarms as soon as we touch the knob." I looked up and down the street as the dogs continued to bark. "This was a marginal idea to begin with; now it's terrible." I pulled my phone out of my pocket and called the man. When he answered, I asked, "When did you get the dogs?"

"What the hell are you doing at the garage?" Spoon barked.

"Use your quiet voice, or I'm going to tell Mother on you."

"She's going to ask the same damn question."

"That's not a quiet voice," I whined, which made Fab laugh.

Spoon sighed. "I'm getting a headache as we speak. What are you doing at my establishment after closing?"

"We came by to use some of your tools, but we're reconsidering if there's a chance we'll get eaten by your two killers."

"I'm going to remind you one last time—no picking the locks at my business," he ground out.

"And the dogs?"

Fab walked the front of the property, and one of the dogs followed along the fence line, barking.

"They won't eat you, but they'll work you over pretty good. I suggest you come back tomorrow."

"Oh, all right."

"If I get a call from the security company, I'm going to let them arrest you," Spoon threatened.

"Good luck running that past Mother. Tomorrow then." He was laughing as I hung up. "I've had enough of this day. How about you?"

Chapter Thirteen

Creole brushed my lips with a kiss. "Do you think you'll be staying out of trouble today?" he asked, pouring himself a cup of coffee.

Glancing over my shoulder, I turned back with a weak smile. "You talking to me?" I asked in mock surprise. "I can't promise because the day's just gotten started."

"When Dr. A initially called, what did he want?" Creole asked, handing me a cup of coffee and sliding onto a stool next to me.

"For me to find him a good lawyer."

"Have you done that?" I nodded. "Then it's time to put an end to your involvement."

"But—"

He cut me off. "You read the police report, so I don't need to list all the reasons why it's a good idea to keep your distance. This case involves a large quantity of drugs, and a dealer is certainly lurking in the shadows. I don't want you in their sights."

I was feeling guilty for not telling him about yesterday's find. "Next time Dr. A calls, I'll tell him," I said reluctantly. Saying no was not my strong suit, no matter how many times I reminded myself to do just that.

"Dr. A or his girlfriend, or both, are neck-deep in something illegal."

"Agreed." I rested my head against his chest.

"So you'll have an uneventful day."

"Now that I can't promise." I half-laughed.

* * *

"As I get each box open, you inventory the contents before I move on to the next one," Fab said, cruising into the driveway of JS Auto Body.

I had called and let Spoon know that we were on our way. He was full of questions, and I told him he had to wait.

"After Didier left this morning, I sat on the bed and counted the money in one of the jars. It had two bundles and took a while." Fab grimaced. "One hundred thirty-three thousand in hundred-dollar bills."

"Nice, but probably illegal," I said. "Don't forget to remove the pictures from your phone." I waved to the man standing at the gates, who closed them after we drove through. "According to the background report, Nicolette had no verifiable work history, which means she had to have another healthy source of income. And apparently she didn't believe in banks." A stack of cash that large presented to a bank teller would trigger paperwork to the IRS.

Spoon ran an appointment-only business

catering to luxe autos and classic cars. It would have been hard to miss the new doghouse in the far corner. It was the size of a studio apartment and even had a porch, where the Dobermans were sacked out on a plush bed.

"Aren't you excited to find out what's inside these boxes?" Fab asked.

I was more excited to get them out of the back of my SUV, which Fab had locked in her garage the previous night. If I told her I didn't have a good feeling, would that change what we were about to do? "It's not too late to put everything back where we found it and mind our own business for a change."

Fab backed into the last open bay. "We'll do that next time."

Spoon came out of his office and crossed the driveway, closing the distance between us.

"I need to use your tools," Fab said, popping the liftgate in her efficient style and shoving it open.

"Don't look at me; I have no clue which ones," I said as Spoon walked up. I filled him on the finds from Dr. A's house.

Billy, a longtime employee and friend of Spoon's, had joined Fab, letting out a low whistle as she handed off the steel boxes. Both men were tall and lean, the kind of quiet guys you messed with at your own peril. We trusted them both. In the past, when we had a problem, Billy would always show up, no questions asked.

Spoon put his arm around my shoulders. "You okay?"

I nodded as we joined Fab and Billy, who had commandeered a workbench. Fab relayed how we found the boxes.

Billy had one of the long steel boxes on end and was examining the lock. "This would be an easy lock to snap open, but it will never work again." He looked to Fab for confirmation that it was okay to proceed. "After that, the box will be useless."

"I've got a nose for trouble," Spoon said. "This doesn't look good for your doctor friend. Going to this much trouble to hide something indicates it must be valuable, illegal, or both."

Billy retrieved a crowbar and hammer off the wall and had the lid open a moment later with one well-placed swing. It was filled to the brim with stacks of cash. Same in the second box.

Spoon picked up one of the bundles and fanned through it. "Damn. All hundreds."

"Same as last night's haul," I said.

Billy popped the top off the fire safe with same finesse as the other two. On the top lay a Glock 22, which he lifted out with a screwdriver, laying it on the counter. Under it was a plastic ziplock bag, containing two driver's licenses from different states, both in Nicolette's name, which lay on top of six plastic zip bags of a white substance marked 1 thru 4, each also labeled 2.2 plus coding of some sort.

A silence fell over the four of us as we stared, inspecting the contents without touching. I wasn't sure what the others were thinking, but I didn't want my fingerprints on any of the bags.

Spoon whistled. "Since it's probably exactly what it looks like, I'd estimate the street value to be roughly a half-million, maybe more."

"Now what?" I mumbled, growing more uneasy at the twists this case was taking. "Nicolette was a drug dealer? Or Dr. A? But if all this belonged to Dr. A, he wouldn't hide it in her bedroom."

"Every time we uncover something about this woman, it leads to more questions," Fab said. "Dr. A is really lucky the cops didn't find this; he'd never have gotten out of prison."

"What are we going to do with it?" I looked inside the box again, shuddering. "If this were found…no one would believe it doesn't belong to us. They'd come to the conclusion that we're dealers."

"Is Ruthie Grace Dr. A's attorney?" Spoon asked.

"They didn't get along—mutual dislike." I wished I'd been there for that scene. "After that, she wouldn't take my calls, so I got Dr. A another attorney." And to think that at one time, I'd wanted the woman to represent Fab or me if we were in need of legal assistance.

"How about I make the drugs disappear without a trace and we pretend we never saw them?" Spoon suggested.

"Show of hands," I said, mine shooting into the air along with the others'.

"Getting rid of the boxes would also be a good idea," Billy said.

"If this all belonged to Nicolette, I'm surprised that whoever she was doing business with didn't do a search once the cops were done." A shiver went through me. "Dr. A's arrest and detention made the headlines, signaling that his house is vacant."

"Considering the shape we found his place in, maybe they did," Fab said.

"On second thought, I think we should return this to where we found it," I said.

"Forget that," Billy said sternly. "You two girls need to stay away from the doctor's place. You have to go back for some reason, you call me. I'll search the place first, then guard the door until you're done."

"I second that," Spoon said emphatically.

Fab winked at Billy, whose cheeks turned pink.

My phone rang, and when I took it out of my pocket, I saw GC's name come up on the screen. I stepped away to take the call.

"What the f—?" GC yelled when I answered. "You go behind my back and contact my brother to represent your skeevy friend?"

"It—"

"I told you I didn't want my brother getting

wind of any association between the two of us," he ground out.

"Could I—"

"You find the doctor another lawyer. Now," he roared. "Your word doesn't mean piss."

I took a deep breath, hoping that when he was done ranting, I'd get a word in.

"I'm telling you now, no one f—s me over like this. No one." He hung up.

My heart beat wildly. I'd never been talked to quite like that, and I didn't relish having GC as an enemy. Or anyone else. I didn't do hate relationships.

I turned, and Fab took one look and rushed over to me. "You okay? Who was that?"

"I'll tell you later."

I knew from the thunderous expression on Spoon's face that he'd heard the angry voice coming through the line. Hopefully, he hadn't been able to make out the words, or he'd want to talk to the man. That wouldn't go well.

I took a deep breath and walked over to the SUV. I reached inside, grabbing my water bottle and taking a long drink to calm my nerves before rejoining everyone.

"You got room in your floor-to-ceiling safe for the cash?" Fab asked Spoon.

He'd recently found an antique safe and had it installed in his office.

"Don't forget the half-mill in the back seat. It needs to be added to the stash." I'd told Spoon about the painted mayo jars, and he said he'd heard of the idea but hadn't thought anyone would actually do it.

Fab related the story to Billy.

"That's an old trick." Billy laughed. "It's typically used to stash a few bucks in the refrigerator. Don't know what good it would do in a plant pot."

"Are you sure about getting involved?" I asked Spoon. "I would understand if you didn't. We're all staring at big-time trouble."

"This way, we're all assured that it will be done right and never come back to haunt us," Spoon reassured me.

Hopefully.

Talking with Spoon had reminded me that I'd forgotten to peruse the contents of the envelope and notebook, which I'd left at home.

"You're the best." I hugged Spoon. "Anything you ever need, we're available at the snap of your fingers." I flicked a hand between Fab and I.

"There's more to this case than an overindulgence in drugs," Spoon said gruffly. "You two need to be careful. It appears that you've stepped into something illegal, and it could boomerang and get dangerous on you fast. Drug dealers don't leave witnesses that can come back on them."

"I agree with the boss," Billy seconded. "In fact, I suggest you cut off visits, or whatever you're doing, with the doctor and keep a damn low profile. You don't know how many pissed off people the dead woman left behind, and if the doctor is involved, he won't make it to trial. Keeps him from talking, telling what he knows."

I shuddered, thinking of news accounts of what happened to people that crossed criminals in general.

"I must be maturing or something." Fab frowned. "I'm not the least bit interested in kicking over a hornets' nest."

Spoon and Billy hid their smirks before Fab saw them.

"We're out of this case," I said, tired of waffling. "I fulfilled my promise and got Lucas Mark to represent Dr. A. As for the rest of this…" I waved my hand at the workbench, where Billy had packed everything back into the boxes. "I say we wait until Dr. A's out of jail, and he can decide what he wants done."

Fab handed Billy her business card and whispered something to him that I couldn't hear.

Spoon growled. "You ungrateful brat, trying to steal my employee…"

"I'm not going anywhere, boss." Billy laughed.

I stepped in front of the big man, hugging him. "I know you'd probably never call on the two us, preferring to handle your own problems, but we're available."

"You're not leaving until we've had a short chat. In my office," he ordered, picking up the boxes. Once inside, he opened the safe, took the bundles of bills out, and put them on the bottom shelf. "You ever want to count it, you know right where it's at."

"How are you going to dispose of the drugs?" Fab asked.

"Just like the DEA—burn them. The boxes are headed to the dump."

Fab clearly approved. I didn't care, as long as I never saw the illegal substance again.

Spoon regarded us with a stern expression. "I suggest that you trust no one, and if you have questions, get your answers from Creole. At least, he won't steer you right into jail."

Creole! Wait until he heard about today. He wouldn't be happy, but as Spoon suggested, he was the perfect person for advice, since he'd built a career as an undercover officer before retiring.

"This is the second time I've agreed with you in a short time. Don't get used to it." Fab's lips quirked up in a smug smirk.

Chapter Fourteen

"Where next?" Fab pulled out of the driveway, and we hung our arms out the window, waving to Billy as he closed the gates.

"I say we stop and get tacos and margaritas and christen that beautiful beach I guess you own. I've had enough of this day already." It annoyed me when she turned in the opposite direction of home. "Why even ask me if you already have something planned?"

"You owe me."

I shook my head, which she knew meant "fat chance."

"You've apparently forgotten about Joseph. I'm doing the good-partner thing by driving by The Cottages. Before this case goes much further, we need to get Butthead to drop the charges."

"You never remember people's names, but this one you remember?"

"It's a start." Fab smiled cheekily. "Almost forgot—who was on the phone? Don't say you don't know what I'm talking about or don't remember. The call made the color drain out of your face."

"GC." I'd forgotten about him for a few minutes, and at the reminder, I got a stomachache. "He found out that Lucas is Dr. A's attorney and flipped out." I relayed the gist of the call. "If Creole knew the language he used, he'd break his face."

"He'll calm down."

I wasn't so sure. I reached for my phone and called, hoping to get a word in this time. "Disconnected." I threw my phone into the back. *What an ass!*

"Breathe," Fab instructed. "We do know where he lives."

"Next door to my brother." I heaved a sigh. "After that phone call, I'm not sure I want to use him again, even if he agrees. I'm telling you, I'm tired of not having reliable resources."

"I've got a couple of connections that can get us information if we need to use them, but they both have criminal tendencies." Fab backed into Mac's driveway.

"I'm happy that all our checking out Nicolette is over," I said. "Next case, can we round up lost cats?"

Fab cuffed my head. "If you recall, even a few of those involved felons."

"It was your idea to come here, so you're running the show." I scooted out of the SUV before she could commit more bodily harm. "I'll follow you like a stalker."

"If you leave my side, I'll track you down," Fab threatened. "I need you to translate drunk talk."

"If you can catch a couple of words, you can usually fill in the blanks."

Mac barreled out of the office, some sort of cape dress flying out behind her. "I'm here to serve." She swept us a bow.

I held my breath until Mac straightened, certain she'd tip over on her head any second.

"Do you happen to have Mr. Butthead's address?" Fab asked.

"As a matter of fact…" Mac whipped out her phone and texted Fab the information. "If you're planning an in-person visit, be careful. He's a sneaky devil and would relish putting another person in the hospital."

"Is he home?" Fab pointed to Joseph's cottage.

"He and Crum are brainstorming ways to raise money to pay his lawyer bills," Mac said with a grin.

"You're going to be held one hundred percent responsible if whatever they're up to turns into another trip to jail," I snapped, wiping the grin off her face.

She jumped around in some kind of ninja stance, leaning forward. "You're no freakin' fun."

"Who's the boss here?"

I wasn't sure how she'd perfected crossing her eyes, but it looked ouchie.

Mac ignored me as though the answer to my

question just wasn't coming to her. She tried to hook her arm through Fab's, but the woman was too fast and stepped away. "You're going to need someone to decipher drunk talk."

"I'll catch up," I yelled to their backs as I shuffled along behind them. I was in a quandary. I didn't want to suck it up and act like the owner of the property. Instead, I wanted to excuse myself and go sit in the car. On the other hand, whatever those two codgers were up to, I wanted to hear it from the men in question.

The cottage door stood open, Fab filling the doorway. "Quiet," she barked.

I almost turned to see if anyone walking by in the street could hear.

I peeked inside as Fab moved to the center of the room, her militant stance letting everyone know she was in charge. Mac plunked down on the couch and put her feet up, ready for the show. On the opposite end sat Svetlana, her calm, cool demeanor never wavering. One of the benefits of being full of air.

Poor Joseph had been run over by a bus, then brought inside and tossed in his favorite chair. His hair stuck up on end, an unlit cigarette wobbling between his lips. Judging by the pile of beer cans that had missed the trash, he was tanked or close to it.

"I don't want to go to jail," he whined, rheumy eyes clouded over.

"You think Madison and I are going to let that

happen?" Fab kicked his foot. "And you..." She glared at Crum, the retired professor still in a 'tude over being ordered to be quiet.

Hands on the arms of his chair, Crum stood up, ramrod stiff and naked. Almost. The too-small tighty-whities were indecent.

"You better not have left your cottage undressed like that." I kept my eyes pinned to his face.

Crum snatched a piece of fabric off the floor. "If you weren't such a puritan, I wouldn't have to tuck this pillow case in the elastic." Which he proceeded to demonstrate.

"Sit back down," Fab ordered. "Whatever is going on here, you're the ringleader, and therefore, you can explain."

"How dare you, missy?" Crum thundered.

"I dare plenty. Now sit, or it's going to get ugly." Fab stared him down. "Start talking."

"Even you should be able to get it through your simplistic mind," Crum peered down his nose, "that Joseph needs cash to keep him out of trouble. But most of the ideas we came up with were questionable. Then..." He preened. "I came up with the idea of selling Svetlana by the hour. It's not like she's going to complain, and I figure we work her around the clock, and in no time, Joseph will have the money he needs."

"That's not going to happen," Fab snapped.

"I second that, and if I hear that Svet's been pimped out even once, you'll both be on the street, your belongings in a trash bag." I dusted my hands together.

"I need to speak to Joseph in private." Fab stared pointedly at Crum.

"You're dismissing me?" Crum's white brows disappeared under the scraggly hair hanging over his forehead.

"If it makes you feel better, I'm leaving with you." I'd already heard the rehash of the so-called fight once.

"It doesn't." He rose and stomped to the door, only prevented from slamming it because I was hot on his heels.

"You're really something," I hissed. "You need to use that high IQ you brag about in less ridiculous ways. Pimping is a felony, and I'm not sure that the fact that the woman in question is a rubber work of art matters."

Crum sputtered, his face crimson. "This will teach me to mind my own business and forget lending a helping hand to a friend." He stormed over to his door and disappeared inside, a faint click signaling that it'd closed.

I scoped out the property as I headed back to the SUV, and all was quiet, which should be a red flag, but it did happen on occasion. I didn't have the key, so I leaned against the hood.

I didn't have long to wait. Soon, Fab strode down the driveway, Mac hustling behind her carrying Svetlana.

"Mac is keeping Svet in the office until I deal

with Butthead," Fab decreed. "I don't trust Joseph not to go ahead with this dicey idea. I also threatened that if I ever got wind that he'd resurrected this scheme, I'd find Svet another soul mate and he'd never see her again."

Once Fab and I were in the car, I asked, "We headed to Butthead's?"

"He's working the closing shift, so we'll have to do it tomorrow."

I groaned. "What's your plan, anyway?"

"A chat about how it would be in his best interest to drop the charges. I may offer up some cash if he's contrite enough."

"Will your Walther be involved?"

"I'll wear it on the outside of my clothes and brag about what a good shot I am. But I promise it won't leave the holster. Just in case he calls the cops after I leave—I don't want him saying I threatened him at gunpoint."

I sagged against the seat, certain we were headed for jail on one charge or another.

"I've got this handled," Fab reassured me. "Don't worry about going. I'll turn this over to Toady."

Judging by the excitement in her eyes as she'd unveiled her plan, I didn't believe her. She was looking forward to scaring the man herself. "You had better not go by yourself, which I can see that you're contemplating. Try and leave me behind—see what happens."

"It's going to be fun. You'll see."

Chapter Fifteen

The next morning, Creole dragged me out of bed, eager to hustle me out the door. "I'm taking you out to breakfast. It's something we never do."

Since he was so excited, I didn't grumble that I wanted to stay home, just the two of us.

He took me to one of my favorite restaurants, The Bakery Café. I claimed our usual table on the sidewalk while he went inside and placed an order.

Only then did I catch sight of GC and Lucas sitting at the opposite end of the walk. Lucas, slightly turned away, hadn't seen Creole and me arrive, but judging by the scowl on GC's face, he had, and his anger with me hadn't abated.

Creole snuck up on me, setting my coffee in front of me. "You look lost in thought."

I flipped off the lid and smelled my coffee. "My favorite." I smiled up at him. "I was worried for a minute that you'd get me decaf."

Instead of laughing, he frowned at me, dragging his chair closer. "You know you can tell my *anything*."

"Have I told you lately that you're the best boyfriend ever?" I ignored his groan. "It seems like there's drama coming from all sides, and I'm certain I've missed a detail or two." I sucked down half my coffee. So much for a ladylike sip. "It's nice to have a lazy day with fiancé extraordinaire."

"Is there something you haven't told me?" he demanded, somewhat playfully.

"You just need to learn to take a compliment." I brushed his lips with mine.

"Do you see this foot?"

"The one you're holding up?" I tossed a glance at the next table. "I'm not the only one wondering what you're doing."

"I'm putting it down." His foot hit the sidewalk. "We've had this conversation once, and we're having it again. This case of yours that's not really a case — give it up. You've done your part."

I puffed out a laugh.

"The dead chick was a felonious hot mess, involved in the get-you-killed kind of activity." He took my cup from my hand, setting it down and clasping my hands in his. "You've gotten the doc jail perks, a first-class lawyer, and arranged bail. He can deal with his own problems from now on."

"Like you said, I've done all I can." Lucas Mark would have his work cut out for him trying to prove Dr. A didn't supply the drugs.

"If he needs a sympathetic ear, have him call me," Creole grouched.

I pressed my hands to his cheeks, kissing him. "Are you extending the same offer to my tenants at The Cottages?"

"*Hell* no!"

I laughed. "There's more on Dr. A's case that I need to share to catch you up. I'd like to do it when Fab and Didier are both present, so can it wait until we're all together?"

"As long as you're not in any danger."

I acknowledged the waiter with a smile as he set down the food, not having to ask whose was whose. Every time I ate there, I ordered the same thing.

"I have a new business idea," I said, changing the subject. "I'd like to invite Fab and Didier to dinner and pitch it to them. I say we flip to see who cooks," I teased.

Ever since she acquired the building, Fab had wanted me to share office space with her and Didier, and now I was ready to take them up on the idea. I was certain that Fab already had her own ideas as to how we'd accomplish that, but then, so did I.

"I'll volunteer. We haven't fired up the barbeque in a while. When you call Fab, tell her that I'll be grilling hamburgers and hot dogs."

"You're so bad." I always loved an opportunity to prank her. "I'd have to tell her *after* she agreed to come, and even then, Didier would have to drag her."

I caught sight of Lucas and GC standing to

leave and hoped they'd cut out to the street and we'd go unnoticed. No such luck.

"Incoming." I nudged Creole's leg.

"I almost didn't see you sitting over here." Lucas held out his hand to Creole and introduced himself. "Lucas Mark."

"The lawyer." Creole shook his hand.

"The man behind him is Brad's neighbor, Alex," I said.

Still annoyed, GC didn't make eye contact.

Lucas turned to me and asked, "Do you mind answering a couple of questions? I'll be quick." He appeared slightly embarrassed by his own pushiness.

"If you don't mind us eating while you talk." Creole's tone relayed that he did mind.

"I'll catch up with you later," Lucas said to his brother, taking a seat.

"Before you leave..." I waved my hand in Alex's direction. He stopped being GC when he turned off the phone. "Lucas, would you tell your brother exactly how it was that you came to be Dr. A's attorney and disabuse him of the notion that I harangued you into taking the case?" I shot GC a dirty look. "Neighbor relations and all."

"Yeah, I called Madison and offered her friend my services." Lucas laughed it off.

"Good to know." GC nodded, then turned and clapped Lucas on the shoulder. "Later."

As much as I wanted to watch his retreat

down the sidewalk to see where the man disappeared to, as he'd done on previous occasions, I instead smiled lamely at Lucas.

"Dr. A is on the court calendar for another bail hearing," Lucas said. "I'm working to get him out, probably on a monitor. I wanted to thank you for the bail referral. They didn't balk at what could be a high amount. Funny thing, I couldn't find a listing for them anywhere."

"That's interesting." I gave him the innocent face I worked on in the mirror from time to time. The only one it didn't fool was Creole.

"Another thank you for the report and video you delivered," Lucas praised. "It surprised me to find it leaning against the door. So much for security."

"I made the first delivery and Fab the second. I followed another owner into the building; probably the same for her." I put my empty cup to my lips to keep from laughing at Creole's smirk.

"The report you delivered was first class. Do you mind giving me the name of the person you used?"

"That guy disconnected his number. They're such an reliable lot."

Creole leaned forward. "Madison has done enough on this case. If you need further recommendations, call the bail bondsman. If it's who I think it is…" He arched a brow at me and I nodded. "He's got all kinds of connections. He'll fix you up...for a price."

The two men sized each other up.

"Got it." Lucas stood. "Thanks again for all your help." He crossed the sidewalk and climbed into a Mercedes.

"Not that I'm planning on needing a good criminal lawyer, but if I did, I'm not sure he'd take my call now."

"Sure he will." Creole snorted. "If not, I'll beat the hell out of him."

Chapter Sixteen

Rather than call Fab and get six hundred questions, I called Didier and invited the couple to dinner, getting an instantaneous yes. Creole and I stopped at the market, where I teased him about how domesticated we looked. He chose a piece of fish to grill, and I loaded up with vegetables and chose an apple tart from their bakery.

"Your idea to have them over for dinner is a good one," Creole said as we walked into the house. We'd stopped at the liquor store, where he'd checked out their newest beer arrivals. "We've all been so busy that we haven't had a lot of time to just hang out."

I still missed all of us living together. "How is the work on my house going? I need to put on my hardhat and go check out the progress." I'd mostly dealt with the loss of my house and wiped away the memory of flames licking through the rooms.

"You name the time and we'll go together."

"I should do it myself, so I can prove to my inner self that I'm stronger than I feel sometimes. It could've been worse." I shuddered. "I confess that I love the added security of living behind gates and no one but family knowing where we live." I'd also taken the advice to get a mail drop. Fab had gone with me, and we signed up at the same time.

"Thanks to Caspian, we have our own private street. If Fab can't talk your family into moving, I wonder what she'll do with the two empty houses."

"Don't underestimate Fab's persuasiveness. I expect to see a For Sale sign at Mother's one of these days. Brad will have to be dragged kicking and screaming." But if the right kind of pressure were applied to my brother, he wouldn't be able to hold out forever.

"I'm happy we already live here and won't be subject to all the drama." He opened the refrigerator, then turned back. "A little wager? The loser signs a personal IOU. Do our neighbors arrive by beach or car?"

"Beach," I called.

"We're here," Fab called from the patio door.

"You saw them coming," Creole growled, his lips turning up. "I'll get my revenge later." He gave me a smacking kiss. "Come in." He waved. "Just getting out the vodka."

"Sore loser." I wagged my finger at him, then squeezed past him to greet Fab and Didier. "We all need to slow down, as Creole reminded me, and do this more often."

Didier joined Creole in the kitchen, and Creole

handed Fab and I our drinks while the guys discussed which beer to drink.

Jazz and Snow woke up, stretching on the large round pillow Creole had found and placed at the foot of the bed. Then they headed straight for Didier and wound through his legs, rubbing their faces on his pants. He opened the refrigerator, pulled out a can, and spooned it onto their plates.

Fab looped her arm through mine and steered me out to the patio. "I assume we're sitting out here?" She nodded at the table I'd set earlier.

We sat in the dark-brown rattan double chaises that Creole had surprised me with after I'd moved in. He had even picked out pillows.

"I got a call today from the insurance company processing Mr. Mott's claim. They want me to come to their office and speak with them about my role in the day's events," Fab said. "I suggested that they ask their questions over the phone, and they said it had to be done in person."

"You can't go by yourself. You need to take a lawyer. Not that you did anything wrong, but we don't want them getting that idea."

"They asked for a number for you, and I gave them GC's disconnected phone number. They didn't call back."

"Neither of us did anything remotely illegal, and we have video proof." I tipped my glass against hers. "You've got two choices—Lucas

Mark or Emerson. I'm thinking ask the latter for a referral."

"Why am I hearing that man's name again today?" Creole grouched from the door, platter in hand as he headed to the barbeque.

"Is this about Fab taking a lawyer to her appointment?" Didier asked, stepping around Creole. "Surprisingly, for once, I'm not the last to know." He updated Creole about the latest in the Mott case. After Fab's visit to Mott's office, the guys had wanted to follow up with a visit of their own, but Fab calmed them down.

Fab set her drink down and flew out of her chair, throwing her arms around his neck and whispering in his ear.

"Stop, you two. We're about to eat dinner." I scrunched up my nose.

"As my assistant, you decide which lawyer to call and set it up," Fab said, a sneaky smile on her face.

I made a show of looking around, as though some other person had miraculously appeared. "That job has yet to be filled, due to your incessant foot-dragging. If you're asking me, then do it nicely."

"Nicely," she blurted with a huge smile.

The guys laughed.

"I'm going to hit up Emerson and see how that goes over." It was an easy choice, since she was so approachable.

The timer went off, and Creole served up

plates of grilled fish and vegetable skewers, setting them on the table. Didier refilled our drinks.

"Did you know the girls have an update for us?" Creole asked Didier. "Can you imagine? There's something they haven't told us."

"Shocking," Didier said sarcastically.

"Shall I flip to see who goes first?" I asked Fab.

"I insist that you be the one."

"Once upon a time…" I started with a half-laugh.

Both men frowned.

"So…at our last visit with Dr. A, he gave Fab permission to search his house, and we did that." I started to tell them what we'd found.

Fab huffed at my lackluster explanation, cut in, and took them on the grand tour. Whatever the guys were expecting, it wasn't this, and they wore their worry openly. She finished by detailing what we found when the boxes were opened at Spoon's.

"Now you know why I don't want you involved," Creole said.

"Case closed. At least on our end." I nudged Fab, who nodded in agreement.

"You better keep your promise," Didier growled at Fab.

To lighten the mood, I said, "You know how, when Mother is up to something nefarious, she invites everyone to dinner? Then waits until everyone has eaten to spill the goods? I think I should pitch my ulterior motive while we're all still enjoying the good food."

Fab clutched her chest. "You tricked us!"

"That's a good one. Something I would do." I mimicked her.

"You could've warned me." Didier punched Creole's shoulder.

"And ruin the proposition? I think not. Besides, it's not like you're dealing with the sneakier of our two women." Creole pulled me to him and kissed the top of my head.

"I'm needing office space; we're out of room here." I waved my arm around. "Since the two of you have offered in the past, I want you to have the first opportunity to share space with me, as long as we can come to terms."

Creole arched a brow. "That's an interesting way to start negotiations on a deal."

Didier smirked over the rim of his beer bottle. "I'm anxious to hear what you've got to say next."

"I hate to turn you down," Fab said without a hint of remorse, "but you rejected our request to join us several times, and as you know, we've knocked out the walls to what would've been your office and incorporated the square footage into our space. So sorry."

"Nonsense. You've still got plenty of room, and that's without disturbing your overly large floor plan. I want the oblong space where you replaced the hideous windows with French doors and have yet to decorate. It's the perfect place for my ten-foot-long desk." Seeing Fab was about to interrupt, I waved her off. "I happen to know that you're only mulling over a few ideas for the space and have yet to decide on anything definite. And since there's no door for privacy, we can talk about a screen for when I have a client. Something modernish. I will forego any suggestion of beachy, except for the large shell that I'll need on display."

"Sold." Didier slapped his hand on the table.

"Hold on a second," Fab hissed. "You're supposed to negotiate. Deal. We can't give in on everything."

"Sure you can," Creole said.

"I second what he said." Didier pointed at Creole.

Fab frowned at both men.

"What do you want out of the deal?" I asked Fab.

Fab was silent overly long. "No flip-flops."

"I won't embarrass either one of you." I winked at her. "I'll keep a couple of changes of clothes and sweats and tennis shoes for when we have a shoot-out to go to."

Both men growled at the same time.

"Just joking." Fab and I exchanged smirks.

"Since Creole cooked, I've got the dishes." Didier stood and picked up plates.

Fab followed him inside, I was certain to supervise his dish-doing skills.

"That was yum, honey." I stood up and leaned down to kiss Creole's cheek, then grabbed the platter and cleaned off the rest of the table.

"I'm impressed with your negotiating skills." Creole relieved me of the platter and headed inside.

Fab came outside a minute later. "I was thrown out."

"You're okay with my deal?"

"It's about time. No furniture shopping without me."

"I found a couple of things already that I'm certain you'll like. I'll email you the links."

The guys were done cleaning the kitchen in short order. Creole flipped on the overhead string of lights that I'd talked him into, which illuminated the deck area with soft lighting, and we settled into the double chaises.

"Now's a good time to bring up what I want," Fab said coyly. "I'm opening new negotiations."

Even Didier was caught off guard.

My partner instinct kicked in, and I was certain I knew what she was about to propose. "So there are more terms?" I asked.

"The office deal is done. This is about you moving in with us. As awesome as this house is, it is small. Besides, we're a proven commodity when it comes to living together."

"Creole and I haven't really talked about it. It's been non-stop these last few weeks."

"I haven't shared my idea with anyone but

Madison, so I'll catch you two up," Creole said. "We agree we could use more square footage, and with that in mind, I pitched building a second story to Madison. Leave this level an open living and dining space, with the upstairs split into two bedrooms with ensuites. I've made a couple of sketches that I can show you later," he said to Didier.

"I suggested a curving staircase in the far corner," I said.

Didier appeared to give the idea some thought. "Do you think you can get the plans approved? Check with Madison's friend in the Code Department and see if you'll be able to get permits."

"It sounds great but still small," Fab said.

I squinted at her.

"Once we decide, we'll be sure to let you know first," Creole said. "If we do decide to remodel, we'll take you up on your offer and stay with you during construction."

"Another thing to think about is doing a complete tear-down—start from scratch," Didier said. "You can't forget the bedrooms you're going to need for the eleven children you're going to have—your half of the soccer team."

Fab rolled her eyes at me.

"I'm not going to start squeezing out my side until you and your wife have produced at least half of your side," I said. That wiped the smirk off Didier's face and got a good laugh.

"Okay Didier, you must have something to share," Creole said.

"As you know, the Boardwalk opening is coming up. I had an idea about that the other day, and Fab laughed so hard, she had to sit down." Didier glared at her, although he was clearly amused.

"Good time to share, buddy," Creole said. "We'll take a vote."

"Why do I get the feeling that this has something to do with me?" I mused. "You, best friend, didn't tell me." I pouted at Fab.

"It's not that bad. You know how you always say that if you can do anything to help..." Didier half-laughed.

I groaned.

"On opening day, load up your tenants from The Cottages and bring them over. Your step-daddy has a school bus connection, I believe."

"Have you lost your mind?" I came close to shrieking. "If you think they'll boost the bottom line, you're mistaken. The only thing they'll part with their cash for is liquor. Then they'll get drunk and pass out, and it will be my fault."

"Blame it on Mac," Fab suggested.

"That's a great idea." Creole grinned. "Load up the bus with your crazy tenants and their like-minded friends, and party on."

The guys laughed their heads off.

"You're in so much trouble," I told Creole.

"Looking forward to it." He winked.

Chapter Seventeen

"Anyone home?" Fab yelled.

"If you're standing in the kitchen, you're lucky that Creole isn't here," I yelled back. I'd brought my laptop out to the patio and was sitting under the umbrella. No better backdrop than the waves lapping on the shore.

"Strawberry lemonade?" Fab stood in the doorway.

"Yum!" I held my hand out. "How did your meeting go?"

Fab settled in the chaise next to me.

It had been a few days since I contacted Emerson for a legal referral. After questioning me about the case, she eagerly told me, "I'll do it." I forwarded her the information and the video I'd shot. She contacted the insurance company and informed them that Fab had legal representation.

"Love Emerson." Fab sipped her iced coffee. "She told me before we walked into the meeting to keep my answers short, which I already knew, but it was a good reminder. At first, I thought they were looking to make a case against me, and then the questions changed to what I knew about Mr. Mott."

"It probably was always about Mott. If you turned out to be the guilty one, you'd do jail time and be on a payment plan after your release — they'd still be on the hook to their client for whatever they didn't recover."

"When the direction of the conversation changed to more personal questions about Mott, Emerson whispered for me to stick to what I knew and avoid any speculation."

"That's a good one to remember." I slurped up the last of the lemonade.

Fab shook her head. "I explained what I was hired to do and that I didn't get much accomplished before security arrived, and Emerson offered up the video as corroboration. I found it interesting that they'd run a check on me and asked why Mott would use a new company and virtual unknown for a security consultation. I was honestly at a loss for an answer; I wasn't about to disclose that perhaps it was because he was an associate of my dead ex-husband. Instead, I told them I didn't have the foggiest idea, which I'm not sure they bought."

"Let's hope that's the last we hear of Mott."

"Emerson's certain that's the end of it, and a time-waster as far as she was concerned. They knew everything I told them ahead of time from the police report. Emerson also told me to run future cases needing representation by her, and if it's something she can't handle, she'll refer us on. She knew of Lucas Mark and was impressed that you got him to represent Dr. A."

"Did you tell her that I'm often seeking legal representation for tenants at The Cottages for bicycling drunk and other such felonies?"

"I did, and she laughed. Once your brother finds out, he'll talk her out of taking our calls. When I dropped her off, I promised a girl lunch."

"We'll invite Mother and Mila," I said.

Fab laughed. "Mila ensures we'll be on our best behavior—no getting drunk or looking for trouble." Her phone rang, and she picked it up off the table, scowling at the screen. Fab answered without saying anything, which didn't bother the other person, whose masculine voice could be heard coming over the line although the words were indistinguishable. "We're on our way," she said before hanging up.

"Was that Didier?"

Fab shook her head.

"I'm not going anywhere with you." I grabbed my laptop, putting it back on my lap. "I put every call on speakerphone, and you can't return the favor? I get second-hand? I don't think so."

"It was Toady." Fab blew out a frustrated sigh. "You have to go; he's got a problem on the stolen-cars job for Brick and says he needs to speak to you. He's at the office, waiting on us."

I scowled at her.

"That's fine." She held her phone up. "I'm

going to call him back and tell him to come to your house."

"I'm calling your bluff. When Creole and Didier find out the Toad was here, you'll be toast."

"You're going." Fab stood, gathered up the trash, and flounced into the house.

I counted to ten, then got up and went inside. "I'm not going in my bathing suit." I disappeared into the closet, coming out in a jean skirt and t-shirt. I slid into a pair of flat sandals, throwing a pair of tennis shoes in my bag, just in case. "Wonder how I can help on Brick's case," I said, following Fab out to the SUV.

"Toady didn't say, and since it's your time he's wasting, I didn't bother to ask." Fab pulled through the security gates. "I needed to go by the office anyway."

I stared out the window as she got on the main highway and took the first exit, curving around down to the docks. We passed Spoon's garage, and as usual, it was hard to tell if they were open for business, but most likely they were, since it was afternoon.

Fab hit a button, and the security gate for her office property opened. She pulled in and waited until it closed before driving into the warehouse garage. There were two warehouses on the property, and thus far, only one had been utilized for office space. The other stood empty.

Expecting to see Toady's beater truck, it

surprised me when he climbed out of a classic baby blue Mercedes. The man never failed to amaze. He'd traded in his ratty jeans and beater shirt for bathing suit trunks, a tropical shirt, and cowboy boots.

"Ladies." He tipped his black straw cowboy hat. "Thank you for being so impromptu." He blew Fab an air kiss as she skirted past him and up the stairs.

The two-story warehouse had storage and parking on the bottom. Once you hopped the thirty-plus steps straight up to the second floor, you came to where Fab and Didier had their offices. The dark and dingy space had been transformed into an open area, Fab's desk on one side and Didier's on the other. He utilized more of the space, with the addition of a drawing board and a long conference table. The differentiation between the spaces was that Fab's was all white, while Didier managed a splash of several colors.

I peered around the corner into the space I wanted, expecting to see it already furnished with the pieces picked out, which wouldn't have surprised me. But it was as I last saw it— awaiting furniture delivery. I'd ordered a couple of accessories that I planned to surprise Fab with once I had them in place.

"Water, drink?" I asked, maneuvering around the island into the strip kitchen.

"I'll have me a Coke." Toady held up his hand.

Fab nodded, which I deciphered as meaning water.

I retrieved the drinks and joined the two at Fab's desk. Toady had pulled up a chair for me and pushed it into the corner where I liked to sit. Like Fab, I had an unobstructed view of the room. I set Toady's can on a glass coaster with a look that said, 'Don't leave a watermark on Fab's desk.' I sat back, tempted to put my feet up, since Fab didn't like it, but refrained. "You've got my full attention." I nodded at Toady.

"Not sure how much you know about the case I'm working on for Frenchie." Toady downed his soda, stomping on the can and getting up to toss it in the trash and fetch another.

"A bunch of classic cars were stolen; that's about it."

"I found them."

His declaration surprised Fab. "Where are they?" she asked.

"That's the problem. Jimmy Spoon's got them in his possession. For a couple of reasons—one being I don't want to get on the man's bad side— I was thinking that, since you're related, you could facilitate the transfer."

"Spoon v Brick—I'd put my money on Spoon being the honest one in this equation. One thing I know for sure, is that Spoon isn't a thief, so there's something else going on here." I certainly hadn't been expecting this news. "I'll talk to him, but it will cost your client money — my intervention services aren't free — and there will be no mention of my name or Spoon's." I looked forward to hearing what was going on.

"Can you do it now?" Toady tapped his watch. "I'll wait."

"That depends." I pulled my phone out of my pocket and called Spoon. When he answered, I said, "If you're with Mother, I have car trouble...some kind of clicking noise."

"If I'm not?" he chuckled.

"I'd like to chat about the hauler of classic cars that's in your possession."

The silence was deafening. "I'm in my office."

"It so happens, I'm at my new office. I'll be there in under five." I hung up.

"No way you're leaving here without me." Fab stood. "Make yourself at home...sort of. Don't make a mess," she told Toady.

"I'll wait in my car. Too clean in here for me. Seriously, this place could use a little dust. It would make normal people feel comfortable." Toady's boots clomped across the floor.

That would never happen. Cook's wife had a cleaning service, which Fab used. They did an excellent job.

The three of us raced down the steps, and at the bottom, Fab said, "I left the door unlocked in case you want another soda or it gets too hot." Once inside the car, she added, "I don't want him peeing on my property but didn't have the nerve to say it." She punched my arm. "Why are you laughing?"

"I'm surprised he hasn't asked to live at The Cottages. He'd fit right in."

Once again, Billy had the gate rolled back when we got there, and Fab pulled in and parked.

"You on gate duty?" I asked as I got out.

"If it's about you two, I'm the man." He grinned. "Heard you were asking about..." He nodded to a twenty-foot-long aluminum storage shed at the far end of the property. "It doesn't shock me that you might be the ones with the missing piece of the puzzle."

Fab and I headed to Spoon's office and seated ourselves in front of his desk.

"You want to go first?" I said cheekily and got a grunt in response. *Guess not.* "This is what I know. Brick Famosa—"

Spoon growled at the mention of the man's name.

"—normally hires Fab, but this time went behind her back and called Toady directly. Brick thinks Fab is preggo and therefore unavailable." Spoon's brow shot up. "Long story, but she's not. So today..." I relayed that Toady knew Spoon had possession of the cars and wanted to make a deal.

"Just so you know, I had nothing to do with the acquisition," Spoon huffed. "One of my guys did a favor for a friend, who said that he needed a place to park the cars, as he'd arrived early for an auction and had no place to store them. It was supposed to only be a couple of days. My guy confessed to taking money on the side and I knew why he needed the cash, so I let it pass but told him there better not be a next time because he smelled illegal just coming down the block."

"The friend is Brick's driver?" I asked.

"Didn't know that ass was involved until just now. Dude didn't show up when he said, and he hasn't turned up anywhere. No missing person report, and even more interesting, no police report on the cars." Spoon flicked through a pad and turned it in our direction. "The cars are registered to a holding company."

"Sounds like something Brick would put together," Fab said. "It wouldn't be the first, or twentieth, job where a client steals from him and he refuses to involve law enforcement."

Spoon's fist pounded the desk. "I don't want either of you any more involved than you already are." He jabbed his finger at me. "Don't you roll your eyes at me."

"What do you want in return for giving them up?" Fab asked.

"I want the red Corvette with the black ragtop at a damn good price. But only if the driver shows back up alive. If not... I'm calling the cops. Another stipulation: Toady handles the negotiations and he doesn't reveal names. Yours, mine, anyone's. Or I'll give the old alligator a taste of his own methods and feed him to his neighbors. Along with Brick, if he's stupid enough to show up here or send some lackey."

"In the spirit of full disclosure, I'm charging a fee for my services in facilitating getting the parties together. I'm charging double, so I can split it with Fab," I said. "I can deal with Toady."

"Send him to me so I can make sure we're copacetic," Spoon barked. "That way, there's no mistaking the terms.

"Have time now?" Fab asked. "He's down the street."

"You do that, and then you should leave. You already know too much." Spoon leaned back in his chair, eyeing the two of us.

Yay! I was ready to go home and sit out on the deck.

We passed Toady on the way out of the driveway. He clearly wasn't happy to see us bailing on him.

"The one to worry about is Toady. Brick isn't going to take this well, with all the anonymity that's being insisted on."

I sighed. "You tell him not to put himself in any kind of danger."

Chapter Eighteen

A 'Grand Opening' banner hung across the road as Creole turned the corner. Parking had become an issue as soon as we found out that the building code required a certain number of spaces be made available for customers. Didier had approached the owners of the lots across the street, which would make an ideal location. One man told him to "blow off," as did the rest of them, only in politer terms. Seeing an opportunity, they'd paved their land themselves and turned it into metered parking, storage for boats, and a mini-RV park. It went together so fast that it was the consensus of our group that they had stellar connections and the plans were already in the works. Hats off to the old guys; they took the idea and ran with it.

"What's the update on the car case?" Didier asked.

"That criminal, Brick, is lucky they weren't ditched on my property. I'd have turned it all over to the cops and let him explain why he didn't file a police report," Creole grouched.

"Last I heard, Toady commented that it takes

'intestinal fortitude' to be the go-between for Brick and Spoon," I said.

A big sigh came from the back seat. Fab had declined to drive, instead wanting to snuggle up with Didier. "Brick is hopping mad about the fee for finding the whereabouts of said cars and has haggled on the price for the Vette, wanting top dollar. Toady finally told Brick, 'You got two days to wind this up or the cars disappear.'"

"It shocks me that Spoon would threaten that. I'd think he'd enjoy having Brick twisting on a string," I said.

"Toady made it up. I can't say exactly what he said—no way to clean it up—but he's over the case and ready for the next one," Fab said. "Here's a good tidbit—Brick threatened to have Toady killed. He thinks that Toady is somehow behind the 'screwing' he's taking."

"I bet Toady didn't take that well."

"Told Brick to go ahead and went on to describe in precise terms how Brick would die if he did, and that he had associates who would definitely make it happen, all the while cleaning his nails with a switchblade," Fab said. "I called Brick and told him nothing better happen to Toady. He blew it off, saying Toady's a sissy and doesn't have a sense of humor."

I harrumphed. "Call Toady a sissy to his face and you'll end up choking on your teeth."

Creole parked in one of the five reserved spaces. Even though the stores and stands didn't open for another fifteen minutes, the lot across the street was at least half-full and many more had found on-street parking and were headed to the Boardwalk.

"Creole and I need to do a quick walk-thru," Didier said. "You two are welcome to come along," he said to Fab and me.

"I think we should go be good customers and check out the stores." I tugged on Fab's arm.

Fab and I split off from the guys and went in the opposite direction. We walked around the area and were impressed that, although it wasn't Disneyland, Didier had done a good job of melding retail, greasy food wagons, one restaurant completed and more to come, and a small boutique hotel. Most of the rides were open, with the exception of the roller coaster. The only one that interested me was the train that ran around the entire property, pointing out the various attractions at a slow speed.

I had lobbied for an arcade room and a fortuneteller machine that spit out your future on a card. I'd had a hand in selecting the machines, which was one of the most fun projects to give input on. If I'd had my way, I would've doubled the space and filled it with more machines. The guys had laughed, but I told them I'd expect apologies for their lack of faith when they started hauling in the money with no room to expand.

Fab tripped and bumped into me, which caught me off guard. The old woman who'd rammed into her apologized and, at the same time, grabbed the strap of Fab's purse, yanking it from her shoulder.

"Come back here," Fab shouted in a tone that showed she expected obedience. She whistled — a sharp, high pitch — then took off after the woman.

I was right behind her, wondering what the heck just happened. And on the other hand, impressed. The old girl was pretty agile for her advanced years.

Fab caught up with the woman, gripped the back of her jacket, and whirled her around, retrieving her purse. The woman ended up in a heap on the cement. Fab reached down and hauled her to her feet.

I huffed up behind her. "She's old," I reminded Fab so she wouldn't clock her a good one.

The old woman glared. In her scrabble to get up, her wig and hat fell to the ground, revealing a boy who appeared to be about fourteen in a floral dress and fishnet stockings.

Fab twisted her hand in the front of the dress, dragging him face-to-face. "You're going to jail."

Panic filled the kid's face and he kicked out, connecting with Fab's leg, which gave him the opportunity to turn and dash down the wharf. He cut around two children fighting with light sticks, weaved and jogged, took a turn around a pretzel-making machine, and disappeared.

"That kid needs a different gig; he's terrible at

purse snatching," Fab said, out of breath. "I think his original intent was to help himself to my wallet, but I felt the nudge against my purse. Once caught, he went for Plan B."

"What just happened?" Didier asked as he and Creole ran up. "Saw you about to get into a fistfight with a little old lady."

"I suppose you two showed up to come to the other woman's aid?" I asked with a hint of sarcasm.

Fab hit the highlights and looked ready to beat the two men for their amused expressions.

"Let's hope he doesn't come back." Didier shook his head. "Pickpocketing won't be good for business."

"Did I hear pickpocket?" Kevin insinuated himself into the conversation. I couldn't believe I hadn't noticed him in his full police regalia. "Doesn't surprise me you two are involved."

Creole growled at him. "Too bad you're in uniform."

"Is that a threat?"

"Take it however you want," Creole snapped back.

I stuck my hand in Creole's back pocket and gave him a soft pinch. "What can we do for you, officer?"

"Description would be helpful. We've had a couple of reports about missing wallets, and it would help to get this person locked up. The sooner the better."

"A woman, seventyish, black hair, ugly hat and dress," I said.

Everyone turned and stared, since I'd just told them it was a kid.

Kevin looked like he wanted to pursue that, but just then, he got called away. "If you think of anything else, you know where to find me."

Once he was out of earshot, I said, "It was a *kid*."

Creole turned my face to his. "You're not going to go looking for him and bring him home, are you? He's not a cat; he's a criminal. And what if he hurts someone?"

"I hear you."

"Don't think I won't notice if some kid shows up, sleeping on the patio."

I shot a pleading look at Fab.

"Let's try out the rides," she suggested, and the four of us turned in that direction.

"While the rest of you are trying to keep from barfing, I'll test the miniature golf," I said.

"I'm going with my girl," Creole said. "Let's meet at the new restaurant for lunch."

Chapter Nineteen

The next morning, I swung through the drive-thru of Fab's and my favorite coffee joint and ordered both our favorites, racing back to Fab's before it got cold. I pulled into her driveway and, because I wasn't about to relinquish the wheel, laid on the horn. Another perk of not having neighbors.

The front door flew open and the irate French woman yelled, "What the devil?"

I was happy that I'd had the foresight to roll down the window so I wouldn't miss a word.

"Hurry up and get in," I yelled back. "Change your clothes. That getup isn't acceptable for going out in public." It amused me that she was still in her silk nightgown and not the least bit pulled together.

"Whatever you're up to, I'm not going." She turned and went back inside, slamming the door so hard, I was surprised the glass didn't break. I laid on the horn again.

The door opened and she stood there, irritation radiating off her face, arms crossed.

I leaned across the seat and held up the coffee cup. "Come get it before it gets cold."

She flounced over and grabbed it out of my hand. "You honk again, and I'll shoot your tires out."

"Then hustle," I yelled at her retreating back.

To my surprise, she was back in under fifteen minutes in jeans and tennis shoes — she'd obviously taken notice of what I had on when she poked her head inside the SUV. It also surprised me that she didn't utter one complaint about not driving.

"Where are we going?" Fab pushed the seat back.

"It's a surprise," I said with a lame smile.

"A perfect morning with my husband and now this." Fab turned her head to stare out the window.

I hit the gas and lurched forward, cutting off another car and receiving a blaring horn and sign language from the disgruntled driver. I returned the gesture, knowing the man couldn't see it through the tinted windows. Checking the rearview mirror, I cut diagonally across the road to make the exit and squealed around the corner.

"Are you drunk?" Fad asked, aghast.

"I thought you'd enjoy my driving more if I emulated yours — all fast and scary." I smiled sweetly.

She straightened in her seat and glared out the windshield.

I turned onto the street that ran along the backside of the Boardwalk and pulled into one of the reserved spaces.

"Nothing's open. Too early. Except the coffee house, and we just had a cup," Fab said.

"I have a hunch I want to follow up on. Our young purse-snatcher disappeared off to the far end and wasn't seen again, even though security was on alert. I think he's around here somewhere."

"So you find him, then what? You do remember your promise to Creole not more than a few hours ago? If not, I can remind you."

"I don't have any intention of bringing him home." I got out and shoved the door closed.

"I'm telling you now that splitting hairs isn't going to keep you out of trouble, and I should know, since I've done that more times than I'm about to admit."

"And how does that end for you? Jungle sex?"

"Not always." Fab sulked, as though recalling those times.

"If we find him, I only want to chat. Don't scuff him up any; puberty's a hard age."

Fab sniffed.

"We're going to retrace his getaway. He cut around the pretzel machine and wasn't seen again. I checked a couple of the construction blueprints last night, and the direction he chose leads to a dead end, the only exit over a chain-link fence. That would've been caught on a security camera."

"So you think he's back here somewhere?" Fab scanned the area.

"Or he made a run for it this morning, but there'd still be a risk of getting caught if he chose the fence route."

"Isn't that him?" Fab pointed to a lone figure making his way across the other side of the construction area, not in any particular hurry. "He appeared over by the tractors."

"This is where your expertise comes in." I nudged my friend.

"He just spotted us." Fab cupped her hands around her mouth and yelled, "We just want to talk. No cops."

He did a double take and took off running.

"I'm not chasing him," Fab said. "If he's at all familiar with this area, he'll be long gone before I can catch up." She tugged on my hand. "We'll check out the direction he came from."

Instead of walking the perimeter of the area currently under construction, we cut diagonally across the dirt lot and around pieces of big machinery over to where a skip loader was parked under an aluminum carport. As we strolled, we surveyed every inch of the area, looking for a hiding place...or possibly a living space.

Fab inspected every crevice of the covered area. She climbed a ladder and continued her inspection.

I whooshed out a sigh of relief when she came

back down. We had one last corner to check out. I'd given up on what I'd thought was a good idea.

Fab peered inside the door of an open shed, giving it a cursory glance since there was nowhere to hide in it. She circled the small building, sticking her head back around the side. "Got him." She disappeared, and when we came back face to face, she had a sleeping bag in one hand and a duffel bag in the other, a jacket slung over her shoulder. "He's clever. He slanted a couple of boards over his sleeping space. If I'd looked in from the opposite end, I'd have missed it." Fab dropped everything on the ground, stepping back.

"No sign of anyone else?"

Fab shook her head. "We've been over every inch of this place, and there's no sign of another person."

"I'd like to buy your phone, triple value, but you have to hand it over right now. In return, in addition to the cash, you get my phone until you replace yours." I held out my hand.

"Before I agree to anything, you need to spell out what you're up to now."

"I'm going to take his belongings and leave behind his jacket, the phone on top with my face smiling at him. All he has to do is push call. I'm going to leave an enticing note, food, cash, and reiterate no cops."

"If it doesn't work?" Fab came close to rolling

her eyes.

"Then I'll feel like the worst human ever. What's Plan B? Wait until the middle of the night and corral him and drag him out of here?"

Fab pulled her phone out and exchanged it for mine. "It's got a tracking chip that I'll activate, so one way or another, we track this kid down. Because… I know you won't give up." She jerked me around the front of the shed. "We've got company."

Workers were starting to show up, one of whom I recognized. "Hey, Riley."

He turned. "Madison," he said, clearly surprised.

I approached. "You got something for me to write on and a pen, by chance?"

"On that metal table over there." He pointed.

"You pretend you never saw me and my friend, and you'll get a free meal and drinks at Jake's. Tell the bartender, 'Madison discount.'"

"Never saw you." He grinned.

On the work table, I found a sticky note pad and a thick pencil that had been shaved to a point. I wrote a message and, just in case, wrote my number at the bottom. I flicked through Fab's phone, found my number, and stuck the note to the screen, then handed it back to Fab. "Put this on top of his jacket where you know he'll see it."

Fab grabbed the jacket and walked off holding it with two fingers, disappearing around the shed.

I retrieved the two bags, holding them away from me. They smelled rank, the scent difficult to define. On par with dead-body stench…almost.

"He's been on his own for a while," Fab said as we met up and backtracked across the lot.

"You've got my phone, so you're going to be the one he makes contact with. Your job is to seal the deal for a sit-down. No threats, got it?"

"The kid is *underage*." Fab shook her head. "You know that old saying about good deeds and punishment? Not turning him in to authorities could land you in big trouble."

"If he agrees to the meeting, then I'll call Emerson and find out what the options are."

Fab rubbed her forehead.

"Let me guess. Another premonition? Just spit it out…without actual spit."

"The line of people that are going to be irked at you is growing."

"There's a sympathy factor here, and don't think I won't exploit it." I opened the passenger side of the SUV when Fab popped the locks and slid in.

Chapter Twenty

Mac's text saying Joseph's court date was in two days was a reminder that Fab hadn't followed through on her offer to broker a settlement between him and Ronnie Butthead Bardwell. Good thing Mac had included his real name in the text.

I relayed the message to Fab. "We're running out of time."

"What's the address?"

"It's the pay-by-the-week motel on the main drag." Mac had sent a picture and labeled it, *Verified*.

You're the best, I texted back.

"The hovel that's set back from the street?" Fab eased back into traffic.

"That would be the place." I gave her a big smile. "He has the unit next to the laundry room."

"Might as well get this over with."

"I feel it important that we go over the plan of action, since I'm assuming that I'm sidekick on this job." I ignored her raised eyebrow. "There's to be no bodily harm, at least to me anyway. Butthead is also a 'no,' but only because I don't want to land in the pokey."

"It can be hard to prove if there are no visible marks." Her blue eyes turned towards me in amusement as she turned into the property and parked.

We got out and cut around to the side gate of the garish, turquoise, u-shaped, one-story building, skirting the pool in the center, which was in bad need of re-plastering. Several doors were held open with old vinyl kitchen chairs, the sounds from various televisions blaring out. Walking by the office, I gave it a cursory glance, noting that the lone woman on the phone wasn't paying any attention.

"Do you know where you're going?" I asked as Fab barreled through the courtyard.

Two men hung over the balcony, whistling. One's cigarette dropped from his lips, landing not far from Fab's foot, and she stomped on it, which garnered laughter.

Fab came to a halt in front of Ronnie's room. The blinds were wide open, which made it easy for her to peer inside. No one was in sight. She knocked.

"Looking for Ronnie?" one of the men yelled. "He moved."

Fab nodded up at him. "Got a forwarding?"

"He lit out of here after two dudes showed up, one practically beating the door down. Packed up and blew out of here...poof." He threw up his arms.

Fab waved. "Let's get the heck out of here." She jerked on my arm.

Two drunks lumbered in the gate, blocking the exit as they hurled obscenities at one another, taking swipes at each other but no real punches. Since there was no way around the pair, I motioned to Fab that we go through the rear gate, which stood open, and circle around through the alley to the car.

After giving my exit plan a quick scan, she yelled at the men, "Knock it off."

The two men untangled themselves and turned on Fab.

The burlier of the two stepped forward, arms outstretched. "Bring it on, sister."

"We don't want any trouble." Fab pointed to the parking lot. "Just want to get back to the car."

A laugh gurgled out of him, releasing a torrent of spit, and he rushed her.

Fab grabbed his arm, whirled him around, put her foot to his backside, and sent him flying into the pool. The other man leaned over the side, pointing at his friend and laughing. Fab's foot connected with his butt, and he landed not far from the first, dowsing his friend, who'd surfaced and was coughing.

They both resurfaced and dog paddled to the steps, spitting out water the whole way and cursing our ancestors.

"If either of you gets out of the pool before we clear the driveway, I'll shoot." Fab pulled up her top, showing she could back up her threat. She motioned to me, and we hustled back to the car, just short of a run.

"That was fun." Fab jumped behind the wheel.

I slid into the passenger seat and clapped. "Just once, I want to be the butt-flinger."

"Practice on Creole."

We both laughed as she sent gravel flying, exiting to the street.

Fab slowed for a jaywalker, who gave her a wave. "We're going to pay our informant a little visit and show her what we think of bogus information."

"If Mac quits because of you, you're working the office until I find a *suitable* replacement."

Fab knew it was an idle threat. The Cottages would be a ghost town under her control.

Rounding the corner, we saw Mac's truck sitting in her driveway. Fab parked sideways, blocking her in, and laid on the horn.

"Stop that." I slapped her hand. "Unless you want everyone at The Cottages spilling out to see what's going on." I checked the property across the street and sighed with relief that all was quiet. I wanted it to stay that way.

Mac clomped out on her porch, sporting croc heels — as if the regular shoes weren't ugly enough, they'd expanded the line. She slammed the door behind her, hands on her hips. "What?" she growled.

I leaned my head out the window and waved.

"It was her," I shouted and pointed over my shoulder.

"I had no doubt." Mac jumped off the steps, executing a brief bow.

Fab got out and met Mac at the front of the SUV. I lagged behind, but still had a ringside seat.

"You gave us bogus Butthead information. He moved. You know what that means?" Fab shook her head with a snarl. "I'm taking back all my IOUs. I'm debt-free." She preened.

Not fair!

"Baloney-ass." Mac jumped forward, hands on her hips. "It was accurate at the time. Not my fault you lollygagged."

The two women engaged in a stare-down. I knew they were both highly amused with themselves, since their body language was more sassy than threatening.

"Any idea where he is now?" Fab cracked her knuckles.

"Ladies do not indulge in such vulgar mannerisms," I said, mimicking her snooty tone while smiling at Mac.

"Let's see." Mac tapped her cheek. "I get my IOUs back, and you get the info."

I bit my lip to keep from laughing.

"Deal," Fab snapped.

"You hear that, boss?" Mac asked.

"I sure did."

Mac pirouetted in her workout leggings,

ending in a convoluted jump that had me holding my breath. "Cooks at Custer's." She made a flipping motion. "Gets off..." She checked her watch. "...in an hour."

"Eww." Fab made a retching noise. "They serve food?"

"They serve a few finger munchies," Mac informed us. The renowned hole-in-the-wall bar did a brisk business selling screwtop beer and wine. "Butthead doesn't work very hard, thereby giving him time to rest up so he can beat up old men."

"I'm going to let him know that I'm the nice one. And if I have to, I'll hand him over to my sidekick. So beware." Fab growled like an animal with a sore paw, then laughed at her antics. "Because of you, I felt it imperative to raise my game on the sound effects. I'm acing it, don't you think?"

"Why can't you just let me be the star of something?" I sighed melodramatically.

"Aww." Fab patted my arm. "You shine. In your own sweet way."

"You're lucky I can't puke on demand."

Mac laughed at us. "One more thing." She pulled out her phone and punched some buttons. "I sent a pic of his car, so you'll know once you hit the parking lot if you're wasting your time."

Fab clapped her hand on the hood. "That better not happen a second time," she said and got behind the wheel.

"Ignore her," I said.

"Already did." Mac laughed.

I got in and waved out the window.

Fab weaved her way through traffic down the main street, pulling into a tree-filled lot that shared the driveway with Custer's. The colorfully painted, graffiti-covered, some would say artsy, building hadn't changed much since the last time we were there. Custer had added a broken-down picnic table or two and a handful of *objets d'art*. If you chose to sit outside in one of the termite-eaten chairs and leaned down, you might catch a glimpse of the ocean through the underground garage of the new condo building across the street.

"There's the car in the pic Mac sent." I held up my phone, comparing image and car.

Fab cruised slowly down the alley before turning around and going back, parking under a tree away from customer parking.

"I've got a plan." Fab flexed her muscles. "I'll meet Butthead at the back door and shove him in the trash area for our one-on-one. As I recall, it's only a few feet from the back door. You're lookout." She nudged me. "I don't want anyone stumbling onto the chance of a fight breaking out. The bar would clear, along with some of the buildings that back up to the alley. If that happens, it won't take long for the cops to show."

I kicked off my flip-flops and shoved my feet

into my tennis shoes. "No guns," I said before getting out.

We couldn't have timed it more perfectly. We'd just reached the back exit when Butthead shoved open the door, more intent on looking at his phone than the two women within arm's reach. "His name's Ronnie," I whispered to Fab.

"Hello, Ronnie." Fab held up her PI badge.

"That's bullshit." He sneered. "I see you've been to the party store. I oughta have you arrested for impersonating a cop."

Not a good start.

Fab grabbed his arm, jerked him around, and sent him flying into the side of the dumpster. "I'm here for a friendly chat. Nod if you understand." When he didn't respond quickly enough for her, she tightened her hold on his arm and twisted it higher up into the middle of his back.

Ronnie nodded, proving he wasn't a complete moron.

"You beat up an old man and then pressed charges," Fab hissed in his ear. "And you...not so much as a smudge of dirt on you."

"What do you want?" he squeaked.

"Drop the charges. Tell the prosecutor you were mistaken and walk away." Fab jerked his arm until he yelped.

"Joseph owes me money," Ronnie whined. "He knew damn well what would happen when he didn't show up with Dilly's cash and only a lame excuse. Now my ass is on the line."

Dilwen Nash, aka Dilly? How the heck did Joseph get involved with that man?

"How much does he owe?" Fab tightened her hold.

"Five large," Ronnie squeaked.

I shrugged at Fab's questioning expression when she looked over her shoulder. I had no clue how Joseph got involved with a loan shark but intended to find out. Ignorance wasn't any excuse. He'd lived in the area long enough to know that Dilwen Nash was bad news.

Fab pushed Butthead up against the fence. "Here's the deal, and it's the only offer you're getting. I'll check out your story, and in the meantime, you know what you've got to do. If Joseph goes to jail, you won't get a cent and you'll live life on the run."

"I guess."

"Heed my warning." Fab banged his head against the dumpster and he yelped. "We're not going to have a second conversation. Instead of me, you'll meet my associate. He brags about enjoying the screams of people fed to alligators." Fab upped the growling noise, directing it into his ear.

Ronnie shook his head.

"Do you understand?" Fab shook him. He mumbled something that satisfied Fab. "Drop. The. Charges. I'd better hear tomorrow, latest the next day, that you've contacted the prosecutor and informed their office of your intent."

"Yesss, I will," he squealed.

Fab shoved his face into the corner. "Count to twenty-five before leaving. Stay away from Joseph's place; the owner shoots trespassers." She gave him one last hard shake.

Fab motioned to me, and we ran back to the SUV and jumped inside. "Scoot down. I don't want him getting any pictures or our tag number."

"Do you think he'll drop the charges?" I asked, peering over the dashboard.

"He peed himself." Fab scrunched up her nose. "I'm thinking he doesn't want another visit and has enough problems with Dilly on his trail. Another thing in our favor, since Dilly's involved, Butthead won't be stupid enough to involve the cops."

"What the heck has Joseph gotten himself into?"

"I'm guessing that Butthead, who works for Dilly, somehow ended up with Joseph on his crew and something went south. Let's hope Joseph wasn't stupid enough to steal from Dilwen, because even if he did pay him back, there would be painful retribution. Likely case, Joseph ends up dead."

Chapter Twenty-One

Fab rocketed into the driveway of The Cottages, pulling up in front of Joseph's cottage, which she'd never done before. Which was probably the reason Mac came running out of the office. That the woman ever managed to get any work done…was a neat trick.

Fab jumped out and beat on Joseph's door with her fist, getting no answer. I rounded the bumper and asked Mac, "Where is he?"

"Sleeping by the pool. What's he done now?"

I breezed by her without answering, walking around the corner and into the pool area. "Why is the gate open? Find the offender and revoke their pool privileges. All I need is for the deputy living here to cite me for unsafe conditions." I stood at the end of Joseph's chaise and kicked his slipper-clad foot.

He cracked open one eyelid. "Go away. I'm tired." Closing his eye, he let out a loud snort. If he thought it came across as a snore, he was wrong, and he wasn't a cat. No human went back to sleep that fast.

I leaned over. "We'd like to have a chat with

you about your relationship with a loan shark. Do you want to do it out here?"

He covered his face with his arms. "One of the conditions of working for him was keeping my trap shut. If he finds out I talked, it will happen sooner and be more painful."

I knotted my hand in his shirt and jerked him into an upright position.

"You're wrinkling my shirt," he whined, brushing his hands down the front of the already wrinkled and stained excuse for clothing.

"I want to know why you're into Dilwen Nash for 5K." I sat in the chair Mac pushed up behind me, Fab on one side, Mac on the other.

Mac gasped. "You're stupider than I thought."

"Five thousand!" Joseph screeched. "You're wrong. It's five hundred." He tilted back in a half-faint.

"That's some steep interest," Fab said.

"Listen," Joseph whined. "It had nothing to do with gambling. It was a legit job. I hired on as a runner, picking up money and delivering it to Ronnie. I'd only worked for him for a couple of days, and the other night, after making my pickup, I got held up and robbed. Reported it right away to Ronnie, who showed up here and hauled me over for a face-to-face with Dilly." He winced. "Dilly told me I let him down and had to make it up by recovering the money, no excuses."

"Good ol' Dilly have any tips for how you

were supposed to accomplish that feat?" Fab asked.

"I just remember agreeing to everything he said, hoping to get out in one piece. And I did, sort of. One of his muscle jerked me up by the scruff of my neck and pitched me out the door. A bunch of scrapes is better than death." He brushed off his sleeves.

"That's one of the down sides of being in the collection business," I said with no sympathy. "How did you hook up with Dilly?"

"I can't say." He continued to moan and groan.

Fab jumped up, jerking him upright and getting in his face. "Oh yes, you will. We've done a lot to help you, and you're not going to brush us off with your lameness. Try it, and I'll stick my shoe up your backside," she said ferociously. "Then you'll owe me because I'll have to trash them." She let him go, and he landed back on the chaise with a bounce.

Mac giggled and held out her foot, smiling at her Crocs. "You could use one of mine."

"Name?" I yelled, loud enough that I expected a guest, or Crum on the other side of the pool, to stick their head out the bathroom window.

"Crum got me the job." He whimpered. "He knew I needed the money. The first night was easy-peasy, and the next, I got shoved face down and the money snatched out of my pocket."

"How many of these pick-up jobs did you go

out on?" I asked.

Joseph held up two fingers.

I rolled my eyes and got even more irked when I leaned back and there was no headrest. "I smell a setup." I looked at Fab.

Fab sniffed the air. "Me too."

"Tell Crum to get out here," I said to Mac.

"Do I have to be polite?"

"No, you do not. If he hesitates in the slightest, shoot off one of his toes. The more he dawdles, the more toes come off. You run out, oops, there goes his foot."

Joseph winced.

Fab shot me a thumbs up.

Mac drew her imaginary six-shooters and emptied the barrels, complete with sound effects, walked to Crum's cottage, and beat on the door with her fist.

If I hadn't been watching her antics, I'd have thought she had a sledgehammer in her hand. When she didn't get an answer, she walked over to the bathroom window and shoved it up, yelling, "Get out here, old man."

The front door blew open. "What do you want, you odious woman?" Crum sneered down his nose, his tall frame ramrod stiff.

"I'm certain that was a compliment, since you know how much I've done for you." Mac bared her teeth. "After all, you still live here."

"Over here." I waved.

Crum clunked over, his bare feet slapping the cement.

"If you'd like to sit down, get your own chair," I said as he shuffled from one foot to the other.

Crum turned up his nose, then turned and walked down the steps into the pool. "Can we make this quick?" He glared at Joseph, which didn't do him any good, since the man had his eyes covered with his arm.

The upside to prancing around in underwear was Crum was always appropriately dressed for an impromptu swim.

"Why would you get Joseph involved with the likes of Dilly?" I asked.

"You're really working for Dilwen Nash?" Fab asked. "Do you know why he thinks Dilly sounds better?"

"You poke around in the man's personal business; I'm not going to," Crum said snootily.

I whistled, which wasn't very impressive, but all heads turned toward me. "Let's get back on track. You remember the question?"

"Job's easy. Money's good." *Duh* implied in Crum's tone.

"Have you ever had any trouble on the job?" Fab asked.

"A couple of attempted attacks; fought them off with my expandable baton." Crum whipped his arms around. "Got in a good whack or two. No police reports."

"Why would you get Joseph involved in

something that sounds like a setup?" I demanded.

"Look." Crum thrust his chest out, throwing himself off balance and off the step into the water. "I'm no nursemaid," he blustered. "I suppose... I could've loaned Joseph the money, but he didn't ask."

"You had other options," I said, my tone letting him know how stupid I thought he was, which had him bristling. "Did you know that Dilly now wants 5K?"

"Now that's impressive." Crum whistled. "I'd put in a good word with Dilly, but the man scares me."

"It didn't occur to you that the runners get set up, and that, thus far, you've lucked out?" I demanded. "You can bet your number is about to be punched. Your stick isn't going to hold off thieves for long."

"I can protect myself." Crum crossed his arms and stuck out his chin.

"Not if it's a bullet," I snarked back. "If you plan to keep your job with Dilly, then you need to move, and I mean tomorrow. Eventually, big trouble is going to show up on my property, and it'll once again be crawling with cops looking to make arrests for felonious activities. It's not happening."

Crum sputtered, which had to be a first.

"Tomorrow. And that goes for you too." I nudged Joseph's foot. "You need to make better friends. Ones that, at least, won't suggest you take a job that could get you killed." I stood and motioned to Fab and Mac, heading to the gate. "I'm going to see if I have a connection who has an in with Dilly. I can't promise anything."

Joseph squeezed his eyes closed. "Thanks," he mumbled.

"Nothing better happen to Joseph before the Dilly situation can be resolved. If it does, I'm holding you responsible," I said to Crum.

The man grouched as he climbed out of the water, shaking like a dog.

As usual, I had to train my eyes on his face.

"If you have a trick up your sleeve to calm this situation down, I suggest you use it and fast," Fab lectured Crum, matching him glare for glare. She had to know neither man was listening. In fact, they'd doubtless concoct some witless idea to get them in even deeper.

"Sorry to leave this party, but Fab and I have another appointment." I wasn't. In fact, it was all I could do not to run back to the car, yelling, *Call me when you've fixed your own problems.* "You're in charge of this nuthouse," I told Mac as the three of us left the pool area. "Try to keep the inmates contained." I veered over to the office to grab a burner phone.

Mac waited outside the door. "At least Joseph's not in any legal trouble for making the collections."

I didn't roll my eyes but came close. "I'm

hoping you're going to use your powers of persuasion to keep everything on an even keel. I'm serious about the two of them moving if I can't come up with a way to defuse the situation. It's going to be your job to boot them to the curb."

Mac crossed her arms over her ample chest and glared. "Just so you know, I'll be calling in sick."

"Don't make me drag you out of your sickbed." I left Mac muttering to herself as Fab and I crossed the street.

Fab gunned the engine down the block.

Chapter Twenty-Two

"You have a contact to deal with Dilly?" Fab asked as she maneuvered through traffic.

I wasn't sure if it was the look on her face, the tone of her voice, or both, but she clearly thought I'd lost my mind.

"Not on speed dial..." My phone rang, saving me from coming up with a Plan B. My own face beamed back at me. I answered and hit the speaker button.

"Want my stuff back," a male voice demanded.

"I was only using it as leverage to get you to call," I said. "Upfront: No cops or anything like that. This is a friendly chat. I'd like to help."

"Do-gooder chick." He snorted.

"I'm thinking you might want to be a little nicer, even if it pains you," I snapped back.

"This better not be some trick." He hesitated. "Meet round the back of the Stop-n-Go and hand my stuff over. Bring the cops, and you'll be wasting your time. I won't be there."

"We can be there in a few." I looked to Fab for confirmation, and she nodded. "I'll be the one with the red bushy hair. It's not nice to laugh. It's not my fault. I blame the humidity."

"That's girl problems I don't want to hear about." He hung up.

"You got the purse thief to agree to a meeting. What next?" Fab pulled a u-turn.

"Considering his age, any help I could give him would be against the law. I'm fairly certain that legally, I should be involving the cops, who'd turn him over to Social Services. I can't see him agreeing to those options, since he's been on the street for who knows how long. I can throw money at him, but that won't solve his problem long term."

We drove in silence to the gas station. Fab circled the lot, and for once, there were no loiterers trying to look like they had something better to do than sit on the planter and drink out of a paper bag. Two men had staked out the bus bench, and neither looked remotely like the teenager we were meeting. Fab parked next to the air hose with an "out of order" sign on it. I got out and opened the lift gate so the kid's personal belongings were visible.

We didn't have to wait long. He strolled around the corner from the neighborhood and cut across the driveway. "Nice ride." He whistled and started to reach for the bag that held his belongings.

"Not so fast." I stepped in front of him. "I'm holding your stuff for ransom until we have a chat."

"I don't have any money." He turned the pockets of his worn jeans inside out.

"You suck at purse snatching; you might want to get a new career," I suggested. "One that's legal. Unless the jail hotel appeals to you."

"It was only my second time, and I didn't enjoy it much." He gave Fab a once-over. "What, she doesn't speak?"

"You're lucky she hasn't shot you for stealing her purse."

"Over-reaction much? I didn't get the wallet, which is what I wanted. Would've left the rest at one of the carts." Despite his bravado, he flushed with embarrassment.

"A real Boy Scout." Fab matched his snotty tone.

"Those were the days." A flash of sadness crossed his face.

"How did you get on the path to the state prison at such an early age?" I asked.

"You think I'm a kid?" He half-laughed with no amusement. "I get it now. Your plan is to rescue the poor homeless child, and then what? Adopt me? I'm twenty, not eleven or whatever you thought. Good genes. Does that make your do-gooder heart feel better?"

"You want your life to change?" Fab challenged. "Suck up your bad attitude. Play your cards right, and this woman will get you a place to sleep tonight, and it won't be on dirty concrete."

"That's a bad idea," he admonished. "Helping people. You could get hurt. I just want my stuff back and, to be honest, a few bucks for food."

I walked back to the passenger side and dug in my purse, pulling out a business card, cash, and the burner phone, and handed them to him. "I want my phone back." I wiggled my fingers, and he dug it out of his jeans and handed it over. "You want a job and can refrain from stealing from your employer, call me. And I can probably find you a place to live…for a short time, anyway."

"Thanks for this." He shoved the money and phone in his pocket. "I'll think about the offer." He walked over to the SUV, reached inside, and grabbed his stuff.

"Do you have a name?" Fab asked.

"Kid works for me." He waved and crossed the highway, headed in the opposite direction from the Boardwalk.

"You can't help someone who doesn't want it," Fab said. "Be proud of yourself. Most wouldn't offer."

"Let's hit up Spoon's," I said once we got in the car. "He can probably help with the Dilly situation. Surely, he'd be happy just to get his money back. He has to know it was stolen by muggers and wasn't a case of Joseph being stupid enough to steal from him."

"Joseph is old enough to handle his own problems."

"If I do nothing," I said in exasperation, "trouble will hit The Cottages in a big way, and that's not good for business. Besides, I happen to like the old coot and don't want him to end up dead." I stared out the window. "He's thus far laughed in the face of the death sentence his doctors dealt him, and the end is not going to be murder, if I can do anything about it. How would I deal with the guilt if I looked the other way?"

"Sometimes you can't save people from their stupid mistakes, and it's not your fault they end up paying a consequence that's steep." Fab swung into the driveway of JS Auto Body and parked in front.

"Wonder if Spoon's even here. Normally, he'd have the door open already."

"If he's not, let's toss his office. We might not get another chance."

"That's such a bad idea, I'm ignoring you." I crossed the few steps to the door and knocked. A buzzer sounded, and I turned the knob. To my surprise, not only was Spoon at his desk but Mila was sitting on top, talking to an open book.

Fab scooted by me and traded exaggerated air kisses with Mila, which had her laughing.

I looked around. "Where's Mother?"

"Hair appointment." He leaned back in his chair, scrutinizing the two of us.

"So, she'll let you take Mila to work and risk her getting greasy, but she sabotages my and

Fab's scheduled shopping day with her." I held out my hands to Mila and pulled her up on her feet. "Stomp through Grandpa's paperwork over here to me."

"That's not ladylike," Spoon said in an annoyed tone, although his lips quirked.

I held her while she jumped up and down a few times, and then I sat and settled her on my lap.

"Look what I've got, Mila." Fab held up a coloring book that had been left on the couch with some crayons.

"Outright bribery." I glared at Fab and set Mila on the floor. She ran over to Fab, who hoisted her into her lap, and the two lay back against the cushions.

"Mila doesn't need to be in the middle of a business discussion," Fab admonished.

Good point. I smiled at the two of them choosing colors, then turned to Spoon. "Do you have any connections to solve a problem with Dilwen Nash?"

Spoon whistled through his teeth.

I went on to explain what'd happened.

"I'll handle it," he said gruffly. "The sooner you get this matter settled, the better. Dilly operates on a *very* short fuse. Money unaccounted for, no matter how it happened, he deals with in an expedient fashion. He does it to save face, and he wouldn't want word to get out that he went soft on anyone who screwed up;

their fault or not."

"I owe you times two." I held up my fingers. "A favor from Joseph would be useless."

Spoon's attention turned to the security screen. "We're not going to be able to hide this one from your Mother. She just drove up." He stood up. "Just tame down the story." He strode over, opened the door, and enveloped Mother in a hug.

"What are you two doing here?" Mother asked suspiciously, bending down to kiss my cheek. She walked over and kissed Fab's cheek, then held her arms out to Mila.

"I don't think so." Fab maneuvered Mila out of her reach. "You constantly encroach on our time with Mila, and we're having fun, aren't we?" Mila giggled and nodded.

"Come sit down over here and settle for my company." I patted the chair next to me.

"I love all of you, and you darn well know it." Mother flounced into the chair.

I reached over and one-arm-hugged her.

"You never answered my question. What are you involving my husband in?"

I told her about Joseph, and that the problem needed to be solved; the sooner the better.

"You need to re-think your brother's idea of turning that property over to a reputable management company and not dismiss it out of hand. The other option is selling it, but I'm certain you won't entertain that idea. It's been one hellish incident after another." Mother sighed in frustration.

"I'll think about your suggestion." *Thought about it and no.*

Mother sniffed. "I know my children, and what I said never even paused as it went through your ears."

"Okay, ladies." Spoon hated drama.

I turned to Spoon. "I have an acquaintance that needs a job, something so he can get off the street and re-start his life."

"Who is this person?" Mother asked, her tone laced with suspicion.

I ignored her and made my plea to Spoon. "It used to be your mission to give people a helping hand, but if that's no longer the case, I'll figure something else out."

Spoon had quite the checkered past, and he'd done an excellent job of cleaning up his act and becoming a pillar of the community; a scary one for those that thought they could take advantage. It was well known that he often gave deserving men a second chance at turning their lives around.

"Send the man around. Not making any promises."

Mother checked her watch. "I've got to go and take Mila home. Brad will be waiting."

"Fab and I can take her." When I didn't get a response, I walked over and nuzzled Mila's nose, then walked out into the garage.

It didn't take me long to spot Billy. We locked eyes, and I headed in his direction. He met me halfway.

"What's annoying you?" Billy cracked his knuckles. "I can take care of it."

"It's my mother."

He laughed. "She's quite the handful. But she makes the boss very happy."

And he her, for which I'm happy. I gave him the Kid story from purse snatch to that afternoon, leaving him with a handful of cash and wishing I could do more.

"He's going to call again," Billy reassured me. "It may take some time, but he'll run out of money, and it won't take him long to figure out he enjoys regular meals. You send him to me. Give him the address. No giving him a ride. He needs to make the effort."

"You're the best. Anything at all I can do... Free meal at Jake's anytime."

"That's not necessary. It won't kill me to do someone a decent turn."

"Hurry it up," Fab yelled across the garage. Two men working on a Mercedes they had jacked in the air turned, *Who me?* on their faces.

"Thanks."

Knowing my aversion to handshakes, Billy held out his knuckles.

I crossed the garage and went through the door, which Fab held open. No Mila made the office seem quieter. "Let me know what happens with Dilly." I hugged Spoon. "As for the other, Billy's going to help me out."

"Billy's a good choice and closer in age to your young criminal. He's apt to listen to Billy more than me." He hugged me and then turned my face towards him. "I'll talk to your mother about lightening up in her new role as grandmother."

"It's Gammi now," I reminded him. "No worries about that either. Even though she annoys me at times, I know she worries about all our safety."

"Just know, no matter what, I'm always available to help you out," Spoon said firmly.

I waved and followed Fab to the car, filling her in on my conversation with Billy.

"Are you going to tell Creole?"

"Of course."

* * *

As it turned out, we didn't have to wait long to hear back from the Kid; my phone rang while we were on our way home from Spoon's.

"I'm going to take you up on your offer of a job," he said. "I'm not cut out to be a criminal, especially if there's another option."

"I found someone who's willing to take a chance on you. His name's Billy. Do with the opportunity what you will."

"You've got me on speaker; who's listening in?" he demanded.

"The woman whose purse you nearly stole," I answered. "How did you know?"

"I'm not stupid," he huffed.

Fab and I exchanged amused smiles.

"Here's the deal..." I went on to tell him he had to contact Billy on his own. "I'll text you the info. Billy's a good guy, so don't take advantage of him because I'm telling you now that he won't take kindly to it and you won't like his response." I hung up and texted him the information. "I'm happy he called because never hearing from him again would have plagued me."

"Wish we knew more about him," Fab mused.

"Isn't wanting to know the answer to every question what gets us into trouble?" I asked.

"I wasn't that way until I met you. Some days, I miss my old 'I couldn't care less' attitude."

"No worries." I flashed a sad face. "Your old persona isn't far from the surface."

Chapter Twenty-Three

It had been a quiet week, during which I waited to hear news on several fronts. Right after my morning coffee, my phone pinged with a message: *Pecan roll?*

Heck yes, I typed back.

Then open your door. Beachside.

I almost tripped rolling off the couch, catching myself to stand and race to the patio doors. Fab was climbing the stairs in her bathrobe.

Fab laughed at my "what the heck" expression and thrust out a pink bakery box.

"You're the bestest, besty, best," I squealed, still annoyed after Creole suggested that I cook breakfast; his next helpful hint being boxed cereal when I whined, "What am I going to eat?"

"Some mornings, there isn't enough coffee in the world for you." Fab took off her robe, tossing it on the chair. "Just wanted to see your face." She was decked out in workout gear.

I walked into the kitchen. "I've got your favorite coffee." I pulled a Turkish blend out of the cupboard and made her coffee and mine while she got out plates.

"This feels like the old days." I handed her a

mug and slid onto the stool next to her.

The phone rang, and Dr. A's face popped up. I showed it to Fab.

"Guess that means he's out...or someone stole his phone." Fab took a long drink of her coffee without making a face. I'd followed the directions the man at the coffee bar gave me. Guess it worked.

"I'm out on bail and leg monitor," Dr. A said when I answered. "I want to thank you for all your help and finding me a good lawyer."

"I'm happy you were sprung, and as for the lawyer, luck played a role." I hoped his release would be more than temporary.

"I'll be keeping a low profile, but if there's anything I can do for you, you know where to find me."

"If you'd like, Fab and I can stop by tomorrow for a friendly chat. Update you on a few things we found out about your girlfriend."

He groaned. "I imagine it's not good, considering the amount of drugs found in that damn briefcase. I know it looks damning, but I had nothing to do with it showing up in my house."

"I just thought you might want to know. You can share with your lawyer or not, depending on the plan for the case."

"My lawyer's warned me not to talk about the case, but I want to hear everything you've found out."

"Tomorrow, then."

"What about the money and drugs?" Fab asked after I ended the call.

"I vote for honesty and telling him everything. He says the drugs aren't his, so he shouldn't be too perturbed that they've been disposed of."

"Somebody might be." Fab refilled her mug. "Can't help thinking there's another party involved, or more than one."

"As for the money, that's his decision. He won't be able to go and spend it all in one place. That would be a red flag. If the cops had found it, it would've been another piece of damning evidence, especially if he couldn't document where it came from. Finding a large stash of cash seems like a dream come true until you figure out that spending it could land you in cuffs."

Fab finished her coffee, and I pointed to the pot if she wanted another refill. "To spend in any quantity, you'd have to deal with the shiftiest of people, and that brings on a different set of problems. Living your life with one eye over your shoulder isn't living."

"Next time, I'll remind you that you don't need to know everything, as much as you won't like hearing it." I caught Fab's smirk, even though she tried to hide it.

"That's rich, coming from you."

"Wasn't I the one to suggest some manner of restraint in our actions?" I asked. "At least, I thought it was me, since I'm usually the sensible one."

"Is that your way of saying I'm the bad influence?" Fab asked in an amused tone.

"In a word — yes." I picked up the bakery box and turned it upside down. "No extras?"

Fab laughed at my antics. "Almost forgot." She put her tennis shoe-clad feet on a stool, and I shoved them off. "Ran into Emerson at the bakery this morning. Red-rimmed eyes, pale, the little makeup she does wear only making her appear paler, and she's lost a few pounds. Not a hint of her usual smile. I got out of her that she lost a big case and the children wound up in the custody of the wrong parent, in her opinion. She hadn't slept since the decision."

"I imagine that's a drawback to the legal profession. You lose when you think you should've won, and it probably isn't easy to shake off." My phone rang again. "Busy phone," I said, answering it. "Hey, bro."

"Where are you?"

"Home. Watching Fab do dishes." I shoved her hip with my foot.

"Favor? I have a last-minute meeting, and Mother had an appointment. Would you watch Mila for about an hour? Mother can pick her up at your house."

"You're in luck. Both of us have a free schedule today. Bring her over."

"See you in a few."

"This is payback day," I said conspiratorially to Fab. "Go get dressed for shopping. We're going to party with Mila. As long as we don't stay here, Mother will never find us."

"I predict..." Fab paused melodramatically. "Your mother is going to have a flippin' fit and so will Brad, because he *hates* getting caught between the two of you."

I jumped up and ran for the bathroom. "Hurry," I yelled before closing the door.

When Brad buzzed the gate, I went out to meet him, having gotten dressed and ready in record time. He'd pulled up in front and had the back door open, where he was unhooking Mila from her car seat.

Mila waved frantically. "Auntie," she yelled.

Brad handed her to me clad in an empire-waisted floral dress and red tennis shoes and slipped a bag over my shoulder.

"Thanks for calling me. We're going to have so much fun." I kissed Mila's nose.

"You're the best." He kissed his daughter and got back in his SUV, waving as he turned around.

Mila and I waved back until he drove out of sight.

Fab roared up in her Porsche, also gotten ready in record time, her hand out the window, waving as Brad drove away. "It's Mila," she yelled. She and Mila squealed at one another, and Mila waved back.

Fab parked next to the SUV and got out. I handed Mila to her. "I'm going to get my stuff and be right back out." By the time I got back, Fab had Mila strapped into the back of the SUV. Everyone in the family had a car seat, courtesy of Mother.

"Half-hour." Fab pointed to the dash clock. "Your phone is going to blow up with Granny calls."

"First stop, Party Palace. Mila wants a cape for her princess outfit." I looked over the seat, and she was stretched back, her eyes fluttering. She hadn't quite given up to sleep.

Fab stuck to the speed limit and took the direct route to the strip mall, avoiding alleys and shortcuts. She'd barely got the engine shut off when my phone rang. She grabbed it from the cup holder and smirked after looking at the screen. "Mila and I will meet you inside." She handed the phone to me.

"Coward," I said, staring at Mother's face on the screen. I got out of the SUV and went around to Fab's side and out of Mila's earshot. It stopped ringing.

Fab could win a contest for getting a kid out of a car seat and disappearing inside a store in record time.

My phone rang again. "Hi, Mother."

"I got done with my appointment early. I'm at your house to pick up Mila."

"There was this window of opportunity that

presented itself, and I suggested to Fab that we take Mila shopping. I'm certain you don't mind. It makes up for our last missed outing."

The silence was deafening. A loud sigh crossed the line. "Spoon warned me this would happen. Well, not exactly this, but something like it. I need to learn to share, but I just don't want to."

"I love you." I laughed softly.

"Please don't make me feel any worse. Promise me that you won't take her to any shoot-outs or similar activities."

"You know we save that kind of fun for you," I said in a faux huff.

"Which we haven't done in a while." Her pout could be heard through the phone line.

"Thank you for being so understanding."

"It's hard for me. So you need to behave."

I blew her a kiss before she hung up.

Next time, I admonished myself. *I won't be so sneaky. Sure.*

I went inside the store and found the two of them in line for the cashier, having decided on a mermaid outfit. "You couldn't slow it down a little?" I arched my brow.

"They were out of stock on most of the princess accessories, and this outfit caught Mila's eye." Fab tweaked her cheeks and got a smile. "It's all the sparkles. There was only one, and another woman wanted it."

"Is the woman okay?" I looked around.

Fab laughed. "I didn't commit bodily harm, but I cut her off...politely."

I picked Mila up out of the cart and swung her around. "What next?"

"My turn to choose. We need to stop at the shoe store. Mila needs mermaid shoes." Fab wiggled her tennis shoe-clad foot.

"I'm fairly certain finding fin-shaped shoes will be impossible."

"Don't suck the fun out of our shopping excursion. You should be happy that you're still in one piece after confessing to your double-cross."

"Mother took it well." I chuckled.

"Uh-oh."

As we left the store, angry voices floated down the sidewalk. Two men stood arguing on the patio of a restaurant at the far end.

Fab stood at the front bumper and watched as I put Mila in her car seat. "That's Lucas Mark, exchanging a difference of opinion with that thug in a suit."

"Get in the car. We're not getting involved." I forced myself not to look until I got in the car and could check them out through the tinted windows. The two had already lowered their voices, but the conversation was no less intense if body language counted.

The dark-haired man with Lucas turned slightly. His dark beard was neatly trimmed, the black designer suit fit his frame, and his tie matched. He looked the part of a respectable businessman, but something about his demeanor said that wasn't an apt description. In contrast, Lucas was decked out in tropical attire — shorts and a short-sleeved shirt.

Fab drove by the two men slowly. "The suited one has a shoulder holster."

"Let's get out of here."

"You recognize that man?" Fab asked, pulling into traffic without another glance.

"He looks vaguely familiar. Let's hope we never run into him. What I find interesting is that Lucas hasn't been in town long, and he's already hooking up with thugs." I stared out the window. "Where are we going after the shoe store?"

"It's a surprise for you and Mila. And before you start, you're going to like it."

I flipped down the visor and used the mirror to look at Mila in the back. "You ready for more fun?" I asked her.

"Yes," she cheered. I rolled down the window, as we were about to drive by Jake's, and thrust my head out, a huge sandwich board out front catching my interest. "Turn around." I pulled my head back inside. "Twinkie Princesses has two half-naked middle-aged men in front, hoses in hand, spraying each other with water. What the heck is going on?"

Fab made an eww face. "It's almost lunch time." She tapped the dashboard. "We're not eating any food from the food truck."

I horked up an imaginary furball. My cats would be proud.

Mila laughed and clapped from the back, then mimicked the sound.

Fab and I exchanged 'oh no' looks.

"That will teach me," I said quietly. "Mila loves her sound effects."

"I wonder who she gets that from?"

"Maybe the Princesses are finally going to open for business. You'd think they might have given me a heads-up."

"You serious?" Fab pulled into a parking space. "I can't wait to meet these two. Have you ever met them?"

"No, and seriously, I like the relationship we have. They send their rent check on time, and their continuously closed shabby chic roach coach gives the property a little more character and zero customer issues."

"Wonder what's up today?"

"I'm about to find out." I climbed out, leaving Fab to free Mila as I headed around the front of the coach. "Hey," I yelled, hoping not to get my clothing soaked.

Both men turned.

"You came to the right place to get your buggy washed," the shorter of the two paunchy specimens boasted. It was by only an inch but was probably a bone of contention when they'd been drinking.

The other stepped back, craned his neck around the back of the coach, and whistled. "Nice ride."

The sandwich board again caught my eye. Who knew they were built with drink holders in each side? They were currently holding cans of beer. On the board, it said, "Git your car wased" in chalk. So much for spelling. "Bucks go to poor folks."

"What the hell is going on?" I said, out of patience with a pair of locals working some sort of scam. "Make it snappy or I'm calling the cops."

"We got legal rights." The spokesman reached over, grabbed a beer, downed it, and smashed the can under his flip-flop-clad heel. The other man reached inside a cooler leaned up against the side of the coach and tossed him another. "We got hired to give Princesses a good wash. It was my brainchild to offer car washes on the side."

"You mean bilk people for a fraudulent cause?" I returned his dumfounded stare with a glare.

"Don't get your shorts in a wad; we ain't made jack yet."

"Why is the cleanliness of this..." I pointed. "...suddenly an issue."

"It's getting sold, and the owner wants top dollar."

Good luck to that. "I suggest that you finish the

job you were hired to do and stop wasting water."

"We're done. We're waiting on someone who wants to see the inside, and then we're leaving."

The other one had already started to clean up, rolling up the hose and tucking it under his arm, trying to drag the sign in the other until it clattered to the ground. He snorted in disgust and stomped over to a pickup truck.

A grey testosterone-size truck gunned its engine into the driveway, coming to a stop.

"We'll be out of here in a few," the man said to me as he hustled over to the latest arrival, his partner meeting him.

The driver hung out the window. The conversation that took place was short.

I noticed that there was an exchange of envelopes and slid my phone out of my pocket, snapping a picture of the license plate. I'd text it to Doodad, who'd put a stop to illegal transactions in the parking lot. And another text to myself as a reminder to contact the Princesses.

"We're leaving," the man told me after the truck left.

The men each grabbed a side of the sign and dragged it over to the back door of the coach, heaving it inside and locking up. They jumped in the truck and backed out, not making eye contact.

Not sure what I was looking for, I walked around the coach, but nothing seemed out of the ordinary. I made a mental note that when I contacted the owners, to tell them that the location wasn't included in the sale, stressing that the coach would have to be moved. The last thing I needed was for someone to think it was an ideal location for illegal activity.

Mila's laughter had me hustling over to join the twosome. Nothing was going to spoil our outing. Mila stood on the bench outside the lighthouse, clapping her hands as Fab locked up, having finished a tour.

At Fab's raised brow, I said, "I'll tell you about it later."

"You ready for this?" Fab asked.

Not sure what she was talking about, I was hesitant to answer.

Fab scooped up Mila and, before putting her back in the car, asked her, "What do you want to eat for lunch?"

"Ticos." Mila air-boxed.

"From where?" Fab asked.

Mila pointed to Jake's. "U Hen."

Mother was going to kill us.

Chapter Twenty-Four

"It doesn't take much to entertain Mila," Fab said, glancing in the rearview mirror at the little girl sleeping in the back. She'd zonked out not long after leaving Jake's.

"I'm not going to feel guilty for taking her to Jake's, since she knew everyone in the kitchen. It obviously wasn't the first time she'd met them." The crew was as happy to see her as she them. "Did you notice that she got better service than we did?"

"She loves her ticos." Fab half-laughed. "We should give her a bubble bath before returning her to Madeline, so she won't detect any food crumbs."

Fab handed me my ringing phone.

"Hey, babe," I said.

"In case you didn't know, family dinner at your mother's," Creole said.

"Is Brad coming?"

"Since you kidnapped his daughter, he'd probably like to get her back." He laughed.

"How about you stop by the house, pick up Mila, and take her to Mother's?"

"No chance." He laughed again. "See you later."

I hadn't been paying attention to where Fab was driving, but it only moderately surprised me when she pulled up in front of her door.

"We're going to try out that new bed of yours." Fab hopped out. "When Mila wakes up from her nap, we can jump on the mattress." She whisked Mila out of her car seat and into the house without disturbing her sleep.

I lagged behind and made a call. "You busy tonight?" I asked when the call connected.

"What's up?"

"My mother is tossing a family dinner, and I'm setting you up as my brother's date."

From the laughter that rolled through the phone, I knew she was amused by the idea. "I don't know what you're up to, but I'm in."

"It's set for six, so wait at least fifteen minutes before knocking."

She laughed and hung up.

Fab had left the door open, and I walked in and glanced around, then walked down the long hallway to *my* bedroom. All the doors I passed were closed; Fab had told me they hadn't started to decorate those rooms yet. Fab and Mila lay in the middle of the big bed. I kicked off my shoes and sat on the side, then rolled over and over, meeting them in the middle.

"I'll be back." Fab got up and disappeared into the hall.

I curled up against Mila and was soon fast asleep. I didn't wake up until I heard Fab reading out loud about Goldilocks being a thief, having stolen the bears' cookies, and how they weren't happy with Locks. I rolled over and peered out from under my lashes. "You're not going to get away with your plot recreation for much longer."

Fab ignored me and added voices to the characters, which Mila mimicked.

"I'm going to go home and shower and change, then come back and get you two," I said.

"You can do that here. There's clothes for both you and Mila in the closet."

"I'm going to repay you one of these days and go shopping for you." I tried to swallow the laughter.

"Oh, please don't. You'd pick out something really ugly just to watch me struggle to say, 'How cute.'" Fab pointed me to the bathroom. "I'll get Mila and myself ready." She rolled Mila down the bed.

I watched the two of them skip out of the room hand in hand.

* * *

The three of us rode the elevator up to Mother's condo on the third floor, Mila twirling in front of the mirror, dressed in a white net skirt, pink sleeveless top, and sparkly sandals. I copied her and whirled around in my short-sleeved black t-shirt dress, which I'd found in the closet. Fab had also hung a bag of silver necklaces and a matching bracelet over the hangar and left black slip-on sandals on the floor. For herself, she'd chosen a black tunic dress and paired it with gold jewelry.

We got out, and Mila raced to the door and knocked.

Spoon opened the door with a slightly disgruntled look that disappeared as soon as he spotted Mila. He scooped her up and swung her around in a circle while she squealed before setting her back on the floor. "You're cutting it close."

"We're here," I said.

Fab and I followed him inside.

Mother waved from the far end of the living room, appearing happy to see us, which had me sighing with relief.

"Liam couldn't be here tonight; he's got a paper due tomorrow," Mother said. "I overnighted him a big box of cookies."

"He's going to love that," I said.

Brad stepped out of the kitchen and held out his arms to Mila, who was happy to see her dad. He hoisted her up and gave her loud kisses and tickled her. "Kidnapping?"

I gave him a disgruntled look. "It's called possession and comes with rights under the law. Besides, I wasn't in the mood to relinquish my niece, and I've been a good sport about all the times my plans were railroaded."

"Yes, you have." Brad enveloped me in a three-way hug.

I heard the voices of Creole and Didier coming from the kitchen, where they'd been commandeered to lend their cooking talents. Ever since Mother married Spoon, he did most of the cooking, and she rarely dragged out the to-go menus. All the men in the family were good cooks.

"So what did the three of you do today?" Mother leaned over and kissed Mila.

"After the liquor store robbery, there was that shoot-out on the Overseas, and then we needed a nap," I said.

A hush fell over the room.

Creole poked his head out of the kitchen to roll his eyes. Behind him, Didier smirked.

"Really! That was what you came up with?" Brad said.

"It was the best I could do at the last minute. Should've prepared."

The doorbell rang.

I waved my arms. "Let me get that. I have a surprise." I started toward the door, then paused and turned. "Would anyone like a hint?"

Everyone in the room groaned, except Fab, who stared accusingly since I hadn't shared.

I cupped my hands around my mouth and whispered, "I fixed Brad up." I winked at him.

"I'm going to…" Brad started forward.

"No language or threats." I shook my finger. "Mila in the house," I said with a shocked face, rushing to the door.

"Have you lost your mind?" Brad asked, now right behind me. "What about Emerson?"

"I don't see her, do you?"

I opened the door before the woman on the other side could think I wasn't going to answer and poked my head out. "You're going to be a big surprise." I pushed it wider to let her in.

It took a minute for Brad to pull himself together. A big grin lit up his face, and he took a couple of steps in Emerson's direction but was cut off.

"Em," Mila yelled and ran down the hall.

Emerson picked her up and swung her around, whispering something in her ear. Brad caught them both up in a hug.

I'd shut the door and snuck around them. Creole came out of the kitchen and wrapped his arms around me. "That was nice of you."

"I thought inviting Emerson would make Brad happy, and it would give him a kick to include her more, since she fits in so well."

"Your mother said earlier that she'd learned a new trick from you today but didn't say what it was. I'll admit it made me nervous."

I looked around his shoulder. "I'll have to keep an eye on her."

* * *

After dinner, everyone gathered back in the living room. Fab, Emerson, and I cleared away the dishes and stacked them in the dishwasher. Fab, as usual, reveled in telling the two of us what to do.

"I'm happy that you're a good sport and came to dinner," I said to Emerson.

"It wasn't the least bit awkward, and I'll admit, I did worry that it would be. Brad was happy that I came." She smiled.

Once we finished in the kitchen, we joined the others in the living room.

"Did you learn anything today?" Mother asked Mila, who sat next to her on Brad's lap.

Mila gave her a big smile and imitated coughing up a hairball.

All eyes turned to me.

My cheeks flamed. "Good job." I clapped.

Brad looked at me like I'd lost my mind.

I cut him off, certain that whatever he was about to say, I wouldn't like. "Okay Pot—or Kettle, since we never could decide who was who—we stopped at Jake's today because there was activity outside the roach coach and I wanted to find out what was happening." The whole time, I leveled the evil eye at Brad.

"You couldn't just call your tenant?" Mother asked.

"Anyway...it took all of a minute to get my answer, and since it was lunchtime, Fab asked Mila what she wanted for lunch, never in a *million* years expecting her to point to Jake's and request ticos." I squinted at Mother's snort. I'd have to have a talk with her later; if I wasn't allowed to make unladylike noises, then neither was she. "And who else does she want to see? U-Hen. I've owned that dive for how long? Even I don't get to call Cook by his first name. Which is Henry!"

"U-Hen?" Mila looked at the front door.

"He's not here." I smiled at Mila. "Maybe next time. We'll remind Gammi to invite him." That appeased Mila, and she debuted the whistling noise that U-Hen taught her earlier. "The best part was, Hen scooped her up in his arms and they danced around the kitchen, him talking to her in Spanish and her hanging on his every word, nodding in total agreement."

"You left out the part where Mila didn't even have to place an order," Fab reminded me. "Her taco and rice lunch magically appeared. Sorry, ticos. Old Hen pulled out a kid's table and an extra chair and yacked it up while she ate."

"Don't go all high and mighty on me, brother dear, about being a bad influence."

"It's a good trait to have the ability to talk to anyone," Emerson said.

I winked at her.

"Who does that remind you of?" Brad snarked.

Once again, all eyes stared me down.

Tired of being the center of attention, I asked

Spoon, "How is the Kid working out?"

"His name is Xander Huntington, of the Huntington Industries family."

Creole whistled. "What's he doing living on the street?"

"How about why is he a thief?" Didier asked.

"That's a sad story and included in the background report I had him run on himself," Spoon said. "I had him working in the garage doing grunt work, which he hated. He complained that it smelled, it was this or that, and was rapidly becoming a pain. Second day, he stomped into the office when I was swearing at the computer—thing has a mind of its own— looked over my shoulder, and his exact words were, 'Dude, you're way behind the times. Get up. I can fix the problem.' And he did."

"When he was done, did it work or go into complete melt down?" Fab asked.

"So far, so good. Xander offered to bring all my records up to date, and I wasn't about to turn him down. Billy had told me he was smart, and I figured he meant smart a-s-s. That's when I suggested the background check and told him if he did a good job; he could have a job as my secretary. I have a copy for you." Spoon got up and retrieved his briefcase off the floor, reaching inside and handing me the report. "Check it out for yourself. He's about done with project 'bring Spoon out of the dark ages' and needs a much better place to put his talents to work. I think it's worth helping him find his footing."

Mother came over and sat on the arm of Spoon's chair. "It's sweet of you to take an interest in this young man." She kissed the top of his head.

"Totally agree with Mother." I slid the report in my purse and leaned my head sideways against Creole's shoulder. "Didier, did Lucas Mark end up renting space from you?"

"He came by and checked out the area, but it wasn't up to his standards," Didier said. "Told him that if he was looking for a chrome-and-glass high-rise, he'd need to go up to Miami."

"What did you think of him?" Creole asked.

"If you're thinking he's going to represent Madison's *special* clients, he's not," Didier said. "He went out of his way to impress me with his credentials, which *are* impressive."

"Madison and Fab don't need him when they have me." Emerson smiled devilishly. "I've already volunteered to find them an attorney when needed."

"Oh, no you're not," Brad growled.

Emerson patted his arm and beamed at him. Whatever code talk the two were engaged in, my brother calmed considerably.

My phone rang, which had me whooshing out a breath of relief, hoping that the right interruption would change the direction of the conversation. Seeing Mac's face, I tried to stand, but Creole tightened his hold.

"Turn that thing off," Mother said.

"Right after I answer," I said and pushed away from Creole. "Hello," I whispered, heading to the patio.

"No one got hurt," Mac said in a frantic tone.

"Okay," I said noncommittally, knowing I was being listened to.

"Kevin was home, and his friends in uniform just left."

"Can you get to the good part?"

"Someone unloaded a firearm into Joseph's door. If you'd like me to speculate, I'm thinking Dilly is tired of waiting on his money."

"And Joseph?"

"He moved out to the pool." Mac whooshed out a sigh. "To sleep anyway. Pushed a couple of chaises together behind the bar. You don't even know he's out there unless he starts snoring."

"I'm on my way. By the time I get there, I expect Joseph to be relocated. Crum's would be a good option," I said.

"No need to come until tomorrow. It's quiet here now. You can see the bullet holes better in the daylight."

After promising to come the next morning and hanging up, I slipped back inside and sat next to Creole, and once again, all eyes turned to me. "The Cottages were shot up, but all is quiet now."

"Really, Madison," Mother scolded. "She likes to be shocking," she explained to Emerson.

Me? I pointed to myself. Fab laughed.

Spoon's eyebrows had shot up. I nodded slightly, and his smile turned to a grim line.

Chapter Twenty-Five

I had gotten up early, having decided it was my turn to surprise Fab with coffee, but I didn't make it out of the house until after Creole left. I headed to her house, crossing paths with Didier on his way out the door. Everyone had had a late start that day.

"What are you doing?" Fab asked, walking into the kitchen. "You know I can see you on the security monitor in the bedroom."

"Good thing I held off on ransacking your cupboards." I plugged in the coffee pot, saying a silent prayer that I'd got the concoction right.

"So what was that Cottages call last night really about?" Fab set two mugs on the counter.

"Do you have to know everything?" At her half-laugh, I relayed the details I'd gotten from Mac and added that I'd called her on the way home and there had been no more action at the property.

You'd think such activity would put the property on the list of rentals to avoid, but it didn't. We always had folks clamoring to get a reservation, and when news of the gunfire got around, the phone would be ringing off the hook.

"I thought Spoon was going to intervene, broker some kind of deal."

"Creole had me call Spoon this morning with an update and to let him know that he needed to speed up his intervention before someone got killed, which might be me if I keep involving Spoon and Mother finds out. He assured me he was already on it and would call with any news." I filled the mugs, picking them up and carrying them outside to the patio. It was time to christen the chaises by her pool and enjoy the view of the sun glistening on the water. "So beautiful out here." I sat back in the chaise.

"Didier asked about our plans for the day, and I told him we were meeting Dr. A to share what we found out about Nicolette. He wasn't happy, agreeing with Creole that we need to stay far away."

"Creole wanted me to call him instead. I had to remind him that Dr. A was a friend and it would be my last visit." I didn't tell her that he'd offered to come along and I assured him that it would be short and I'd call him as soon as we left.

"Follow the case in the news?" Fab mused. "Maybe we'll get some of our questions answered that way. The last thing you want is to find yourself in the middle of the case, which would make your boyfriend unhappy."

"You're right." I smiled weakly. "What's on

your schedule? I'm thinking you need a billboard featuring your lovely mug, and the calls will pour in for your PI services."

Fab threw her head back and laughed. "I can imagine the kinds of calls that would come in. Probably not a single lost-cat case," she teased. "Didier objects to most of the cases I get already, especially the ones where they think it's a great idea to frame me for a felony."

"Speaking of...any update on Mott? Jail perhaps?"

"I'm staying far away from that mess."

I fished my ringing phone out of my pocket. "Emerson," I said, looking at the screen, then answered, pressing speakerphone.

"The court hearing didn't go as planned." A loud sigh came through the phone. "Mr. Bardwell, aka Butthead, got on the stand and testified that Joseph had sent goons to ambush him outside his job and threaten him to drop the case or he'd be killed."

"That's horrible."

Fab covered her mouth and laughed.

"Thankfully, Butthead had zero proof. His first description was sketchy. When he blurted out that two women were the attackers and someone in the courtroom laughed, he changed it to men. You wouldn't know two women who would scare the holy-moly out of him, would you?"

"He did change it to men," I reminded her.

"Yeah, right. Only because he didn't want to come off as a pussy."

"Did you just use the 'p' word?"

"You just morphed into your mother," Emerson accused, and we both laughed. "The good part is that it gave me the opening I needed to question Butthead about his side job working for a loan shark." She laughed evilly. "The color drained from his face when I brought up Dilwen's name. The prosecutor jumped up and objected, but at least I got it in."

"What's the status of the case?"

"Back on the calendar in two weeks. The hearing got cut short when Joseph clutched his chest and went into a swoon. The judge stared for the longest time before ordering the paramedics called; probably, like me, he wondered if the old goat was faking."

"Joseph okay?"

"He's in the back of my car...snoring. Can't you hear him?" Emerson asked, annoyance tingeing her voice. "Paramedics rolled him out to the curb and he refused a ride to the hospital. I stepped up because I'd brought him after he whined about having to take the bus."

"I so owe you. Better me than Joseph; he won't come through."

Fab shook her head.

"I'm driving a hard bargain and using my favor for something more than a free meal at Jake's."

"My brother's been coaching you," I accused in an amused tone.

"Once Brad got over his annoyance at my offer of help, he gave me some handy tips. I'll have to thank him later," Emerson said. "I did speak to the prosecutor, and she's still insistent on jail time, since Joseph's a serial nuisance."

"I suppose that means it would probably be a good idea if Joseph doesn't disappear."

"For a lot of reasons…" Emerson paused. "You're not my client, so we shouldn't talk about felonies in the making."

"Fab and I could remedy that," I said hopefully.

"We'll talk."

I groaned. "You know, that's the same as when your mother tells you 'maybe.' It isn't happening."

"I suspect having you two as clients would at times be highly entertaining," Emerson said. "We'll be back in the Cove in a few; we're at the city limits sign. You need to come to The Cottages. I'm going to need help wrestling Joseph out of the back seat."

"Don't bother coming up with an excuse," I said after hanging up. "You're coming with me. We'll get Mac, and if each of us grabs a limb, we can get him inside his cottage."

"I'm bringing gloves."

Chapter Twenty-Six

We had great timing, as Emerson's SUV pulled into the driveway just behind us. Joseph threw open the back door and lurched out, somewhat assisted by Mac, who'd run over. It got awkward when he tried to launch himself into Emerson's arms, spouting tearful thanks. Fab twisted his shirt, hauled him back, and gave him a gentle shove towards his cottage.

Emerson thanked Fab profusely and jumped back in her car to go make an appointment back at her office. I suspected she'd had enough and couldn't wait to get away.

Saying our good-byes, Fab and I were right behind Emerson. After turning onto the main highway, we parted ways from her, going in opposite directions.

"You're doing all the talking," Fab said, pulling into Dr. A's driveway next to his car. "I'll agree with whatever you say."

"I'm giving Dr. A the straight skinny, and he can deal with it however he wants. I'll be making it clear that he can't rely on my help, and I'll happily blame Creole if necessary. I'm certain he'll understand when I explain." I climbed out. "He's got an excellent lawyer, and that's what he's for."

We walked to the door and rang the doorbell. Nothing. I rang it again.

"That's weird," I said. "He's expecting us."

"Shall we flip to see who picks the lock?" Not waiting for an answer, Fab reached out and turned the knob. To our surprise, it was unlocked. She pushed the door open.

The living room was a disaster, far worse than when the cops had been through here.

"Dr. A?" Fab bellowed and got no response.

I grabbed her arm as she stepped over the threshold. "Why does this place suddenly give me the creeps?"

"Get your Glock out," Fab said and pulled her Walther.

I followed her, maneuvering around overturned furniture, artwork lying haphazardly on the floor, and broken glass everywhere. Fab poked her head in the kitchen. Stepping back with a shake of her head, she headed down the hall.

Not sure which of us was the first to see the man's legs extending out into the hallway from Dr. A's bedroom. I screamed.

Rushing forward, I gasped at seeing Dr. A, his head down and hands tied behind his back, the belt around his neck hooked around the doorknob.

"I'm calling 911." Fab went room-to-room with her Walther in one hand, phone in the other. "Is he alive?" she asked, coming back.

I dropped to my knees, placing two fingers on the side of his neck, attempting to find a pulse. "I think so. It's faint." I leaned up against his body to give him support, so he wouldn't suddenly fall one way or the other and unbuckled the belt. Wrapping my arms around his torso, I laid him gently on the floor and turned him on his side, then sat next to him, holding his hand.

Fab relayed the information to the operator.

I gently pushed his blood-drenched hair out of his battered and bruised face. He was barely recognizable, his eyes swollen shut. His shirt was ripped away, his torso discolored and showing signs of bruising.

"Paramedics are on the way," Fab said.

"Who would do this?" I whispered.

"We definitely don't want to know the answer to that question." Fab surveyed the room. "Whoever it was, my guess is that they were looking for something, and they didn't find it. Another guess would be that Dr. A didn't have the right answers to their questions."

"What do I do for him?" I asked.

"Just talk to him. I'm going to go room-to-room before the law gets here. I'm certain we're alone, but I'm going to triple-check."

"Be careful," I said to her retreating back. I looked down at Dr. A. "Open your damn eyes.

Now." I tried for stern and fell short while squeezing Dr. A's hand and patting it gently. "Help is on the way." I hoped for a flutter of eyelashes, his fingers moving. Nothing. Not getting a response freaked me out. "Don't die," I begged, trying to blink away the tears that were forming. "I'll be really annoyed with you."

The minutes ticked by, interminably slow.

"Paramedics pulled up," Fab yelled. She'd completed her search and was standing at the front door.

Less than a minute later, two men armed with medical bags barreled into the house and down the hall, taking over. They dropped to the floor, and I stood and stepped back and out of the way. When they asked, I told them where and how we'd found him.

Kevin and his partner entered.

"You okay?" Kevin asked. He took me by the arm and led me outside to my SUV.

I nodded, swallowing back tears.

Fab had been pulled away by the other officer and was answering his questions.

"Take a deep breath," Kevin ordered. "Don't you dare pass out on me."

I leaned against the front of the Hummer. "I don't know what happened. We just...found him... Is he alive?"

"The paramedics will do their best to make sure he's got a fighting chance." Kevin patted me awkwardly on the back. "Start at the beginning."

"Dr. A was expecting us," I said tearfully. "When we didn't get an answer...the door was unlocked. His feet..." I went on haltingly to tell him how we found the doctor. "At first, I thought he was dead, then I discovered a faint pulse. I couldn't leave him attached..." I shuddered.

"I'll be right back." He crossed the walkway and met up with the paramedics as they rolled Dr. A out of the house.

The first thing I noticed was that the sheet didn't cover his face. *Good sign.* I watched as they loaded him into the back of the ambulance and backed out of the driveway.

Kevin and his partner engaged in a short conversation; then he came back over. "The doctor's in bad shape, but he's hanging in there. He's lucky the two of you stopped by when you did, and you two lucked out that you didn't arrive earlier or meet anyone on the way out."

"I've got to call his godfather, Doc Rivers." I pulled my phone out of my pocket. "He would want to be at the hospital. I'd like to meet him there." I called his cell and got no answer, then tried Jake's. When Kelpie answered, I asked, "Is Doc Rivers there today?"

"What, no 'how's my favorite employee?' I'm fine, thank you," she huffed, sounding more amused than annoyed. "He's playing cards."

"I'll make it up to you. I need a favor. Would you take the phone back to him?"

"Hey Doo, shake it over here," Kelpie

bellowed, followed by laughter from what I assumed were her regulars. I could hear Doodad grumbling and Kelpie teasing him about it.

After a long silence, I heard her say, "Doc, phone for you. It's Madison."

"What's up?" Doc asked.

I took a deep breath to steady my nerves. "Dr. A... Stan had a mishap and had to be taken to the hospital."

"Well, hell. That boy can't catch a break. I'm on my way." Doc hung up.

Pocketing my phone, I stood and breathed a sigh of relief that I hadn't had to answer questions I didn't have answers to.

"Dr. A is in good hands," Kevin said. His lips formed a grim line. "I know where to find you if I have any questions."

Fab walked up and stood right behind his shoulder, looking as shaken as I felt.

"Thanks, Kevin," I said. "I'm happy that you drew the short straw."

"If you find out anything, pass it along for once!"

I nodded as he turned and went back into the house.

"Take me to the hospital," I said, sliding into the passenger seat. "I want to be there when Doc Rivers arrives."

With a last look around the exterior of the property, Fab backed out of the driveway. "I did a quick walkthrough while waiting for the paramedics and checked the previous hiding places, which were undisturbed." Lost in thought, she didn't notice when the light turned green until the car behind her honked. "If someone were beating me near to death, I'd have handed over the drugs, money, whatever the assailants wanted...or, at least, tried to. Leads me to believe that Dr. A didn't know about the drugs."

"All signs point to the girlfriend being a dealer. Did Dr. A know? I would bet not." I covered my face with my hands. "Dr. A can't die; Doc Rivers would be gutted."

"Being your bestie and all..." I groaned, and she continued, "I called Didier and Creole was there, so I had him hit the speaker. Told them what happened and that, knowing you, we would be headed to the hospital. I promised to call with any update."

"I'm going to stay at the hospital until Doc arrives." I turned, staring out the window. "He'll take charge and make sure his godson gets the best care. I've seen him in action, and he's formidable, retired or not."

"Don't forget, no more involvement," Fab reminded me as she sped across town. "If whoever it was didn't get what they wanted, Dr. A shouldn't go back to that house. Even better, he should find another place to live. Did his attackers mean to leave him alive? If not, they won't be happy that he can ID them."

Fab turned into the hospital lot and parked. We jumped out and hustled across to the building, entering through the Emergency Room entrance. Knowing that hospital personnel wouldn't give a non-family member information, I sat in front of the window, staring out at the parking lot full of automobiles where I could see anyone that entered. Fab stood at the window and motioned when Doc Rivers pulled in and parked. Fab and I met him in the driveway.

"What the hell happened?" Doc Rivers rasped as he ran towards the door.

I started to give him a quick rundown as I ran alongside him.

"I'll take the detailed version."

We slowed to a fast walk as we entered the hospital, bypassing the check-in desk and heading down the hallway leading to the patient rooms. I'd just finished telling him everything when he came to a halt in front of the nurse's station. One of the nurses came over, and they engaged in a conversation so full of medical jargon I couldn't understand a word.

He turned and enveloped me in a hug. "You go home and have a stiff one, soak up what's left of this sunny day. I've got this from here, and I'll call you as soon as I know anything." He hugged me harder. "Thank goodness for you two." He walked over to Fab, who'd followed us, and drew her into his arms for a hug.

Then he disappeared into a room across the

hallway. Before the door closed, I saw that Dr. A had been hooked up to machinery, with a doctor and nurse in attendance.

I turned to Fab with a sad smile. "Thank you for not kicking Doc to the ground for hugging you."

"There are times when I surprise myself." Fab put her hands on my shoulders and turned me around. "Let's get out of here."

We retraced our steps back to the waiting room and out the door. She nudged me and pointed as Creole drove in and parked to one side of the entrance. Didier hopped out, waved, and crossed over to us.

He kissed Fab, then escorted me to the truck and helped me inside. "Dinner at our house," he said before closing the door. Whatever he said to Fab, she laughed and ran in the opposite direction. He easily caught her and twirled her into a hug.

Creole leaned across the seat, and our lips met halfway. "Your friend is in good hands," he reassured me.

My phone rang, and Creole groaned as I fished it out of my pocket. "Now what?"

I held up the screen, showing Spoon's face. "You got good news for me?" I asked upon answering. "I'm putting you on speaker; Creole is driving."

Spoon grunted, which I interrupted as consent for Creole to listen in.

"Good news. Sort of." Spoon half-laughed. "Dilly wasn't the one responsible for the bullets in Joseph's door. It was Bardwell, or as you call him, Butthead. Getting ahead of himself, thinking he's the boss and trying to scare the cash out of Joseph."

"Wait until I get my hands on him."

"There's more..." Spoon huffed. "Dilly seems to think it was Butthead that set Joseph up to be robbed, and he promised it wouldn't happen again. He was adamant that Joseph, Crum, and Butthead were off the payroll—they've been sacked. He called the trio bad for business."

"Reassure me that you kept Madison's name out of your conversation with that criminal," Creole grouched.

"What do you think?" Spoon shot back in disgust. "I said the property was family-owned, hence the friendly phone call, because if I had to deal with it, he'd be out an employee. He thanked me for the call and said, to quote him, 'That kind of shit is bad for business.'"

"I so owe you."

"I'll add it to my growing list," Spoon joked. "It took very little effort to get Dilly to put an end to the drama. He knows his cars wouldn't be accepted for repair work in the future if he didn't."

"You're the best." I winked at Creole, who rolled his eyes.

"You might not think so in a minute, as I'm

going to collect on one of those favors now. Your mother is up to something." He unleashed a growly laugh. "If you could ferret out what the heck it is and tip me off, we'd be even."

"Not a peep so far. I hope she's not ambushing me with another date."

Creole mumbled something unintelligible.

I blew him a kiss, then went back to my call. "There's something you should know." I gave him the quick version of what happened to Dr. A., happy that Creole was sitting next to me and I wouldn't have to repeat the events of the day again.

"Don't like that story. You be damn careful."

I hung up and leaned my head against Creole's shoulder. "I'm hoping this dinner includes alcohol."

"Barbequed hamburgers and beer." Creole grinned.

"I love you." I brushed a kiss on his cheek. "It's probably the last time I'll get to say it because when Fab gets her hands on you, you're a dead man."

He laughed. "Wasn't my idea."

"If I were Didier, I'd totally blame you."

Chapter Twenty-Seven

After a dinner where Fab and I were mostly silent and picked at our food, the guys broke up the party early and Creole put me to bed.

The next morning, I opened my eyes to find Creole staring back at me, sunshine streaming through the windows, his face just inches away.

"Don't go anywhere." He brushed his stubble against my cheeks. "I'll be right back with coffee."

My eyes followed him as he got out of bed, grabbing a pair of sweatpants off a chair and pulling them on.

I reached for my phone and hit the redial button for Tarpon Hospital. I'd called last night after dinner to check on Dr. A, pretending to be his sister, and found out that he'd come out of surgery and was stable. The last thing I wanted to do was intrude until he was ready for visitors, so I again asked for the nurse's station and inquired after Dr. Ardzruniannos.

After putting me on hold, the nurse came back and informed me, "I'm sorry, we don't have a patient here by that name."

"He died," I gasped.

"I didn't mean to imply… He was released last night."

"You're certain?"

"That's all the information I can give you." She hung up.

I stared at the phone as though it might have an answer as to how a man in Dr. A's condition got released. Unless he needed more specialized care and had been transferred to another facility? I set it back on the bedside table.

The sounds of Creole banging around in the kitchen made me smile for the moment. I listened as he moved around, cupboard doors banging closed, the microwave dinging as he prepared my coffee concoction. I rolled over and picked several pillows up off the floor, tossing them over my shoulder, and lined them up against the headboard, then scooted up and leaned back.

Creole returned, mugs in hand, a wolfish grin on his face. He handed me my coffee, set his own down, then slid open the pocket doors. The salty Gulf air permeated the room and climbed back into bed beside me. "How's the doctor?"

"He got released."

Creole's brows rose. "Something's going on there."

"I'll give Doc Rivers a call later. If something bad…" I couldn't bring myself to finish the sentence. "I'd have heard."

He took my mug out of my hand and put it on the table, pulling me on top of him and kissing me. "My guess is, considering the circumstances, it's as simple as Doc not wanting anyone, specifically Dr. A's ass-kickers, to have information about his godson."

I kissed him back. "Doc has the connections to make that happen. Wouldn't surprise me to hear that it was his idea. You're not one to loll around in bed; what's on your schedule today?"

"Didier and I are meeting Brad, and we're headed to Miami to sign closing documents for that piece of property adjacent to the Boardwalk."

"I'm surprised that deal ever went through." It only happened because Brad had been, or still was, friends with Bordello, the owner—I was never sure about the status of that relationship. I did know that the man loathed the rest of the Westin family.

"Bordello told Brad that he hated the idea of a Boardwalk—too pedestrian for him. He was happy to unload it, as he wanted no association between it and his name." Creole half-laughed, conveying that he thought the man was an ass. "We've already got a list of businesses interested in leasing space. That area is going to be more upscale and not as geared to children as the other side." He nibbled on the tip of my nose. "What trouble are you getting into today?"

"If I have my way, I'm going pull a chaise out onto Fab's private beach and catch up on some paperwork. Get her to wait on me. Serve me lunch."

"Take a page from Fab's playbook and just make yourself at home." Creole laughed again. "When she comes stomping out to find out what's going on, place your order."

"I'm hoping for a relaxing day off and hoping that Fab agrees."

"And you'll call me if an unexpected three-alarm fire breaks out."

I placed my finger on his lips. "No drama today."

My phone rang again. Creole reached out and grabbed it, looking at the screen. "Wonder what he wants?" He handed it to me.

It was Spoon. "The call is on speaker," I said. "Creole is here."

"Wanted you to know I uncovered your mother's latest scheme. I'm calling to quash the suggestion of you interrogating her."

"I don't have to worry about an ambush date in the near future?"

"After some intense questioning, she confessed to planning a surprise for me." Spoon laughed. "In fact, we're renewing our vows. I wouldn't have thought of it myself, but if it makes her happy, I like the idea."

Creole covered his face with a pillow.

"Then I'm happy for the two of you."

"How's your doctor friend doing?" Spoon asked.

I told him about the earlier call, and he agreed with Creole that keeping Dr. A's exact whereabouts a secret was a good idea. "One more thing; if you'd let your mother meddle in your life a little more, that would make her happy and me very happy." He laughed and hung up.

"Vow renewal my ass. He's so snookered," Creole said. "My advice to him would be to keep his eyes open. Your mother's a slick one. She could easily be Fab's bio mom."

"Brad and I agreed a long time ago that had Fab been a sibling, we'd have gotten into far more trouble, and she would've skated, leaving us facing the consequences."

He rolled over, taking me with him. Picking me up, he carried me into the bathroom. "Time for a shower."

* * *

After getting a text from Fab that she had appointments and would be over later with lunch, I tossed the duvet haphazardly over the white sheets, smooshed up the pillows, and climbed into the middle of the bed with my tote bag. So much for my plans for the day. I pulled out a couple of reports that I hadn't read yet and the envelope left behind by the elusive Nicolette. I wasn't expecting it to answer my multitude of questions, but any insight would be helpful.

The paperwork in the envelope consisted of an accumulation of receipts and pages of notes that, at first glance, appeared to be in some kind of shorthand known only to the author. Staring at it, I realized that she'd put together a lazy person's spreadsheet. The first column was a list of names, nicknames perhaps, with names like Hawk, Buzz, and my favorite, A-Kisser. The next column, amounts in kilos, with the same coding as used on the packages we found in the lockbox. The last column, total sales. Loosely running the numbers in my head, I reached the conclusion that she'd moved a lot of drugs in the last few months.

Tossing it all aside, I picked up a pink diary with a lock that didn't work, expecting to find the ramblings of a child or pre-teen — something she'd saved that had sentimental value — but was surprised to instead see that it started when she came to Florida. I read on. Nicolette had moved to South Florida two years previous and hooked up with Dilwen Nash, of all people. They'd been a couple up until several months back, when she left him for the good doctor. Dilwen had been the one to introduce her to drugs, but not as a dealer. She was the one who took it to the next step, according to her notes. More surprising entries — she'd purchased a property that she'd kept secret from both her lovers and, to that end, had bought it under the name of a trust she'd formed for that purpose. Halfway through the diary, the entries ended. Flipping the pages, I discovered she'd cut a square into the last half and inside the cubbyhole was a key and a USB drive.

There was a kicking noise on the back door. It opened, and Fab yelled, "I brought tacos."

"You've got to stop barging in," I yelled back. "One of these days, Creole is going to forget that he likes you."

Fab peeked around the corner from the kitchen. "You're still in bed!"

I rolled off the side and crossed the room. "I'm dressed. And hungry." Fab didn't think cropped sweatpants and a t-shirt qualified as clothing, but I did. I slid onto a stool and ripped open the bag she shoved in my direction, licking my lips at the tray of mini tacos.

Fab took the bag out from under my leering eyes and arranged the tacos on a plate, setting it between us and handing me a smaller plate. She got glasses out of the cupboard, filled them with iced tea, then pulled out a stool and sat across from me.

I made a lick-smacking noise that earned me a glare, which I ignored. "I need you to drive me to Islamorada this afternoon."

"What's in it for me?"

"Forget I asked. I'll go by myself."

"You're always tricking me." Fab eyed me like a bug that had appeared out of nowhere.

I reached in my pocket and set the key on the counter.

Fab pushed it around with her finger. "This key tell a story?"

"It does. But since you're busy…"

"You're telling me that you're going to try out what is definitely a door key, and you're going alone? Baloney."

I tried my best not to laugh. "Have you ever even eaten lunch meat?"

Her nose shot in the air. She stood and wrapped the leftovers, putting them in the refrigerator and dumping the trash, then pocketed the key. "You can give me the details in the car. I'm not in the mood for long-winded today."

The cats, who'd been asleep on the end of the bed, jumped down to investigate. The smell of food must have woken them up, since little else did. They wound their way around Fab's legs, which she responded to by opening the refrigerator and retrieving a can of gourmet feline food. They had her trained; no howling necessary.

"Give me two minutes." I crossed to the bed, scooped up the paperwork, and shoved it back in the tote. Then I went into the closet and changed into a jean skirt and shoved my feet into tennis shoes.

When I came out, Fab was remaking the bed, which had me laughing. "You couldn't have done any worse of a job," she said. "It's a duvet; you could've at least gotten it on straight."

I ignored her and stared down at her shoes. "This might very well turn out to be a day for tennis shoes."

Fab tossed the last pillow in place, happy with her job. "I have shoes in the car."

Chapter Twenty-Eight

Fab led the way to the SUV. "Since I'm being so accommodating…" She slid behind the wheel. "I'll need you for a job tomorrow."

"Accommodating? That's not the word I'd use." I entered the address into the GPS.

"A woman client this time."

"Let's hope she's not going to frame you for a crime." I loved how Fab tuned out any of my comments she didn't want to hear.

"It's a stakeout. She has a cheating husband and wants proof."

"So…what? We sit in a hot car and play cards and eat junk food while cheater enjoys himself in air conditioning?"

Instead of answering, Fab said, "Where are we going?" Which I deduced meant I was right, or close enough.

"Nicolette's house." I told her about the diary and everything I'd read.

"Dilwen Nash. Notice his name keeps cropping up lately?" Fab shook her head. "Some women can't stop themselves from choosing trouble. Except she moved on to Dr. A, who seems like a stable guy and definitely on the opposite end of the spectrum from Dilwen. If you found the house, then you can bet Dilwen knows about it, and we don't want to run into him."

"Possibly not. She bought it through a trust, making it harder to find. If, for some reason, he did run a property search, it wouldn't come up under her name, not without some digging. The only reason I was able to get the address was because I had the name of the trust." My phone rang, and it was Doc Rivers. "I'm happy you called," I said upon answering.

"Just wanted you to know that Stan's sedated and recovering slowly. He came through surgery better than I thought he would. I had the name changed on his room, so anyone wanting to visit or calling will think he's been released, or whatever…" Doc's voice trailed off. "Three broken ribs, a punctured lung, compound fracture to the left arm, fractured cheekbones, and a concussion," he rattled off injuries that had me cringing.

Fab listened without a flinch of expression.

"I'm happy to hear the good news." I didn't need to tell him that I'd called and wondered and worried. "I can have a cleaning crew sent over to his house, so he doesn't have to go home to a mess."

Fab slugged me in the shoulder and I winced. She mouthed, "No."

"How bad is it? I thought about going over

but haven't yet."

"Don't you worry," I reassured him. "I'll have it taken care of."

"I'll owe you."

"That's nonsense. You just get Dr. A back on his feet."

"I'll keep in touch."

"I'd like that." We hung up.

"Besides the bit where you're not supposed to get involved, you should make darn sure Dr. A's place has been released as a crime scene before sending anyone over there," Fab reminded me.

"I'd forgotten. What I'll do is suggest that Doc Rivers clear it with the attorney and refer him to Cook."

"Did you happen to tell Creole that you ferreted out Nicolette's secret hideaway?" Fab smirked. "Oh…and that you planned to visit?"

"I'll let you break it to Creole and Didier at the same time, since you haven't called your husband…yet."

"I'm the innocent party," she stated in exaggerated shock. "I had no clue about your harebrained scheme until we were almost to Islamorada. Make that turning into the driveway of the house."

"Nobody would believe you." I concentrated on our upcoming turn, wanting to make sure she didn't miss it. "Once we're on Nicolette's street, I say we cruise it from one end to the other, scope out the property and neighborhood in general.

Then park somewhere else and make our way back on foot."

"It's not the worst idea." Fab flashed a sneaky smile. "I'd say park in the driveway, since we know Nicolette is dead, but it leaves us exposed. Perhaps, across the street between two property lines. Once we get to the door, what's the plan if someone answers?"

"Forget claiming to be friends. Can't risk them knowing we're lying. I've got handouts in the back in support of animal rescue; we can—" At her raised eyebrow, I switched that to, "I can solicit for a donation."

"Using poor animals like that…" Fab frowned.

"You know damn well I'd donate any money we managed to shake out of someone. Most likely, they'll slam the door in our face."

"If the latter happens, then what?" At my shrug, she suggested, "A stakeout, perhaps, and wait until they leave the property."

"That's breaking and entering and certain jail time."

Fab turned onto a narrow street, manicured houses on each side. "If we manage to get inside, what are we looking for?"

"Since it's clear that Nicolette was a dealer or, even stupider, stealing drugs off someone, I'm hoping to find something that will clear Dr. A and point the finger at her. I should've asked Creole what kind of evidence it would take to get the charges against Dr. A dropped. But I chickened out, since I'm not supposed to have any interest in this case." Creole wasn't going to be happy to find out about this excursion.

"You could ask Lucas, since he's Dr. A's lawyer." Fab made a face. "That's another thing the guys won't like. Creole took an instant dislike to the man and shared his opinion with Didier, who, after meeting him, shares the opinion."

Fab cruised slowly down the residential street, and we checked out the multi-story houses that lined the road, staying alert in case we attracted unwanted attention.

Nicolette's property was the last one on the dead-end street, which ended in front of a boat launch area with a small parking lot. The grey wood frame house, which sat on stilts, had white trim, a red front door, and a large deck that wrapped around it and overlooked an inlet. The house was small in comparison to the rest on the block but didn't lack for curb appeal.

Fab turned and circled the block, coming back and parking at the boat ramp. She powered down the backside window, scoping out the area.

"Cute house," I said. "Location, location, location. She bought extra privacy, being at the end of the block, and the other houses aren't stacked on top of one another. It's a plus when the neighbors can't peer in your windows." I turned in my seat and stared out the back window. "Do you think we'll attract attention parking here?" It appeared that the residents each had their own dock and this area was seldom used.

"This isn't the kind of neighborhood where we can park randomly and have it go unnoticed." *Duh* in her tone. "Got your plan worked out?"

"I can handle it from here," I said. "You stay in the car. Call me if anyone shows up." I slid out and shut the door on any response.

A car door closed behind me, and Fab walked alongside me, ignoring my attitude. "Some days, you make me want to tear your hair out."

"Not today. We've been spared frizz-inducing humidity, and it looks halfway decent."

"I say we cut around the bushes." Fab grabbed my arm and detoured me to the side. "Since I'm certain, due to your 'tude, that you don't have a plan, I've improvised. We'll knock."

"On the back door? That's where this is leading...that's if we get on our hands and knees and crawl under the hedge." I whipped out my hand. "You first."

"It was worth a try." Fab hip-bumped me, and we reversed course. It was a hundred steps to the driveway and one last look at the street before turning in. "Assuming we get no answer, we go in and have a look around. If someone does open up, you take over and improvise."

"No noises when I launch into my missing cat story."

"I admit it—it works. The whole pet thing. No one has ever questioned us."

"I like this house," I said as we climbed the steps. I eyed the cute patio furniture and approved of Nicolette's choice. The chairs looked comfortable.

Fab knocked politely, avoiding the brass knocker. Both of us listened intently, not hearing a sound. She knocked again, taking the key out of her pocket. It fit. The door opened.

Before stepping over the threshold, I turned and got the elevated view of the block. All was quiet. I closed the door behind me.

We stood in a living room/dining room that encompassed the large space, an open kitchen to the left. It was decorated in comfortable-looking white oversized furniture, all the pieces placed to take advantage of the view of the deck and water below. She'd chosen a nautical theme, which I loved.

A short hallway led to two bedrooms, one outfitted as an office. At the end was a large bathroom — recently renovated, judging by its appearance — with a walk-in shower and claw-foot tub.

"Who gets this house?" Fab pulled gloves out of her back pocket, tossing me a pair.

I snapped on the gloves. "I'd buy it as is," I said, admiring the view.

"Over your dead body," Fab growled.

"I'm just complimenting the woman on her choice and her taste in decorating."

"Did the family claim her body?" Fab asked

over her shoulder, heading to a large shuttered cabinet.

"I didn't hear anything about a funeral, but then, we didn't come into this until after Dr. A. was arrested and there would've already been a funeral."

Opening the shutters, Fab whistled, looking over Nicolette's computer setup, which included a large-screen television, a stand-alone processing tower, and two computer monitors. "Nice setup." She pulled out the chair. "The mystery deepens. What was she into?"

"I'll leave you to your electronic snooping, since it's over my head." I turned and headed back down the hallway, stepping through the first open door. At first glance, due to the desk overlooking the window, I'd assumed it was an office, but it did double-duty as a guest bedroom, and she'd continued the nautical theme. The bed was dressed in navy and white, and the only touch of anything personal was the bookcase. No houseplants. I chuckled to myself, opening the closet doors. Empty.

I headed to the bookcase to check out the framed photos. None were of her and Dr. A. I bent down and perused the bottom shelf, which held a set of leather-bound encyclopedias reminiscent of two editions that I'd scored at a flea market. I'd bet that hers had the same secret feature as mine. I sat cross-legged on the floor, taking one off the shelf, and opened the cover, finding a safe box inside. Inside was a black diary. Thumbing through the pages, I saw that the woman kept meticulous notes of her business dealings. It wasn't unlike the one I'd already found but in more detail. No code names this time — she'd written down first and last names. I put it back exactly as I found it.

I pulled out the rest of the books one by one, opening and replacing them. The first three held diaries, and the rest were crammed with hundred-dollar bills. The woman had a preference when it came to cash. I pulled out my phone, snapping pictures, unsure what to do with the finds. This time, we weren't taking possession. When I was done, I double-checked that everything lined up where I'd found it.

Fab appeared in the doorway. "At a quick glance at Nicolette's files, the woman documented everything she did in life and who she interacted with, complete with pictures and some video. She's got several external drives stacked on the shelf, and if they're even half-full, it's a lot of information. What do you want to do?"

"Just had the same thought. I need to find out if the discovery of all this could work in Dr. A's favor. Let's not disturb the evidence any more than we have."

"Based on the files I perused, she was in league with Dilwen — I'd say big time — and collected info on the man as an insurance policy.

Just in case...and in the end, her illegal activities did her in."

"Not sure why I didn't do it before, but I did a little research on Dilwen earlier and pulled up some photos, in case we saw him on the street, so we could turn in the other direction." I shuddered at the thought of the man connecting either of us to the case in any way. "For a criminal, he doesn't keep a low social profile. Remember when we saw Lucas in an argument with a man? Well, that was Dilly. Now what was that about, do you think?"

"I know that my first choice is usually to rush in and think about it later, but not this time," Fab said. "I say we get some legal advice before wading in any further, and not from Lucas Mark."

"Agreed. I'm going to get advice from the person I trust the most—Creole. After you, of course." I smiled at her. "He was an undercover cop for years; he'll know what to do."

Fab went on down the hall.

I made sure everything was back how I'd found it and stood in the doorway of the master bedroom, watching as she scanned the room and poked her head in the closet.

"Let's get out of here." Fab led the way back into the kitchen. She opened one of the shutters on the kitchen window, checking the street before opening the door.

We walked down the stairs and back to the SUV.

Headed back to the Cove, I shared what I'd found and that I'd taken pictures.

"I'm rubbing off on you."

Chapter Twenty-Nine

"Let's stop by Tropical Slumber and see what our two favorite funeral diggers are up to." I waved frantically at the next exit.

Fab swung out to hit my arm, not amused by my antics. I grinned back. "That would be gravediggers, and Raul and Dickie would be highly insulted to be referred to as such, since they don't actually dig up anything. And since when do you volunteer to go see them?"

I met Dickie Vanderbilt at the funeral of my Aunt Elizabeth when I first came to town, and that, as they say, was the start of a sometimes awkward and weird friendship.

"Yes, I know...they're artists. Dickie, anyway." He dressed the dead, and his partner, Raul, handled the business end. Fab and I were in agreement on who had the better end of that partnership. "I'm interested in what happened to Nicolette's remains." I ignored Fab's humph. "You know that anyone who's anyone wants to have their final shindig at the old hot dog drive-thru."

Some clever person had thought it would be a

good idea to take the old fast food restaurant and, after extensive remodeling, turn it into a funeral home. Two owners later, Dickie and Raul came along and expanded the operation to include anything and everything for one's final send-off needs.

"Are you going to be nice?" Fab smirked.

"You've got some nerve. But now that you mention it, I could be even nicer if they have some leftover funeral food for me to share with the dogs." The best day ever for the twin Dobermans was the day they were re-homed with the guys.

Fab careened into the driveway, where the parking options were completely open, the only other car was the hearse parked under the awning. She straddled the red carpet that ran from the parking lot into the entry.

"That Hollywood ambiance," Raul had told me once and laughed his head off.

We got out and were halfway to the door when it opened and Raul stuck his head out, a big smile on his face. Necco and Astro squeezed by him and skated over, skidding to a stop in front of me, knowing I was good for a head scratch, which I obliged them with.

"To what do we owe the honor?" Raul opened the door wide.

The dogs followed me as I took my assigned plastic-covered seat by the door and camped at my feet. I surveyed the table in the center of the room and was disappointed that there wasn't any food; in particular, the tea sandwiches.

Fab pointed to me.

Dickie could be heard shuffling down the hall, and in a moment, his tall, lean frame entered the room. His skin was ghostly white, and the two men couldn't be more opposite looks-wise. Raul was tanned, with a physique that could have made the cover of a bodybuilding magazine.

Dickie exchanged nods with Fab as she went on her usual trek, peeking into viewing rooms, checking for...? Maybe she was taking a dead-body count. No one ever asked her.

"Did you handle the funeral for Nicolette Anais?" I asked.

Dickie nodded, his lips curled in a faint smile. "Beautiful woman." He paused, as though reminiscing. "I went easy on the makeup to bring out her natural beauty."

"It was a quiet affair," Raul said solemnly, seating himself in one of the chairs that dotted the entry.

"What does that mean?" I asked.

"No one showed." Dickie sniffed and straightened his posture, if that was possible. No slouching for this man, ever.

"We got a call from her brother, who ordered us to pick her up at the morgue," Raul said. "He then instructed us to choose a top-of-the-line casket and made arrangements to have us host the service here." He waved at the main room.

"We were the only two in attendance. And graveside."

"No expense spared for a funeral no one attended," I mused.

"How did the brother pay?" Fab asked, having finished snooping.

"That was interesting," Raul said.

Dickie nodded.

"The next day, a messenger showed up with an envelope full of cash," Raul said.

"That's the way I prefer that *my* clients pay," Fab said, the sides of her mouth turning up.

"You didn't find that...shady?" I asked.

"Wouldn't be our first cash funeral," Raul said. "All these questions... Are you about to tell us we buried the wrong person or... Because the brother's name matched the next of kin on the report from the county and on the death certificate."

"Tell her the weird part," Dickie prodded.

"The brother... Theodore Anais, that's it. Anyway, we had several phone conversations regarding the details prior to the funeral. I called and gave him an update the day of the services, though there wasn't much to tell."

Dickie cleared his throat—translated: hurry up.

"A few days later, I called to make sure Mr. Anais was satisfied, and the number had been disconnected," Raul told us.

"You get any good details about the case from

your friend at the morgue?" Fab asked.

"When Miss Anais overdosed, it wasn't the first time she'd used drugs," Raul said. "Toxicology reports confirmed she was a long-time user."

Bored, Fab moved to stand in the doorway to the main room, poking her head inside. "And no other calls?" she asked over her shoulder.

"I'd appreciate your telling me now that we're not going to have a problem. We did everything by the book." Raul twisted his fingers.

"We honestly had no reason to think anything was amiss," Dickie said. "The reason Mr. Anais didn't attend was that he lives on the west coast. It didn't occur to us that anyone would spend thousands on a bogus funeral." He looked for confirmation to Raul, who nodded.

"No one could ever accuse the two of you of shoddy business practices," I assured them. "It's me grasping at straws, and the reason we're here is that Nicolette was the girlfriend of a friend of mine."

"Dr. A called here after we picked up the body, seeming surprised that we'd already done so and wanting to know by whose order," Raul said. "Dickie took the call and referred it to me, as I'd handled the paperwork. We engaged in a couple of rounds of phone tag, and then read in the paper that he got arrested."

"In the short conversation I had with him," Dickie said, "I got the impression that he'd planned to make the arrangements himself."

Fab had disappeared inside the main room and was now back standing in the doorway. "What's going on in here?" She motioned me to come look inside.

I quirked my head and returned a blank stare. I didn't want to know, and I didn't understand Fab's fascination with all things dead.

"We're having a funeral tonight for an older man with a fascination for glitter." Raul stood and crossed the room to stand next to Fab. "We special-ordered a casket and had it decorated in purple glitter, his favorite color."

"Several members of the family showed to make the decisions and couldn't agree on anything." Dickie winced. "It almost came to a brawl. Thank goodness Raul has a knack for defusing such situations."

Raul encouraged Fab's ghoulish streak. They'd ditched me and Dickie to make small talk and run out. I stayed seated, not having any interest in glitter or funerals, nor any intention of disturbing the dogs sleeping on my feet.

Breaking the silence, I asked, "Are you expecting more trouble tonight?" I didn't want to volunteer for guard duty, but couldn't leave them stranded after the times they'd helped us out.

"Fab didn't tell you?" Dickie appeared confused. "Since she had prior plans, she sent over Toady. He presents a formidable presence at first, but once we got to talking, I was sure there won't be a problem. He was a good sport about wearing the glitter suit we got him, so he'd fit in as a guest."

"Did you tell Toady exactly what you expect from him?" Glitter suit? Toady? It would be rude to ask them to take a picture.

"Raul was quite clear that if things get out of hand, family fight and all, and shots are fired, Toady firing back should only be in self-defense." Dickie shuddered. "Word would get out, and it might be bad for future business."

"It brings the customers into Jake's, but I imagine the funeral business would be different." I added the latter point at his look of shock.

"Don't mention it to Raul; my nerves can't take it." Dickie's tone was pleading. "He's already loath to turn down anyone's crazy idea."

I smiled sympathetically.

Fab and Raul reappeared, laughing over a shared joke.

I'd bet on funeral humor. I gave Fab a *hurry it up* stare and nudged the dogs awake. They jumped up and went to stand by the door, ready to make a run for it when it opened. "Thank you for the info." I stood and followed the dogs.

"We're happy to share information with you anytime." Raul escorted us outside.

Dickie waved.

Once Fab and I were in the Hummer, I said, "Toady for funerals?" I turned and waved to the guys as we drove out.

"It's better than us. Besides, Toady told me they got along like three peas in a boot. He's outfitting himself with a pair of six-shooters strapped to the outside of his suit, advertising he's the guard."

"This is one of those speechless moments."

Chapter Thirty

Fab had made the decision that it had been too long since we'd enjoyed morning coffee at our old haunt, the Bakery Café, and sent me a text to get ready. She arrived at my house to pick me up right as Creole was leaving.

"How is it that your timing is so impeccable?" I asked, grabbing my bag and sliding into the passenger side of the Hummer.

Fab shot down the road like a rocket. Too much coffee already. "I've got a telescope."

No, she didn't. "You better have ordered two."

Fab laughed, pulling into a space in front of the restaurant. "I'll get the coffee; you evict those people from our table." She flicked her hand in a "get on it" motion.

Sure. "I'd rather get the coffee."

"I'm not in the mood for jail, which is what would happen if I had to shoot one of them to get them to move." She was gone before I could respond.

I eyed the table at the end of the sidewalk, our favorite spot for people-watching and a bit of privacy from being overheard, and was relieved to see the couple getting up. I moved in before someone else got the idea to take it. Sitting down, I surveyed the occupants at the rest of the tables and groaned at the sight of GC at the opposite end, then kept my eyes averted.

Fab came back with a tray, serving our coffee and setting down a plate with one pecan roll and two forks.

"I don't like to share," I whined, scowling at the plate.

"I only want a bite."

"That's what everyone says, and the next thing you know...eaten. And I'm the one who only got one bite."

"I'll get another one. Happy now?" Fab shook her head and sat down. "Don't look now, but GC is bearing down on us. He just graced me with something he probably considers a smile but falls short."

"Hello, you two." He put his hand on a chair to pull it out.

Ready for him, I hooked my foot around the leg and jerked it out of his grasp.

GC peered under the table. "That's not friendly." He tsked and lifted the chair in the air and put it back on the ground before sitting. "I came over to smooth the waters over the misunderstanding about my brother repping that murderer friend of yours."

"Is that your idea of an apology?" Fab sniffed. "If it is, it stinks. And while we're on the subject, you ever talk to Madison like that again and I'll shoot both your friends off," she threatened, complete with sound effects.

"I'm certain we can get through this conversation without the histrionics." He leveled a glare at Fab.

"I'm happy that you now believe that your brother was the one to contact me and not the other way around." My phone rang, thankfully getting me out of this awkward conversation, even if only for a moment. Liam's picture popped up. I stood and stepped away. "I'm honored," I answered.

"You might not be when I tell you I'm calling for a favor." Liam sighed. "I'm fairly certain I don't have any IOUs to cash in but will be working on that in the future."

"Please...in my book, you have a million."

"When you find out what I want, it'll probably use them all up." Liam laughed. "I'm here in the Cove. Can we meet somewhere?"

"Fab and I are at the Bakery Cafe, having coffee. I can ditch her, and we can meet up." I winked at Fab, who'd stopped trading glares with GC and turned her attention to my conversation at the mention of her name.

"Two of you is good. Be there in five." Liam disconnected.

I groaned inwardly. He was in college, and I didn't want whatever he needed to be serious.

I returned to the table and sat, staring at GC. "Sorry to have to break up this reunion, but we're meeting a client."

"Glad we got things straightened out." GC stood. "Call if you need anything." He waved and walked down the street.

Fab craned her head to see where he went. One would assume he was on foot, but my guess was his ride was hidden somewhere nearby.

"Do you suppose he remembers that he disconnected the phone number he gave us? Wonder if we're reconnected?" Fab mused.

"If my Plan B goes according to plan, which is to hire us an assistant with computer skills, we'll only use GC as a last resort."

"I don't recall any interviewing for the job."

"And you're not going to," I said adamantly. "It's going to be hard enough to get someone to take the job without them meeting you in advance."

"New client? Old? Or was that a ruse?" Fab fired the questions at me.

I pointed as Liam's pickup truck pulled into a parking space that had just been vacated.

"He needs our help?" Fab asked surprised. "Girl trouble already?"

"His entire life, he's been surrounded by men who made poor choices in women; it's my hope that he learned a trick or two for how to weed them out." I sighed. "No snoopy personal questions either. It's none of your business."

Liam got out and crossed the sidewalk, kissed us both, and sat in the chair GC had vacated.

"Anything you tell us is confidential," Fab said.

"It's about my Uncle Kevin, and you can't tell him I told you. You might have to tell him at some point, though, and that will be awkward."

"We're not Kevin's favorite people," I reminded him. "He tolerates us; that's about it."

"Kev needs help and isn't going to ask himself. I thought I'd test the waters before I suggested that he contact you two."

I didn't tell him that Kevin agreeing to our help on anything had zero chance of success.

"Kevin's on vacation this week. He planned to spend the week with his latest girlfriend, Rain, except last night, they went out and she got drunk and instigated a bar fight. He managed to get her out of there before the cops got called."

"What did he do with out-of-control drunk chick then?" I asked. "Please, don't tell me he took Rain to The Cottages."

"To sleep it off." Liam grimaced. "Kevin decided that she wasn't worth the drama, and when she woke up after sleeping off her drunk, he ended the relationship."

"While the chick was hung over?" Fab asked. "That probably wasn't a good time. I'd lay odds that she didn't take it well."

"I realize I'm not the most experienced one in the family..."

"Thank goodness," I mumbled.

At Liam's raised eyebrow, I zipped my lips, to

his amusement.

"If I'd been around," Liam continued, "I'd have told him to get her out of the cottage first. Although a breakup speech in the driveway is rude, too. Is there a good place? For basically 'get lost'?"

"She destroyed the cottage?" I groaned. It had been a while since I'd had to renovate due to vandalism. I didn't miss those days.

"Not exactly," Liam said. "When Rain finally got the message that the relationship was over, she went into a screaming fit. He finally got rid of her, she hauled butt down the street, and he went to take a shower. He thinks she grabbed his keys on the way out, doubled back, let herself in, and stole his wallet, badge, and firearm."

"She bought herself a whole bunch of trouble," Fab said.

"How do you know all this?" I asked.

"I stayed at Grandmother's last night, and on the way back to school, I stopped by Kevin's with coffee and got there just as he realized she'd helped herself to his stuff."

"What do you want us to do?" I asked, wincing inwardly at the thought of meddling in Kevin's personal life, about which he'd have a fit. "Track her down and get everything back?"

"That's what I was thinking," Liam said. "He's required to report things like this to his boss, but once he does, he'll be lucky to have a job."

"How did you leave it?" Fab asked.

"I waited at his place in case Rain came back while he went over to her apartment, but there was no sign of her," Liam said.

"That would be too easy," I said.

"We'd have to have Kevin's agreement to get involved in any way. Okay, we don't, but in this case, I think it would be a good idea," Fab said. "The last thing we want to do is make a bad situation worse."

"Doesn't sound like there's a lot of time if he's planning on reporting the incident," I said.

"Could you at least talk to him?" Liam asked. "He loves his job, and I don't want him to lose it. It wouldn't be good for him to drag his feet on reporting it either; that could land him in more trouble."

"The woman's probably banking on him not filing a report," Fab said. "If he had, she'd be in jail by now. Maybe...do you have her address?"

I was happy when Liam shook his head, saving me from saying, *bad idea.*

"Well..." Fab mused. "It would be easy to get his stuff back...if she still has it and didn't do something stupid like hock it. If she did that, most pawnshops would call the cops. They wouldn't want the headache if they didn't and it was found out. If Rain has any sense, she'll return the stuff."

I stared at Liam intently. "You want us to go somehow push our help on Kevin?"

"Pretty much."

"Where is he now?" I asked on a sigh.

"At home. He was going to go for a swim to clear his head and then head into the office. Then who knows what will happen."

"And you want us to keep your name out of it?" Fab asked.

"Not sure how you'll be able to pull that off." Liam made a face. "I just don't want him to hate me."

"No way he's going to hold a grudge," I reassured him. "Not against you. We'll go over now and offer our help. I'll call you later with an update."

"You two are the best."

The three of us stood and hugged, then split up and got back in our cars.

"Are you forgetting that we're not Kevin's favorite people?" Fab asked, turning in the direction of The Cottages. "He barely speaks to me. Don't ask me what my plan is because I don't have one."

"I've got a plan...we make it up as we go." I ignored Fab's laugh. "We'll offer to hunt the woman down, scare the you know out of her, he'll refuse, and we'll leave. Try to be civilized; no snarky comments. After that, you'll call Liam and update him. Tell him we tried."

Chapter Thirty-One

Fab cruised down the highway and, thanks to light traffic, made it to The Cottages in record time. She pulled into the driveway and parked in front of the office. "I'm thinking we shouldn't involve Mac," she said in response to my raised eyebrow when we passed our usual parking space—Mac's driveway.

"Except she's standing over by Miss January's cottage, poking her head around the side." I pointed. "Which means trouble's afoot."

We got out of the SUV. Fab whistled and motioned Mac over. "What's going on?"

Mac ran over, decked out for a day at the gym she didn't belong to—she'd told me once she'd only go to if pigs flew. "I was just about to call. Not sure how to handle this one."

I motioned for her to get to the good part.

"Kevin's current girlfriend, Rain—actually, I'm not sure of her status; his women don't tend to hang around long—just climbed in his bathroom window," Mac blurted.

"I'm going to take a leap here and assume that Kevin's not at home," I said, scoping out the driveway. The place was quiet. For now.

"He took his paddleboard and headed to the beach."

"How long has Rain been inside?" Fab asked.

"Not long. She climbed in right before you drove up." Mac eyed us suspiciously. "You two are taking this well."

"Got your passkey on you?" I asked.

Mac fished it out of her pocket and handed it to me.

"Let's go surprise Miss Rain," I said to Fab.

"You…" Fab turned to Mac. "Keep a lookout and when Kevin shows, give him a heads-up about what's going on." Fab and I started down the driveway. "Get your Glock ready," she ordered. "Kevin's straight-laced, except for his taste in women."

"In his defense, it is hot down here, and that tends to bring out the emotionally unsettled."

"I'll take the lead. Stand to one side, in case she shoots at us." Fab waved at me.

"You make sure you don't get hurt, either."

"In case it hasn't occurred to you yet, Kevin's not going to be happy, no matter how this turns out," Fab warned.

We got to the door, and Fab drew her Walther, hip bumped me farther to the side, and tried the knob. Locked. She inserted the key, turned it, and kicked the door open. It banged against the wall.

A woman screamed.

"Eww," Fab said. "Pull down your dress, top, whatever it is."

I looked around her shoulder, and the woman in question was bent over, going through a plastic container, her butt hanging out. She didn't have on underwear.

Maybe it was laundry day.

"Where's Kevin?" The woman straightened, her blond hair tousled, and wiggled the dress over her ample hips, the top half stretching tight across her enormous chest. The front mid-section had a piece missing, as though a dog had taken a large bite out of it. On second look, I decided she bought it that way.

Breathing room?

"Rain, I assume," I said. That caught her by surprise, but she didn't answer.

"Give me a good reason not to shoot you," Fab growled at the woman. "Entering a private residence through the bathroom window is a crime, and don't give me some yarn about living here. I already know you don't."

"I was surprising my boyfriend with a little sexy-time," she whined.

"By going through his stuff and boosting his watch and…" Fab glanced briefly at the pile on the floor. "I can't see what else interested your thieving fingers from here."

Catching sight of her tote bag, I moved forward, which caught her attention.

"Not so fast," Fab barked.

Rain jumped sideways, squealing, but caught herself before tumbling over and managed to remain upright.

I grabbed her bag by the handles and upended the contents on the floor. Amongst the personal items were a police-issue Glock, a badge holder, and a man's wallet, all of which I assumed belonged to Kevin. I toed them away from the rest of the pile.

"Those are mine," Rain said in a huff.

"Why don't we let Kevin make that call?" I said, dropping her bag at her feet.

"I assume you're done?" Rain bent to retrieve her things, tossing them back in the bag. "Do you mind if I use the bathroom?"

"As a matter of fact, I do," Fab said. "I'm not in the mood to chase you down the street."

Rain huffed out a loud dramatic sigh and flung herself in the closest chair, slinging her long legs over the side. "Kevin and I had an argument. I handled it badly and wanted to make it up to him."

That's swell!

"By stealing from him?" I asked, incredulous at her lack of remorse or embarrassment at being caught.

"I thought strippers made good money," Fab said, eyeing her from head to toe.

Granted, Kevin had a type, but to assume... *Have you lost your mind?* I telegraphed to Fab. She shrugged slightly, which most people would miss.

"I'm not a stripper," Rain said indignantly. "I'm a businesswoman."

Fab choked out a laugh. "Sorry," she said, not sounding the least bit sincere.

Kevin appeared in the doorway in swim trunks, his hair slicked back, looking like he spent his days on the beach. "What's going on here?"

I had to hand it to him; he was calm in an awkward situation.

"Miss Rain here was caught crawling in your bathroom window," I said. "She had those in her possession." I indicated his gun and the other items with a glance. "They fell out of her bag."

He walked over and picked them up, locking them in a desk drawer. "Are you pressing charges?" he asked me.

"Kevie," Rain screeched. "She does that, and I'm pressing my own charges. They pulled guns on me."

"I know these two, and you're lucky that they didn't shoot." Kevin zeroed in on Rain, anger radiating across his face. "Skip the victim act. You and I both know that the last thing you want is for the police to get involved. Plus, the property belongs to Madison, who has a right to defend it against trespassers and criminals, which you are, having committed breaking and entering to get in here."

"You're not going to back me up, with everything we mean to one another?" Rain asked in shock.

"I'm going to leave and let you handle this situation," I said to Kevin. How was up to him. "I'm not going to press charges." I stared at Rain, who refused to make eye contact. "I'm assuming that you won't be making up any cockamamie charges."

"Rain has enough on her plate," Kevin barked.

"Just so we're clear, you're banned from the property," I said to Rain, who appeared to be planning to make a run for it. "If you come back, I will have you arrested. Probably by Kevin here, since he draws the short straw and answers all disturbance calls at The Cottages."

"I'll call you later." Kevin shot me a half-smile.

Fab and I crossed the threshold, and I was closing the door when Rain said, "Kevie, I can explain." I closed the door, uninterested in anything she had to say.

"Do you want to put money on whether we see Rain again?" Fab asked as we walked back to the office.

"That's not very sympathetic."

"I'm not known for my sympathetic side. Are we wagering or not?"

"Not." I turned at the sound of someone whistling, which turned out to be Mac. She waved frantically for us to join her and Crum, half-hidden behind a palm tree at the front of the property.

"I'm going to wait in the car," Fab said.

"Get your ass over here," I hissed.

"What did you say?"

"You heard me. Do you need a refresher on being a best friend?"

Fab growled.

Now that was a sound I needed to add to my repertoire.

We reached Mac and Crum and interrupted an argument. "I almost didn't recognize you," I said to Crum. "You have pants on."

"Don't get used to it." He stretched out his arms. "A man my size needs all the room he can get."

I heard a barfing noise in my ear and didn't have to turn around to know who the culprit was.

"This better be good," I said testily to Mac. "We were close to a clean getaway." As close as one gets after all heck breaks loose.

"Butthead is dead," Mac announced.

"Found in the dumpster behind Custer's," Crum blurted, not wanting to be left out of the breaking news. "He took a cigarette break, and when he didn't come back, Custer went out to ream him a new one and found his body."

Fab poked me in the back, and I knew she and I were both thinking that we had our confrontation with him in the same area.

"Anyone arrested?" I asked.

"Not so far," Crum said. "I hung around as long as I could but didn't want to attract too much attention. The last thing I wanted was for the cops to find out that I worked for Butthead; technically, anyway. Any asshat should know Dilly is the head honcho." The big man shuddered.

"I thought you'd given your notice," I said.

"I quit all right," Crum confirmed. "Butthead owed me a few bucks, a personal loan I meant to collect while reaffirming that he not contact me again."

"What do your sources say?" Fab asked Mac.

"Butthead took a bullet to the head and died." Her head slumped to the side. She opened one eye and said, "No suspects."

"If you're going to simulate a dead person, next time, you might want to throw yourself on the ground," Fab said.

"And get my skirt dirty?" Mac huffed. "I don't think so." She smoothed down her lasso-decorated cowgirl skirt, which she'd thrown on over the workout clothing.

The tennis shoes didn't add the right flavor, but I suspected she wore them to climb or run, knowing that on any given day it was a possibility.

"Does Joseph know?" I asked.

"I broke the news." Crum made a face. "He puked on my feet. Good thing I was barefoot at the time." He looked down and wiggled his toes in his flip-flops. "Hosed them off pretty good."

"Joseph's back to snoozing behind the pool

bar," Mac said. "Told me if he's going to die, he wants to do it in the sunshine."

Except that the area was covered by a tiki umbrella, which pretty much shaded that section.

"You." I stabbed my finger at Crum. "Keep an eye on the man. I'm still blaming you for his involvement in a crime ring."

"It wasn't a ring," Crum snapped. "I'm surprised that you don't blame me for it being too hot."

"If I thought it would have any effect on our weather patterns, I would," I snapped back. "I'm afraid to ask if there's anything else."

"Don't you worry, Bossy." Mac curtsied. "I've got everything under control."

"That's reassuring." I turned and grabbed Fab's arm, practically jerking her over to the SUV. "Why do you insist on standing behind me?" I asked after she slid behind the wheel.

"I don't want anyone thinking I'm in charge."

That won't happen.

"*And* I'm protecting my shoes from vomit."

I covered my face and laughed.

Chapter Thirty-Two

Fab backed out of the driveway, waving. "Good riddance."

I laughed. "Reminder — we've got tinted windows, so they can't enjoy your antics." I fished my ringing phone out of my pocket and saw Spoon's face on the screen. "This can't be good. Step-daddy never calls just to chat; he only calls when it's important."

"Stop calling him that," Fab admonished. "It's so icky. Your mother probably needs bail money."

"I'm going to tell her what you said."

"Answer it already." Fab jabbed her finger at the phone.

"Fab thinks you're calling for bail money," I said when I answered.

"Neither of you is the least bit amusing," Spoon growled, a hint of amusement in his voice.

"That's such a bold lie."

"I'm not admitting to anything. Enough of this already. I'm firing the Kid. His whining about working in the garage has snapped my last nerve. And I don't have enough office work for him."

"Why are you telling me instead of him?" I felt a headache coming on. Where was a margarita when a girl needed a cool one? "I just put you on speaker before Fab punches my arm one more time. Then we'd need to pull over and duke it out."

"No fighting on the road, you two," he grumped. "I'm giving you time to find him another job. But not much. I don't want to toss him to the curb. He thinks he's tough, but he's not."

"He's old enough to find his own job," I said testily. "I have a thought up my sleeve about a possible opportunity, but he will have to prove himself first. It won't be available until next week."

What? Fab mouthed.

I shook my head. "If it doesn't work out, he needs to hit the streets and start applying. In the meantime, can he use your computer?"

"What are you up to?" Spoon asked.

"Just think about it. Fab and I will be stopping by your office in a few to pitch the deal."

We hung up.

"Let me guess..." Fab's voice dripped with sarcasm. "Your hot idea is to give the pickpocket a job in *my* office."

"*Xander* can sit in my little area, if that makes you feel better. All he needs is a desk and a chair."

"It doesn't."

"Do you want to know why this might not be the worst idea ever?" I didn't wait for a response. "If you'd read his background report…"

"I might have if you'd given me a copy," Fab snapped.

"Sorry?"

She squinted at me.

"Before his life fell out from under him—"

"And he turned to crime."

"We should not be tossing stones in the 'what's illegal and not' arena." Another glare. "If you'd let me finish…"

"Keep in mind that I have a short attention span for sob stories."

"He was a junior at NYU with a 4.5 grade point average in computer science when his dad died. His mother having died when he was young, his only remaining family was a stepmother who gained control of the finances and cut him off without so much as bus fare…and without a word to him. He got a delinquent notice on his tuition and was forced to drop out. His stepmother refused to take his calls and sicced the lawyer on him."

"That's cold," Fab said. "So the father wrote him out of his will?"

"He didn't leave one. In the end, step-mommy will end up having to share, but who knows how long that will take."

"And this makes him a candidate for employment, how?"

Hopefully, the idea was growing on her. "Xander's smart enough not to screw up this opportunity. Let's not forget that he has a bad attitude and moxy and will fit right in."

"Don't blame me when Didier flips and fires both of you." Fab pulled into the auto body shop and parked in front. "Don't think that I won't have a few questions of my own."

Spoon had the door open before we got out of the car. In his office, he motioned us to take a seat. I sat in front of his desk, and Fab claimed the couch.

"Do you know what you're doing?" he asked.

"Probably not, but that hasn't stopped me from plowing forward before, and it won't now."

Spoon picked up the phone, pushed a button, and boomed, "Kid, get up here."

A moment later, Xander opened the door and didn't cover his surprise at seeing us sitting in the office.

"Have a seat." I motioned to one by the desk. "I've got a job offer. Maybe. If it works out." I told him Fab was a private investigator and that I backed her up on most of her cases. I left off the parts about not backing her up on the ones where she snuck off on her own and my owning other businesses.

"I'm interested," he said, sounding unconvinced that it was even a remote possibility.

"Fab and I need someone to work in the office."

He shook his head like he hadn't heard me right.

"Answer phones, put your computer skills to work doing background checks, and deal with the occasional eccentric person."

"She means weirdo." Spoon half-laughed.

"In other words...one of us asks, you do. Nothing illegal. If any of the background checks I ask for encroaches on that area, I'll get over my annoyance with our regular guy and use him."

"What about you?" Xander asked Fab, clearly certain he knew the answer. "You okay with this idea?"

"As long as you know that if you even *attempt* to steal anything, I'll find you and break both your arms." Fab gifted him with a hair-raising glare. "You got off easy the first time."

"Got it."

"In lieu of a job app, I want you to run a report on a Dilwen Nash," I said. "Heads-up: his public persona would suggest that he's not a dangerous criminal, but he is. If that makes you uncomfortable, you can pass."

"There's no chance that this Nash character is going to find out what I'm doing unless someone tells him or he has someone tap your computer." Xander was definitely interested. "I know a program I can run to block most hackers...slow them down, anyway."

"If you don't have people-rapport, then you're going to have to develop it," I said.

"She's talking weirdos again." Spoon smirked at me.

I started to glare back, which ended up a smile. "You'll have dealings with my renters, and there's not a one of them who has all their oars in the water. I don't want you stomping on their feelings. If in doubt, smile lamely."

"You're leaving out the part where, for the most part, they'll be drunk and unintelligible," Spoon said.

I hissed a sigh at him, which made him laugh.

"Do you have an office or what?" Xander asked.

"Down the street. So, if you miss your old friends, you can stop back by here and socialize."

"This is a business," Spoon grouched.

"Do you have any self-defense skills?" Fab asked.

"I can run."

Spoon and I laughed.

"You need to sign up for a class," Fab said. "Madison and I have found that it pays to be prepared. Not that we're expecting any trouble at the office."

"Billy mentioned the same thing about self-defense," Xander said. "I'll talk to him. He'd love a good reason to kick my butt."

"Do a good job on this report," Spoon told him, "or think about working at the Stop-n-Go."

"I know you've been wanting to wring my neck. Thank you for your restraint," Xander said sincerely to Spoon. He turned to me. "Any reason I can't have my own clients?"

"This isn't one of those jobs where if you have nothing to do, you need to look busy," I said. "You'll have free time to fill, and you can do what you want, as long as you keep it legal. Can he monopolize your computer for a few days?" I asked Spoon.

He nodded.

I grabbed a notepad off Spoon's desk and handed it to Xander. "In addition to a background on Dilwen, I'd also like you to find any information you can on Ronnie Bardwell's death."

"When did that happen?" Spoon yelled, leaning forward in his chair.

I repeated the conversation I'd had with Crum.

"Dilwen's the kind of bad that doesn't take kindly to those who screw him. He's not going to leave witnesses and risk getting caught," Spoon said, unhappy with the turn of events. "You can bet there's not a scintilla of evidence that would lead back to him."

"I'm hoping that this doesn't have anything to do with the missing money debacle," I said.

"I made it clear during our short conversation that your property was off-limits," Spoon said.

"Thank you again for making that call and

exerting your influence," I said.

Fab's feet hit the floor, code for "time to go."

"I'll work you a deal to keep your files up to date," Xander said to Spoon. "Not that you can't go back to doing it yourself, but you shouldn't."

"Works for me," Spoon said.

I stood, rounded the desk, and hugged Spoon. "You're the best," I whispered in his ear.

Chapter Thirty-Three

Creole had come home late, tired, and just wanting a shower and to go to bed. I didn't think it was the right time to tell him about my day. I did tell him that I'd be setting the alarm, as I had a stakeout with Fab, chasing a possible cheating husband. He shook his head.

Fab was waiting when I walked outside the next morning.

"I need coffee," I gasped as I got in the SUV.

"That's not a good idea, since there's no bathroom in here."

I scrunched up my nose at the thought. "Is the neighborhood so swanky they'd object to me using the bushes?"

"You're good practice for when I have children."

I laughed. "You're going to look back on these moments and realize I'm quite tame in comparison."

"I told Didier that I'd prefer our children to be little hellions and not grow up always concentrating on the right thing to do for fear of being reprimanded," she said in a wistful tone.

"Just wait until we have our little hellion get-togethers."

We laughed.

Fab caught a break all the way to Miami Beach — the traffic was light, and everything went in her favor. She pulled up to a secured condo building across from Miami Beach, entered a code that opened the gate, then backed into a visitor parking space. "Damn," she hissed. "I almost missed him. Next time, we need to be earlier."

A black Mercedes sports car pulled through the open gates and barely braked before pulling out onto the road. Granted, it was quiet, even for early morning, but geez, he needed to look before he jammed on the gas.

Fab pulled out and sped after the Mercedes, following at a discreet distance. She turned into a quiet neighborhood off the main drag, which went north through South Beach, and stopped in the middle of the street while the Mercedes parked. "Get out and watch to see where he goes."

I jumped out and stepped behind the bumper of a car, and Fab sped off. She slowed at the corner and hung a u-turn, pulling over.

Six feet of twenty-something sexiness got out of the Mercedes — dark hair, a bit of a shadow on his cheeks, in well-fitting jeans. He walked across the street and entered a pink art deco fourplex.

I ran over to the sidewalk and attempted to

keep him in sight without being obvious. When I got closer, I bent down and pretended to tie my shoelaces while watching him through my hair.

He knocked on the door of one of the downstairs units. The door opened, and he pulled a long-haired brunette woman into his arms, laying on a long kiss and walking her backwards, banging the door shut.

Not sure what Fab wanted me to do and unable to ask since I'd left my phone in the cup holder, I strode down the middle of the street. Spotting the car pulling away from the curb, I stuck out my thumb. I got in, and she claimed a space that opened up across from the building. "He went into the downstairs unit on the right. So, what's my role?" I flipped down the visor and fluffed my hair. "I need to look cute for when I — "

"You sit there and try not annoy me."

"That's it?" I pouted.

"We're here to get the goods on Mr. Cheater." Fab reached into the back for her camera, screwing on the lens. "I need to answer the question of 'is he or isn't he' for my client. He's not very smart. He leaves the house for the gym three times a week, and the wife tried following him, but thinks he spotted her and lost her every time. So, she tried another tack and stalked the gym, and he never showed up."

"Did she confront him?"

"Since she burned my ear on and on about her

dignity and pride, I would suppose not," Fab said. "Any more questions?"

"I wouldn't have to subject you to a grilling if you'd spill the details instead of making me drag them out of you one at time," I said testily. "Expecting your *backup* to sit here in ignorance is ridiculous. I'm not happy."

"We can't have that." Fab smirked. "The lovebirds have been married three years—his first, her fourth. What else...?" She tapped her cheek. "Wifey is sixty-seven. Hubby—twenty-four."

"Let me guess; she's filthy rich."

Fab nodded. "Another thing she went on about was how the marriage was a love match of soul mates."

"How do you plan on proving his infidelity? Since he traded spit with the chick at the door, they're probably doing it now. You're not going to peek in the windows, are you?" I scrunched up my nose. "If you do, take pics, since I'm certain your client asked for proof."

"Do you have to reduce the situation to the lowest common denominator?"

"Which part? The spit? Insinuating that they're banging bones? You wanted me to be more direct?" I asked, wide-eyed, trying not to laugh.

"When Cheater comes out, I can get some good shots from here." Fab adjusted the lens of her camera and took a couple of pics of the neighborhood. "It would be better if it were the two of them. If not and he leaves by himself, we knock on the door and get a picture of her."

"You're never going to pull off taking someone's photo when they answer the door. If I were her, I'd call the cops."

"That's why you're going to do it. You'll be looking for that cat you can't keep track of, and I'll get the photos. Make sure you stand to the side and don't hog the doorway."

"Yes, ma'am." I saluted. "Then what? You get a picture and…?"

"I turn it over to my client; she gets her divorce." Fab brushed her hands together. "Apparently, he signed a pre-nup—no dough if he cheats."

We didn't have to wait long, which surprised me. Mr. Cheater came strolling out with the same long-legged woman I'd seen him kissing. They made a picture-perfect couple.

Fab hopped out of the SUV, crouched behind the hood, and got a couple of shots. I climbed into the driver's seat. When the Mercedes pulled away from the curb, Fab got in on the passenger side and lowered the window, ready for any opportunity.

"I want just a couple more pictures to prove the relationship to my client beyond a doubt."

The Mercedes cut over to the beach and stuck to the speed limit, which with the help of traffic signals made it easy to follow. Thankfully, he hadn't taken a page from Fab's driving manual and squealed through the streets. "Where do you suppose they're going?"

"Pull up alongside them, and I'll ask."

The blinker on the Mercedes flashed, and it turned into the driveway of a popular restaurant, pulling up to the valet stand. The couple got out, he put his arm around the woman, and they went inside.

I slowed and Fab got out, hot on their heels. Less than a minute later, she was back. "They requested a table on the patio." She grabbed her camera. "Out," she ordered. "I've got a plan."

"You're going to attract all kinds of attention," I warned.

Fab held up her hand. "Don't ask. It's better to spring it on you at the last minute. Do I need to remind you that sidekicks do as they're told?"

"I got demoted?" I made a sad face. "What happened to partner?" I followed as she headed to the street. "I should move the car so I don't get towed for not being a customer."

"We'll be out of here before the truck shows up. That's if you don't dawdle." Fab snapped her fingers, her impatience showing. "Go hug that dirty pole." She pointed.

"No! I'll stand close, and that's it." If she laughed, I swore I was going to jump her in the street.

Fab aimed her camera in my general direction and snapped one picture after another. Most people wouldn't notice that I wasn't in most of them. "Pose, turn, right, then left."

It was a great idea. No one was paying us any attention.

Fab closed the distance between us. "Let's go. I've got enough here to make my client happy."

"They looked like they were totally into one another," I said as we walked back to the car. "What an icky situation."

"The upside is that we can tell the guys we had a job where we didn't pull our weapons and didn't get arrested."

Chapter Thirty-Four

Fab made a couple of calls before getting back in the car and informing me that we'd be going to the office, but stopping at Spoon's first, though she was secretive as to the reason. She pulled into the auto body shop and laid on the horn.

"Spoon's going to kill you," I said.

"He went home early," she returned smugly.

The front door opened, and Xander waved, then ran over and slid into the back seat. "Happy to help out."

Whatever that meant. At least, he looked happy to see us, which was a first.

Fab pulled out and up the street, cruising up to the security gate at her building. She hit a button, and the gates rolled back.

"Nice." Xander whistled. "Both buildings yours?"

Fab nodded and hit another button; the steel doors of the bottom-level garage went up, and she pulled in and parked.

"Whose ratty old truck?" Xander asked when he got out, staring at the white pickup.

"Don't let its looks fool you. In this line of work, you sometimes need a less conspicuous ride than a Hummer," I said. "What did you get on Dilwen?"

"Not a whole lot, and not from lack of trying," Xander said. "Dilwen owns a string of cash advance places. If you're breathing, you can get a loan. Some require collateral; all come with high interest rates. I had to dig some to uncover them, since he bought everything under a corporate name."

"Find any evidence of criminal activity?" I asked as we climbed the steps to the office. I noticed that Fab was listening to his answers.

"His internet profile is pretty clean," Xander said. "Could be he hired someone to scrub it for him. I did find his name linked to two murders from over ten years ago. One associate's body was found at a landfill, and another died in a drive-by shooting—shot in the head. The other two guys in the car were unharmed and claimed amnesia."

"Bullet in the head and body in the dump seems like a pattern." I shuddered, thinking of Butthead.

Fab unlocked the door, then turned and grabbed my arm. "Close your eyes."

"Do I have to?"

"Just do it."

Xander laughed.

I looked down and peered under my eyelids, so I could see where I was being led.

"Open. What do you think?" Fab pointed to

the oblong space I'd claimed, which was now decorated. "Do you like it?"

"It's prettier than the stuff I picked out."

"Toady has a friend that built the table to my specifications." Fab pointed to the desk—at least, ten feet long and made of white shiplap—which she'd placed in front of the French doors, knowing I'd enjoy the view. "The rest, I ordered." On the opposite wall were two shelf ladders with drawers below. She'd even found a white louvered divider that would offer a little privacy if needed. "The space still needs accessories. Didier held me back, insisting you needed to have input."

"There's enough room for another desk for our assistant." I spun around, admiring what she'd done.

"I'd prefer the title of vice president." Xander laughed. "What is this place anyway?"

"This side is a design/real estate company and belongs to her husband, Didier." I held out my arms to the chrome and glass side with flashes of color. "The colorless side is a private investigation/security company. And you're standing in Madison Enterprises."

"Really?" Fab asked.

I shook my head. "It's nameless for now. I needed a space to work in, and my best friend graciously offered one." I turned to Xander. "We can share my desk until yours arrives. We probably won't be here at the same time a lot.

You'll have semi-regular hours, a little bit of beck and call."

"Works for me."

"Another assignment," I said to Xander. "I want you to go to The Cottages, a property I own, introduce yourself to Mac, who's the manager, and have her show you around."

"You won't be disappointed you hired me," Xander said, sounding cocky. "I'll be the best VP, and you won't be sorry." He half-laughed, enjoying himself. "I asked around about you two. Everyone had mostly good things to say."

"Mostly?" I raised my eyebrow. "Any good advice?"

"Yeah, screw you and you'll shoot me. Her for sure." He pointed to Fab.

I crossed my arms and stomped my foot. "Why do you always get to be the badass?" I asked Fab.

"It's a lot less stressful than handling the nice stuff all the time." Fab unleashed creepy-girl smile. "If you're as smart as it says you are on paper, you should make friends with a cretin named Crum, a retired college professor who lives at The Cottages." She poked her finger in Xander's direction. "But you show up in your underwear, and you're out of here."

"Just remember this weird moment," I said. "It will make sense to you soon."

He didn't look convinced but stayed quiet.

Xander and I grabbed cold drinks, sat at my

new desk, and went over plans for the space, and in particular, the office equipment he'd need. Fab called her client with a report.

Chapter Thirty-Five

I arrived home later that afternoon before Creole and ditched my work outfit for a sundress and bare feet and stretched out on the couch.

The door banged closed.

"I love you," I yelled.

Creole groaned. "What have you done now?"

"That's so un-romantic." I sniffed, covering my amusement. I had already put off my confession an extra day and it couldn't wait any longer.

"I'll make it up to you later; if I don't have a headache."

"Grab a beer, make yourself comfortable." I blew him a kiss. "You know how you love my little updates."

He grabbed a beer and walked over to me, leaned down, and brushed my lips with his.

I grabbed his arm. "Don't sit on Snow."

"Animals are supposed to sleep on the floor."

"Says the man who lets them sleep on his chest."

"How many people died?"

I held up my index finger.

"You're kidding."

I shook my head.

He banged his beer bottle on the table. "You better be okay." He sat by my side and ran his hands down my arms.

"I got the news secondhand, for which I'm grateful." I told him about the demise of Butthead and ended by telling him that I'd hired Xander.

My phone rang, and Mother's smile popped up. I tried to hand it off to Creole, who scooted backwards.

"How much is your bail?" I asked.

"You're not the least bit funny." Mother sniffed.

"That pains me." I winked at Creole, hitting the speaker button.

"This is a reminder phone call. I'm double checking to make sure you have it on your calendar that Spoon and I are going to renew our vows in two weeks. No excuses for not showing up. It's going to be a family affair."

Creole and I had received an invitation and readily RSVP'd that we'd be there.

"I'd like to make certain that this invitation isn't some lame setup," I said.

"I'm reformed."

Creole's blue eyes filled with humor.

"Yeah, okay." There wasn't anyone in the family that would believe her. "If there's anything I can do to help, let me know."

"I've got it all handled." Mother hung up.

"I wonder what's she's up to." I looked at Creole.

"Don't look at me. At worst, she's setting you up on another date, but since she knows I'm coming too, maybe she's setting me up."

"I would kill her."

"You say the word, we can elope and announce our news at the get-together. Perfect timing. We can shock everyone at the same time."

"Okay." I knew I'd surprised him. "How does your calendar look?"

Creole pulled me into his arms. "I—" He was interrupted by a kicking noise at the kitchen door. "You want to bet who that is?" He stood, stomped through the kitchen, and flung open the door. An arm shoved two pizza boxes in his face.

"At least, you brought food." He took the boxes and held the door for Fab and Didier. "I don't know why you can't control your wife."

"Because I find it's more fun not to."

The two men exchanged a conspiratorial grin.

"While I get out the good dishes," Fab grabbed the roll of paper towels, "open the link I emailed you."

"We're rubbing off on you, princess." Creole smirked, grabbing the roll from her and putting it on top of the boxes, then heading to the patio.

"What's everyone drinking?" Didier had the refrigerator open.

"Water," Fab and I yelled.

I grabbed my laptop off the table and followed everyone out to the patio, setting it down and flipping open the lid. I found the email in question and clicked the link. The headline made me gasp. "Socialite's husband gunned down in a Miami neighborhood," I read out loud.

Creole sat down next to me, scooting closer, and read over my shoulder.

I recognized the guy in the photo as the cheater that Fab and I had followed. Reading the article, I found out that the girlfriend or "friend," as she was called in the article, also took a shot to the head. According to police, someone walked up and shot them point-blank. The grieving widow, Kelly Brandt, couldn't be reached for comment.

The cops' first suspect was always the spouse or significant other. I wondered if Kelly was crazy enough to whack her husband.

"Do you know the dead couple?" Creole asked.

"It's connected to that surveillance case I mentioned — the cheater." I told him about the stakeout. Didier nodded, indicating that he'd already heard the details. "I'm hoping the wife didn't off him and the girl over the information in the report Fab handed over." The thought made me nauseous.

"Believe me, I thought the same thing," Fab said.

"Listen, you two, it could be as simple as

wrong place, etc.," Creole said gruffly, although his tone of voice said otherwise.

"Enough of this case until we finish dinner," Fab said.

I snapped the lid shut, and Creole took the computer from my hands and carried it back inside. It was quiet around the table as Didier opened the pizza boxes and we helped ourselves.

Fab broke the silence. "I refereed a fight between Brick and Toady."

"This is the first I'm hearing of this one." Didier turned her face to his.

"I wasn't hiding it," Fab assured him. "Just saving it to tell everyone at once."

"Brick is a word we should ban while eating," Creole grumped.

Didier nodded.

"Not until after we hear what happened," I said.

"Toady was in the process of recovering a sports car for Brick, and they got into some kind of one-upmanship on the phone that degenerated into name-calling. Brick called Toady a stooge. After a few choice unrepeatable words, Toady told him to shove the job. Instead of returning said auto, he texted Brick that he left it parked behind a gas station, keys in the ignition." Fab was enjoying every word of the retelling.

The guys grinned. I laughed.

"You three aren't very supportive," Fab said with a smile.

"Let me guess," I said, "Toady dumped it in a hideous neighborhood, and Brick wants you to go get it. I'm going out on a limb…" I ripped off one of her tricks and rubbed my forehead. "…it's gone already."

Fab nodded. "I called the station manager, and he informed me it'd just blown out of the parking lot."

"I don't know why this is your problem," Didier said. "I thought your only involvement is getting a cut from Toady."

"I'm indispensable."

"She says with a straight face." I smiled at Fab.

"Brick wanted to know when the baby was due."

Creole choked.

"How did you handle it?" I asked.

"I hedged while he peppered me with questions," Fab said. "I couldn't remember when I first told him I was pregnant. My new mantra is, when in doubt, morph into Madison, so I made a barfing noise."

"No inappropriate noises while we're eating." I shook my finger at her.

The guys laughed.

"It worked. He hung up. Good thing I pay attention to you sometimes."

"Yeah, good thing. I'm about to offer some free advice that I suggest you not ignore."

"It's eye-opening watching the two of you interact," Creole said.

I winked at him. "Have Toads find the car, return it when the lot is closed, and stop taking Brick's calls. You too. Tell Brick that Bongo made his entrance into the world and you're going to be a full-time mother. Insert a few cooing noises."

"You're not naming any of our children," Didier said in a horrified tone.

"We'll save that for our kid." Creole grinned. "Creole Bongo Jr. Let people think he's named after his old man."

Fab's phone rang. She took it out of her pocket, groaned at the screen, and held it up. "Speak of the devil."

Seeing Brick's face, I held out my hand. She handed it over, and I answered. "Mr. Brick, what can I do for you?" I asked with faux sweetness, hitting the speaker button and putting a finger to my lips.

Dead silence.

"Where is she?" Brick barked.

"Fab started cramping and her husband rushed her to the doctor. Wouldn't it be exciting if they came home with a baby?"

More silence.

Guess not.

"Get ahold of that cretin, Toady, and tell him to get my car back here. Same terms as before, and we'll forget we had words," Brick growled.

"I'll relay the message. A tip for the future: hold back on the name-calling until you get what you want." Silence. I checked the screen. "He hung up on me."

The guys roared with laughter.

"I owe you," Fab said.

"I'll add it to the thirty-nine hundred other IOUs."

"I'm certain there aren't that many."

I humphed. "Now that I've solved that problem, we've got another one. Back to Mr. Cheater and girlfriend." I made a gun with my fingers, pulling the trigger, complete with sound effects. "Murdered. Point-blank. Right out in front of where the girlfriend lived."

"I don't want to think…" Fab said.

"I'm certain the wife is suspect number one and will be until the cops check her alibi and clear her," Creole said. "If she's as rich as you say, she probably hired it done—wouldn't want to get her hands bloody."

"How easy is it to hire a killer?" Didier asked.

"It's not," Creole answered. "Some people make the mistake of approaching men on street corners and end up in jail."

"Not to be insensitive," Fab said. "But should we be waiting for a cop to knock on the door?"

"Not unless the missus tells the cops she was having her husband followed, and why would she?" Creole asked. "Her knowing about her husband's infidelity gives her motive. Not to mention the timing. She gets her report, and he's murdered the same day."

"If those people were murdered because I gave her the information..." Fab shuddered.

"Stop." Didier put his arm around her.

"Listen to me," Creole said, his tone sympathetic. "Investigators run down cheating spouses all the time without them ending up dead."

"You're not responsible," I tried to reassure her. "It's not like you knew what she'd do with the information, and that's assuming that she killed him."

"Maybe we should talk to a lawyer," Fab suggested.

"Emerson is going to regret offering us help."

Chapter Thirty-Six

The next morning, Creole woke up at dawn, and I rolled over grumpily to try to go back to sleep. Doc Rivers had called the night before, wanting a recommendation for someone to investigate his godson's beating. It worried him that Dr. A couldn't remember what happened that day and nagged at him that whoever was responsible could be back. If there was a next time, Dr. A wouldn't survive.

"I'll see what I can do," I reassured the man.

I'd relayed the conversation to Creole, who'd been sitting there, arms crossed, short on patience, frustration pouring out of him. "You promised you weren't getting any more involved in this case," he said after I hung up. Noting my lack of immediate response, he held out his pinkie. "Covering my bases. Now swear."

I hooked my finger with his, leaned in and kissed him.

Creole was making an inordinate amount of racket making coffee, and I knew sleep was a lost cause.

"I'll take mine in bed," I yelled. All I got back was laughter, so I climbed out of bed, pulling his t-shirt over my head, and joined him in the kitchen.

As soon as I slid onto a stool, he set a mug down in front of me. At the same time, his phone vibrated on the countertop. I leaned in to get a look at the screen, but he snatched it up.

"You available for lunch?" he asked me after answering.

I nodded.

"Yeah. Later." He ended the call.

"That was a scintillating conversation."

"You remember my old partner, Stephen?" Not waiting for an answer, he went on, "He's agreed to make a few inquiries into the Dr. A incident. After I offered to bribe him with food, he chose to meet us at Jake's."

The jury was still out as to whether Stephen was his real name. Fab and I suspected it was an undercover name, and not a very cool one, so we'd renamed him "Help," as he always showed up when we called. We had to put up with a certain amount of grumbling that came with his irascible personality, but it was worth it.

"Doc Rivers is going to want to be part of this conversation." I picked up my phone. "What are you doing for lunch?" I asked when he answered. "Thought you'd like to meet your new investigator. He might have questions that you'd be better able to answer."

"That was fast."

"You have Creole to thank."

"He wants to keep his girlfriend out of harm's way, and I don't blame him," Doc groused. "Works out good—this is the regular afternoon for the poker group."

"I'll commandeer the patio. So ignore the 'Keep Out' sign." I put my phone down.

"I'm hoping that both your doctor friends get their questions answered, but I fear that it will only open the gate to more trouble," Creole said. "Just so we're clear—I'm coming with you. I want to make sure you don't offer any more help. I called Fab, but she ignored the call, as though that would stop me. She really wasn't happy after I talked to Didier—it derailed their lunch plans in South Beach."

"If they're a no-show, you'll know she's driving. Heads-up: there might be a tidbit or two that you'll be hearing for the first time." I flinched.

"That's not going to happen, because you're going to come squeaky clean on the way over." He slapped the counter. "Got it?"

I saluted.

* * *

Arriving at Jake's, I took over the deck and pushed several tables together, then grabbed a cart from the kitchen, filled a large oval bucket with ice and assorted beers and cold drinks, and pushed it outside.

Creole was helping Doodad haul boxes from the storage room to the front so he could get the bar stocked before opening. I slid onto a barstool to watch.

"Margarita?" Doodad asked.

"I need be stay sober for my guests, so I'll take my other usual, and don't be stingy on the cherries." I looked around. "It's quiet without our boisterous bartender."

"It's her day off," Doodad said. "The regulars will be disappointed, but they'll get over it."

"Anything new?" I asked. "Now would be a good time to update me, before the early drinkers get here."

Creole slid onto a stool next to me. "That's code for 'anyone arrested lately?'"

"No shootings or fights," Doodad said, clearly disappointed. "Last night's beer pong matches were successful. Not as popular as theme nights, but I've run out of ideas, so I've been forced to recycle. A few of the customers had the nerve to complain when we did that."

"It would be sad if you did away with all the fun and stupid games," Creole said, not meaning a word of it.

"I guess I won't hold my breath, waiting on any good ideas out of you." Doodad smirked.

Fab and Didier came through the door just then, interrupting any response. They came in holding hands, and she raised both in the air, yelling, "We're here."

Help was behind them, and whatever he said had them turning and laughing.

"Drinks on the deck." I waved and cut across to open the doors, then slid into a seat.

We'd all claimed seats when the door opened and Doc Rivers and Chief Harder came through. Creole stood, shaking hands and clapping his old boss on the back. He took the men's drink order and shouted it to Doodad.

I was caught off guard, and judging by the look on Fab's face, she shared my sentiment. Did we dare discuss felonies in front of the chief of the Miami Police Department?

"Do you know the secret handshake?" I joked with the chief, and we exchanged a quick hug.

Harder patted my cheek. "Take a deep breath and your color will come back." He unleashed a growly laugh. "I'm not here in any official capacity. Since two of my employees are here— doesn't matter that one's retired and the other is about to skip out on me—I'm not going anywhere."

My cheeks burned at being read so easily.

Creole made the intros around the table.

"Harder assured me you were all old friends," Doc said to me. "We've known each other for a dog's age. Since we've got an empty chair at the poker table today, who better to fill it than an old friend? I also thought his input would be invaluable on this."

Who indeed? That would assure that the money

stayed in the players' pockets...hopefully. Gambling was frowned on in Florida.

"I'm sorry for the circumstances that meant I got an invite to this little get-together, but once I heard who was on the guest list, I would've changed my plans to be here." The chief winked at me and then Fab, who screwed up her lips. "You're always entertaining. And so is your friend."

"Not sure you know, but Fab and Didier got married," I said.

The chief clasped his chest. "I didn't get invited."

It wasn't that Fab disliked the man; it just unnerved her that for the longest time, he'd wanted to put her in jail.

The door opened, and Doodad set down the drinks. "You need anything else, holler."

"To an arrest in Stan's case," Doc toasted. "He's been released from the hospital and is healing nicely, but slowly. He's a pain in my backside. Two know-it-all doctors trying to outsmart each other."

Everyone laughed.

"I'm happy to hear that he didn't go back home." I shuddered.

"Oh hell no," Doc said. "I got him tucked away in a stash house."

"That would be a safe house," Creole said, and the three cops at the table laughed.

"How about you tell me how you got involved

in this case," Help said, a glint of amusement in his eye. He knew my penchant for sticking my nose in where...well, others would have opted to mind their own business. "I know you were instrumental in getting Dr. A to the hospital, but start from the beginning."

I told him about my jail visits and that my services had been requested in finding a lawyer and a reliable bondsman. I left out searching Dr. A's house. Help seemed to know there'd been a gap and zeroed in on me, his eyes flicking to Fab. I ended with finding Dr. A and calling 911.

Creole put his arm around me as I started retelling how we'd found Dr. A, knowing that the what ifs still haunted me.

"You did everything right," Doc Rivers said emotionally.

"I hear there's a new legal eagle in town, and he's representing Dr. A," Harder said. "How did you meet him?"

"I met him while having coffee at our local bakery," I said. "Turns out his bro lives next door to mine."

Help stared again, as though trying to read my mind and figure out what I wasn't saying.

"What did you find out about Nicolette Anais?" The chief stared in the same penetrating fashion as Help.

"Nicolette?" I cocked my head as if confused.

"You know, the dead girlfriend?" The chief shook his head, not impressed with my stalling.

"And don't tell me 'nothing.' That particular innocent face is a new one I haven't seen before, but you're not fooling me."

Creole chuckled.

"You can take it from here," I said to Fab.

"I'd hate to interrupt when you're doing such a good job." She glared back at me.

Didier whispered something, brushing the top of her head with his lips.

"Feel free to chime in, should I forget something." Guess not, considering her pursed lips. "Feelings, I've got. No proof. I think Nicolette bought and used drugs." I couldn't tell them how I knew...or could I? This wasn't the audience to disclose the large amount of cash and drugs we'd found to. At some point, Help would corner me, judging by the fact that he was back to staring. "Did you know that her ex-boyfriend was Dilwen Nash?"

"Who's that?" Doc Rivers asked.

"A drug dealer we'd like to put in a prison cell," Harder said. "So far, we haven't got any hard evidence, and every time we've gotten close, one of his thug associates steps up and takes the blame and then mysteriously ends up dead."

"He's also a loan shark," Creole said. "Not sure if you heard, but one of his runners recently turned up dead."

"What kind of evidence would it take to get the charges against Dr. A dropped?" I asked.

"Proof that Nicolette either bought or sold drugs," the chief said. "Far as I know, there's nothing that links Dr. A to the drugs, not even fingerprints."

I had to be careful how much I said; Fab and I might need a lawyer if I went any further. "I know Dr. A; he doesn't do drugs, and I can't imagine him supplying them to his girlfriend," I said casually.

"They hadn't known each other long," Doc said. "Nicolette moved her clothing in one day, and since they were getting along well, Stan didn't object."

"Do you mind if I have a look around Dr. A's place?" Help asked Doc. "Is it still in the same condition as the day he was found?"

"Yes, it is. I can get you a key," Doc said.

"That won't be necessary."

"You've associated yourself with a lock-picking crowd," I said to Doc. "Some of us, anyway."

"That sounds like a useful skill." Doc laughed. "I'm thinking I need to learn."

"I'm on the case," Help said. "Having the chief's approval will make things easier and make it unnecessary to bring in other law enforcement. It will take a few days to interview witnesses and do my own investigation, and I'll keep the chief updated."

That pleased Doc Rivers. I knew that Help would also keep Creole in the loop.

"How do you feel about anonymous tips?" Fab asked the chief. "And could that person stay anonymous?"

His eyebrow rose in question. "I'm assuming you're asking for a friend. Did said person witness a crime?"

"On the drive over, Didier and I discussed telling Help, who could pass on the information, but since you're here..." Fab hesitated.

"I'm all ears."

"It's about the double murder of a young couple up in your jurisdiction," Fab said. "Mrs. Brandt, the wife, had just had her husband investigated to provide proof of his infidelity and the identity of his lover."

"Really?" The chief rubbed his chin. "Did Mrs. Brandt get a report of said activities?" Fab nodded. "How long after she received the report did the duo end up dead?"

"Same day," Fab said.

Doc Rivers choked on his drink.

"We've expressed an interest in having a chat with Mrs. Brandt, but she lawyered up," the chief shared. "We gave her a pass while we investigated other leads. That just expired."

"I want to assure you that the investigator had no clue that the case would end in death," Fab said.

"I'm certain of that," the chief reassured her. "You can tell your friend that there's a low percentage of cheating cases that end in murder."

"Be interesting to know if she made any large payments to anyone—such as a hitman," Creole mused.

"Miss the action?" the chief asked. "I'd hire you back tomorrow."

"I'm enjoying the real estate gig. Besides, I'll soon be a father to eleven, and I want to be hands-on." He grinned. "And Didier's also going to father eleven."

I covered my face and laughed.

Creole told them the joke about us starting our own soccer team.

"You might want to think about tennis." The chief laughed. "That way, you could start with one each."

There was a knock on the door, and Doodad stuck his head in. "Your friends are arriving," he told Doc Rivers.

"I want to thank you for meeting us." Doc stood and hugged me.

"Don't let the cardsharps pick you clean." I showed them the patio entrance to the game room.

When I sat back down, Help said, "I'd like to hear the parts that you left out. I'm assuming that they might include a felony or two."

"There's that." I sighed. "And there were some details having to do with Nicolette I didn't think Doc should hear."

I picked the story back up where we searched Dr. A's house and detailed everything we found.

I told him that the money was being held in a safe for Dr. A and the drugs had been burned. I didn't divulge any names. And I told him about how, after finding Dr. A that fateful day, I'd remembered the paperwork that I still had in my possession and how reading Nicolette's journal led to our discovery of the house she'd kept secret.

"I'd like to see that journal," Help said.

"I've got pictures on a drive that you can have," Fab said.

"You can probably find answers to the mystery of Nicolette at her beach house." I told him what we'd found there, letting him know that we'd left everything undisturbed, figuring that at some point, it might all be evidence.

"Once you get a look at the files Nicolette collected on Dilwen, I'm thinking that might get your chief the arrest he craves," Fab said. "She was pretty thorough. If I were to venture a guess, I'd say she was preparing her insurance policy."

"Your significant others are right to insist that you keep a low profile," Help said. "If anyone knew what you've uncovered and it were to get back to the wrong people, you'd be dead in a blink. A lot of people have ended up dead for a lot less."

"We've already agreed that we're out. Creole would kill me if I offered my brawn." I flexed my arm. "I'm available anytime to answer questions if you need clarification on anything. And I always know where to find Fab if you need to talk to her."

"You agree that you're out?" Didier asked Fab.

"Definitely."

Chapter Thirty-Seven

The next day, I got a call to meet Fab at the office and bring my tennis shoes. Before I could get any details out of her, she hung up. I deciphered it to mean a new case and we'd be lucky to get out alive; couldn't rule out a trip to jail, either.

On the drive over, my phone rang, and I was surprised to see it was GC calling.

"I've got a deal for you," GC said when I connected.

"Can't wait to hear the details."

"I'm not hearing any love in your voice." He laughed.

"I have to be at an appointment in under five. So…"

"My brother needs someone to run background checks and the like, and he's bugging me to ask you who you use. He's impressed with what you've been able to produce."

"That must be awkward, since he's complimenting you."

"Here's the deal—he uses your services, and you forward the requests to me. This isn't a freebie; you'll be getting paid. I'll work for him for a discounted rate, but you'll charge the full amount and keep the difference."

"As long as I can call for my own searches and get the discounted rate too."

"Got it."

"One more thing. Fab and I have an assistant now, and you'll probably have some contact with him. Don't be bitchy."

"I'd never…" he said with amusement. "This paragon have a name?"

"He'll tell you if he wants you to know."

"Be expecting a call from my bro." GC hung up.

Arriving at the office, I hit the button on the dash. The security gates opened and I drove into the garage, surprised to see more cars than usual; all ones I recognized. By the time I got to the top of the stairs, Creole was framed in the doorway. He leaned in and kissed me.

"We're having a meeting," he said in response to my confusion.

Didier was in the kitchen, making coffee, and Fab had set a platter of Danishes on the kitchen table.

Toady and Xander had been included in this little sit-down. *What a motley crew*, I laughed to myself.

"It was my hot idea to invite the guys," Fab said. "That way, they get firsthand what we're doing today."

"Anyone?" Toady held up a bottle of water.

I was the only one to raise my hand. The rest were drinking coffee.

Creole pulled out a chair, and I sat next to him. Fab and Didier sat across from us and Xander and Toady on the ends.

"I call this meeting to order." Fab banged a spoon on the table. "Got a surprise for you," she said to me. "You get it when the meeting is over."

"Yay, a surprise."

"You're going to like this one," Creole said in my ear.

"We've got two jobs for today," Fab said. "Got a call from an old client…"

Didier smirked, so he knew what was coming.

"His son borrowed a friend's alligator, and he would like us to return it to its rightful owner."

"N. O.," I shot straight up and practically yelled. "Have you lost your mind?"

All the guys were smiling.

"I hate to be a downer here," Creole said, but he clearly didn't. "But if said brat took the animal without permission, it's theft. Not to mention that there are wildlife restrictions. Fairly certain you need a permit to keep a gator, so you should make sure the owner has all the appropriate paperwork before returning it."

"Not doing it." I stared at Fab.

"I'm on it, Frenchie." Toady raised his hand. "I know all about gators, and I'm pretty certain this one will have an attitude from being moved around. He'll need his mouth taped so no one ends up losing an arm. I can also have a chat with the owner and point out that it's better to let the gator go back to its natural habitat."

"Can't wait to hear about your second job," Didier said.

"Serving an eviction notice on a commercial property," Fab said in a matter-of-fact voice.

"And?" I asked.

"What? We get easy ones from time to time."

"Name one." I shook my head. "While you're trying to come up with an answer…" I told them about my phone call from GC, asking me to field investigation requests. I didn't divulge that they would be from his brother, since his identity was still a secret from everyone but Fab. "I was thinking you could be the go-between," I said to Xander.

"I can start day after tomorrow," Xander said. "Tomorrow, I'm going to The Cottages and spend the day with Mac. She sounds cool on the phone."

"These two," Creole waved a hand between Fab and me, "are going all out for you and doing a lot more than I would, considering how you met. You screw it up, and I'll hunt you down."

"You've got my word," Xander said. "Before I was busy being a dick, and a criminal one at that, I was a decent person. I like having regular meals and a roof over my head again—one that isn't provided by the state. I plan on paying all this back."

"Just don't screw over my wife," Didier said.

"Since there's nothing else." Fab stood. "Surprise time."

"Wait," I said. "How did the Brick job end? Or did it?"

"Brick got his car back," Toady said smugly. "It cost him. I got paid double and collected before delivery. Also warned him if he expected me to work for him in the future, to keep it civil or I'd quit, and I wouldn't be changing my mind."

Fab moved over next to my chair. "Follow me."

I stood and followed her, and she moved the screen away from my portion of the office. It was now official. Even the electronics had been set up, and it was ready for me to sit and get to work. "Great job. So over-the-top...and so you." I smiled.

"Didier and Xander got all the details figured out, and then got everything set up," Fab said.

"Thank you both."

"The two-foot conch shell is from me." Creole laid his arm across my shoulders. "It's for your business cards."

"Love that idea." I turned and kissed him. "I'll share my desk anytime."

Toady cleared his throat. "I'm going to go locate that alligator before someone gets hurt.

Stupid people." He waved and headed to the door.

"You be careful," I said.

"No worries about me. Me and the wildlife are simpatico." He closed the door behind him.

"He's scary," Xander mumbled.

"Don't screw him, and he won't kill you," Fab advised.

"Come on, sister. Let's go kick people to the curb." I shook my finger at Creole and Didier. "You two stay out of trouble."

Chapter Thirty-Eight

Fab drove to Homestead and easily found the address, which belonged to a small commercial building with four storefronts. The business in question, according to the sign, was a real estate office. Next door was a nail salon, and the other two were empty.

Parked in front of the real estate office was a nondescript white van with two men loading boxes in the back.

I motioned for Fab to drive past, not wanting her to pull in and go into confrontation mode. "With any luck, the occupants are in the middle of moving out, and we don't need to bother serving the notice."

"It's not that big a deal." Fab took a quick look over her shoulder. "I'll get out and hand one of them the notice, and if they won't take it, I'll tape it on the door."

"You know darn well that that scenario is inviting a fight, especially if they refuse the notice and tell you to get lost in succinct terms."

Fab had pulled to the side of the road and checked the rearview mirror for the fifth time.

"What's going on?" I turned in my seat as she hung a u-turn.

"The SUV that just went by has passed us twice and is now parked across the street from the strip mall." She parked behind them about half a block back, which gave us a good view of the property in question. "If I'm not mistaken— and when does that happen?" she boasted. "There's a couple of guns sticking out the windows on the passenger side." She'd no sooner got out the words than the SUV screamed away from the curb, tires squealing, pulled into the parking lot, and opened fire.

The man behind the wheel of the van hopped out and returned fire from behind the car door. The two loading the boxes dropped them, drew their weapons, and fired. One more man came out of the office, gun in hand, and hit the ground, rolling toward the van.

Fab and I had drawn our weapons.

I wasn't getting out of the car, but if trouble came our way, I'd defend myself. "Now would be a good time to leave," I whispered.

The exchange of bullets went on for a minute but seemed like an hour. Not sure if one side or the other ran out of ammunition, but the SUV's parting shot was a canister that barreled through the air and right through the plate glass window of the office. Flames leapt up. The SUV squealed back into the street and down the block.

The driver of the van lay on the ground, not

moving. Two of the other men raced over and hauled him to his feet, dragging him around the back and slamming the doors. The third man hopped into the driver's seat and blew off the lot, going in the opposite direction of the SUV.

Customers and employees flew out of the nail salon.

"I should've followed the SUV," Fab lamented.

"Long gone." *Thank goodness.*

Fab coasted up to where the van had been parked and surveyed the damage, her phone out the window, snapping pictures. "What the heck just happened?"

"You might want to ask your friggin' client," I said in disgust.

"I know what you're thinking…" Fab sighed.

Your client set us up for an ambush?

"Mr. Todd is eighty years old and told me straight out that he was afraid of the tenants." Fab exhaled heavily. "Told me that a guy in a suit showed up, made a good impression, and he couldn't get the lease signed fast enough. Said the ink was barely dry when the riff-raff made an appearance."

I was familiar with that con.

"He saw people come and go, and in his opinion, they didn't stick around long enough to transact any business. He just wanted them gone and no problems."

"Wait until Didier hears the details you left

out," I said. "And he *will* hear because Creole will be fuming mad."

"I gave him most of the details." Fab pouted.

"When rodents fly. If you had, he would've spoke up and I wouldn't be here now. Creole would've dragged me home." Which I wouldn't have been averse to. "Sirens are getting closer; I suggest you step on it and not a mile over the speed limit."

Fab cruised slowly away from the curb, not wanting to miss anything.

My nerves were strung out at what we'd just witnessed. I picked up my phone and texted Creole, "Love you."

Fab picked up her phone and, after connecting, hit the speaker button. "Mr. Todd, this is Fabiana Merceau. I was unable to serve the notice. There was a fire, and the building has suffered severe damage." The firefighters had arrived and begun to hose it down.

"Damn criminals," he shouted. "What the heck happened?"

"What kind of criminals?" Fab demanded. "You held out on me once, and I suggest that you not do so now."

"They liked to pay in cash…"

First clue that something shady is up.

"Turned out to be counterfeit. My bank caught it. Thank goodness I knew the teller and she didn't report it. I confronted them and they denied it. Liars," he spat out. "In the meantime, I got one of those pens that can detect funny money. The next month, I went in person to collect, and they shoved me out of the office. Turned out none of it was any good, either. I tried spending it twenty at a time but got paranoid about getting caught. Now, I've got a stack of phony greenbacks."

"Take your loss and stop trying to pass it off around town," Fab lectured. "You could land in jail."

"That's why I stopped," Mr. Todd insisted. "Jail scares me. I haven't ever been and don't want to start now."

"Do you have fire insurance?" Fab asked.

"I'll need to call them, won't I?"

"The good news is that you can rebuild. And get all new tenants."

"I...uh...thank you."

"Before we hang up, it would probably be a good idea to claim ignorance about the events of the day, and whatever you do, do not share your tenants' criminal tendencies. That could invite more trouble."

They hung up.

"I don't suppose that you're going to triple bill an old man. But you do need to decline any further business from him," I offered my two cents. If I heard Mr. Todd's name again, I would refuse to ride along. "I'm crashing from the adrenaline rush. You need to buy me a lemonade."

"Make that two, and I'll take mine with a shot of vodka."

Chapter Thirty-Nine

A week later, Fab called and threatened to hunt me down if I didn't show up for yet another meeting at the office. She was vague on the agenda and who would be in attendance but clear that I needed to stop at the bakery and pick up the lunch she'd ordered. I scored a parking spot in front of the cafe and caught sight of Lucas Mark, then did a double take, recognizing the man sitting next to him as Dilwen Nash. My first sighting of the two men together a couple of weeks ago had left me unsettled. It appeared that the lawyer had no standards when it came to choosing clients, and I was rethinking being involved with the man in any way.

I backed out of the space before he noticed me and pulled around the back of the building, parking and going inside. It didn't take me long to fill two of the famous pink boxes with cookies, adding them to the order. I slowed going out the side entrance and saw the two men still engrossed in conversation.

It was a short drive to the office building. Hitting the gate opener, I drove inside and paused, waiting for the gate to close. Fab and I had agreed that would be a good idea, here and at home. My phone had rung on the way over, and I'd ignored it. Glancing at the screen, I saw the missed call was from Lucas, and my neck hairs stood on end, which was something I tried not to ignore. For now, I didn't have a plan, and that bothered me. I grabbed the shopping bags and started the hike up the stairs.

"Hey, boss." Xander bolted out the door and relieved me of the bags, taking them inside. "What should I call you? Mrs. Westin?"

"That used to be my mother." I laughed. "Call me whatever you want, as long as you're nice about it. No name-calling."

"Gotcha."

"How did your day at The Cottages go?" I asked, taking the bags from Xander and setting them on the table. "Mac was entertained by your visit. Says you have a sense of humor." I waved to Fab, who was in conversation with Toady.

"It was a bit overwhelming. Lots of odd personalities. Not knowing what to say, I made jokes, and the more stupid stuff I said, the more your tenants laughed. Doesn't take much to keep them entertained."

"Learn anything?" I asked.

"Brushed up on my people skills." Xander grinned. "Spent most of my time in the office, updating Mac's computer. There were a few things she'd ignored, only because it overwhelmed her, so I passed on a few tips. Told her to call with any questions."

I went into my own space, admiring my new desk before setting down my bag.

Xander followed me. "Got along really well with Professor Crum."

Of all people. "Did he have any words of wisdom?" They'd better not be something illegal.

"He said he was surprised I'm not the stupe he'd expect you to hire." Xander rolled his eyes. "Wanted to know if I had a title. Said otherwise, I'm just a stooge. I told him I was vice president. He burst out laughing."

"No laughing without my permission," Fab grouched with amusement. She'd crept up and now stood on one side of the screen.

"That's no way to talk to the new VP," I admonished, then waved everyone over to the kitchen area, eyeing the table, which was strewn with cards and a pile of pennies. "Gambling at work?"

"Toady and I got here early," Xander reported. "I finished up the Dilwen report and put it on your desk. Rather than stare at one another, we played a few rounds. I won fifty-five cents." He grinned.

"What's my title?" Toady blustered.

"Chief Muscle," I said without a pause.

He smiled wide, his gold tooth front and center, and flexed his arms, displaying an impressive amount of muscle. "You betcha."

His antics reminded me of the stolen reptile. "What's the update on the alligator?"

"Stupid kids." Toady snorted out a breath of air. "A prank gone south. Once they had the gator in their possession, what to do with it rapidly became a dilemma. Afraid of it, which they should have been, they let it go, and it crawled into a neighborhood lake."

Toady had everyone's attention, and we were all wide-eyed.

"Called animal control and they relocated it." Toady cracked his knuckles. "As for the thieves, I scared the hell out of them. Told them I better never hear their names mentioned in connection with another crime."

Xander let out a nervous laugh. "That's the last you'll hear of them, unless they're even more stupid than they sound."

I turned to Fab. "I'm assuming you have a written agenda for this meeting?" I couldn't imagine why a meeting was necessary, except that she was relishing her role as dictator boss. "Rolling your eyes will give you wrinkles." I patted my forehead.

"Your mother made that up." Fab motioned for us to sit.

I laughed at her. "That wouldn't surprise me." My phone rang — the lawyer again. All eyes were on me. I put my finger to my lips and answered, putting it on speaker and hoping he didn't notice. "How can I help you?"

"Two things. I'd like a more in-depth background check run on Nicolette Anais," he said in a brusque tone. "Dig into her past. I want to know everything there is to know."

"And the other?" I asked, hesitant to hear the answer.

"It would be more expedient if I dealt with the information guy directly, so if you could pass on my request..."

"We're like-minded on that one. I planned to speak with the man in question later today." I jabbed my finger in Xander's direction. "He doesn't do friendly, so you'd have to agree to do everything electronically, no meet-and-greet. Otherwise, he won't agree."

"In the meantime, pass along the other request with a rush on it."

We ended the call.

"I'm perfect to be the nerdy guy in the basement," Xander said with excitement.

"My regular guy wants to use me as a middle man, fielding these information requests to maintain his anonymity, and I thought maybe it would be a good side gig, but now I'm not so sure." I shared what I'd seen at the bakery.

"Dilwen again," Fab said in disgust. "I'm sick of hearing that name."

"The cops don't have anything new on Butthead." Toady tossed his soda can, missing the trash. He got up and slam-dunked it, then grabbed another. "You'd think it was an everyday occurrence, finding a body in a dumpster."

"No mentions online, either," Xander said.

"Update on Brick," Fab said.

Why couldn't he just go away?

"Toady was offered a contract to repo cars— Brick's branching out and acquired several new accounts. The catch: he doesn't want me finding out. He's using the baby as an excuse."

"Fab's pregnant," I said for Xander's information.

Xander looked shocked, eyeing her up and down.

"Put rent-a-baby on your 'to find' list," I said. "Fab's going to need one unless she fesses up to her mammoth lie. Which I doubt."

"Got it covered." Fab looked quite proud of herself. "If Brick asks, which I doubt, I'll say Didier's babysitting."

"I was going to say, the only kids I know are in their twenties and live hundreds of miles away," Toady said as he got up and disappeared into the bathroom.

Xander and I laughed.

The door flew open and hit the wall. Two suited men, each with one hand inside their jacket, walked in, bodyguards for the man behind them—Dilwen Nash. Even the bodyguards didn't own the space the way their boss did. One stayed by the man's side; the other moved around the office, kicking a chair out of his way and sticking his head behind the screen that separated off my area.

"Hello, ladies," Dilwen said, dominating the room with his mere presence. "And whoever you are." He nodded at Xander. "I'm certain no introductions are necessary. You know me by reputation anyway." His dark eyes were cold and mean, and his smile sent a chill down my spine. There was something deadly about him.

We'd made a point of staying off his radar, yet here he was, icy calculation directed at Fab.

Let's hope she doesn't provoke him.

"How did you get in?" Fab demanded.

How in the world did he even find the office? It wasn't under Fab's name and no one had followed me there.

Dilwen ignored Fab's question, eyeing her in a way that would have Didier blacking his eyes if he were there. "Imagine my surprise when my lawyer informed me that he's using your company for investigations."

"How can I help you?" Fab seethed.

"I want everything you have on Nicolette Anais." He flashed his perfectly white teeth. Moving over to her desk, he flicked a file open with his finger, giving it a cursory glance. "Including pictures, videos, and any and all files on the woman from the doctor's house and her apartment in South Beach. I've heard you're thorough. Don't disappoint me."

No mention of the beach house.

"I gave everything I had to your lawyer." Fab had partially unleashed her creepy-girl smile.

Xander pushed his chair back.

One of the men whipped out his gun and aimed it at his forehead.

The blood drained from Xander's face. "Would you like a cold drink?" he stammered.

"Shut up. Don't move," Dilwen ordered. "Sorry, kid, you're in the wrong place, etc. Bad timing." The silent menace in his words was loud and clear. "Madison Westin. I hear you have interesting connections."

"I have friends in the alternative rung of society." I felt fairly certain he had a passing acquaintance with at least a few of the same quasi-criminals.

"I'm not certain how much information you two managed to dig up on Nicolette, but it's a loose end I can't afford."

My stomach churned and settled in a hard knot. "If that's a threat, I'm certain you're aware that I'm related to Jimmy Spoon. You wouldn't want to make him unhappy."

"Something to do with his old lady."

If I weren't so nauseous, I'd have laughed. Mother would kill him.

"Spoon needs to be put in his place," Dilwen said, his voice as cold as his glare. "I'm the man for the job. Now that he's a leader in the community, he thinks he don't stink like the rest of us entrepreneurs."

Fab and I were packing but didn't have the remotest chance of drawing our weapons and getting a shot off. That left Toady and the pair of shooters he never left home without. I hadn't noticed before, but the bathroom door was cracked open.

"If you're worried that your name came up during our investigation of Nicolette, I can assure you that it didn't," Fab told him. "Her history was pretty much a bore. I'd be happy to copy the files to a drive for you. I don't keep paper files on anything." She smiled grimly. Fab's ability to stay calm during a life-threatening situation was something I admired.

"We'll take your laptop." He motioned to one of his men, who walked over to her desk, slammed down the cover, and shoved it under his arm. "I'm certain it's a fount of interesting information."

Let him discover for himself that he'd find little of interest. Fab kept everything on an external hard drive. I knew because she continuously harped on the subject.

"Take it and leave," Fab said with a flourish of her hand, annoyance tightening her face. "We'll pretend this little meeting never happened." Her easy acquiescence only confirmed what I knew about how she stored files.

"We won't be seeing one another again. Not in this life." He unleashed a hair-raising laugh. "My men will clean up. No one will know we were even here." His voice was frigid, devoid of emotion.

How many times had he ordered someone's death in the same matter-of-fact way?

Xander's hands twisted in his lap, and he appeared ready to puke, his eyes focused downward.

The bathroom door opened. Toady stood in the doorway, an ad for a tropical Wild West cowboy, with a gun in each hand and a deranged, maniacal sneer on his face. Shots rang out. Before the bodyguard who had his gun out could shoot back, Toady blew a hole in his shoulder. The gun clattered to the ground, the man grabbing his arm.

"You and your goon, drop your guns," Toady ordered.

Dilwen opened his suit jacket and drew his weapon, handing it to his guard, who leaned down, laying both guns on the floor.

Fab, who was already on her feet, kicked them under her desk.

"No one, and I mean no one, threatens my girl," Toady ground out. "You want to walk out of here with your balls intact, I suggest your men not do anything more stupid than they've already done."

"Do you know who you're threatening?" Dilwen's voice lowered to a growl and cracked like a whip.

"I could ask the same question." Toady

matched his arrogance. "Frenchie, what do you want me to do?"

"Go ahead, call the police," Dilwen taunted. "You'll be the one on your way to jail. Calling me here, threatening me, and then shooting one of my men..."

I wondered how he was planning to prove that we'd made a call we never made. The phone company kept logs, after all.

"Let them go," Fab said. "No one's going to jail."

"You sure?" Toady asked in disbelief. "I can make them disappear. It would be my pleasure to grind them to bits that would never be recovered...and if the cops managed to find a spoonful, it wouldn't be enough to test."

"Threats and more threats," Dilwen sneered.

If they walked out the door, we'd be forever looking over our shoulders.

"You boys caught a lucky break." Toady's voice dropped in a low warning. "Word of caution—one hair on either of these women's heads is disturbed, *ever*, and you'll die, one body part at a time." He cackled, which drew wide-eyed stares from the bodyguards. "This better be the last *any* of us ever sees of you, if you value your lives."

Dilwen face was red with anger as he stomped out. The uninjured bodyguard helped the other to stand straight and wrapped an arm around his shoulders, leading him out the door.

An engine roared to life below. Fab peered out the window. There was a loud crash and scraping noise, and she winced.

"That ass just hit the gate, even though it was standing half-open." Fab grimaced. "The only good part was that it took out the passenger side of his ride. Good luck getting the doors open."

"I'll figure out how they got the gates open," Toady assured her. "It will not happen again."

"They'll be back," I warned. "A man like Dilwen, always in charge, it will eat at him until he gets even."

"Listen up, ladies," Toady barked. "No. One. Is. Coming. Back. I promise you. And I always keep my word."

"I thought Help had Dilwen in his sights. You hear anything about a warrant?" Fab asked me.

"Once Creole hears about today, he'll be in contact with Help and the chief, and you'll be my first call," I said.

"It can't happen soon enough." Fab shuddered.

I grabbed my water bottle and held it out to Xander. "You okay? Put this on your face."

He rolled the bottle across his cheeks and took a long drink. "I thought I was going to puke. Then die." He made a strangled noise. "That was intense."

"I apologize." I patted his arm. "I'll understand if you want to quit, and I promise to help you get a tamer job." I smiled weakly.

"You've grown on me. The last thing I want is for anything to happen to you."

"I'm staying."

"Think about it. You change your mind, let me know," I said.

"For now, everyone stays put," Fab ordered. "We don't know that Dilwen and his friends aren't lying in wait. They had to have backup weapons inside the vehicle." She pointed to Toady. "That includes you." To Xander, she said, "You watch out the window, and if *anyone* shows up, yell." She grabbed her phone and went into the bathroom, then came back out in jeans and tennis shoes and went out to the patio.

I grabbed my phone and sought out my desk, sitting back in the chair as I called Creole. "How far away from the office are you?" I asked when he answered.

"Didier and I are here at the Boardwalk."

"We're all right. But there was a problem."

"We're on our way." I heard him yell, "Didier, we've got to go."

"You need to be careful." I told him what happened.

"I'll call Help and find out what's taking so long in arresting this bastard. Though it would be better all around if he ended up dead."

Fab came back inside and went into drill sergeant mode. She contacted Billy to get the gate closed, passing off the damage as a hit and run. He knew it wasn't the whole story but didn't question her. He'd get the details from his roommate, since Xander was still living at Billy's place.

Creole and Didier showed up right behind Billy.

I went downstairs with Xander, asking Billy to keep an eye on the young man. He nodded and enlisted his help, reassuring me that he'd see Xander got home.

"Talked to Help," Creole announced. "His crew is waiting on a warrant for Dilwen. He'll be in custody in a few hours."

Toady pulled Fab aside and whispered something, and she nodded. He waved and left.

"Toady was pretty much a superhero today," I told Didier, who'd come over and put his arm around me.

It wasn't until a couple of hours later—when two armed guards arrived, courtesy of Caspian— that I realized how busy the guys had been on the phone.

"Caspian's not happy that Dilwen's still alive," Creole said as we watched the men roll through the gate.

"Once he's in jail, a whole lot of people will be a lot happier."

Chapter Forty

The week leading up to the re-wedding of Jimmy and Madeline Spoon had been unnerving. Mother was hinting at a big announcement. I felt fairly certain she wasn't pregnant, so it was anyone's guess. The invitations had gone out, along with a threat from Mother that if anyone attempted a weasel trick to get out of showing, it would shorten their lifespan.

"If this is what my wife wants..." Spoon had said when I questioned him about them renewing their vows. I felt certain it wasn't another date setup. Creole grumbled, hoping there wouldn't be a ton of people we didn't know. I reassured him that it was family only, and he snorted. "Sure."

Mother went into her usual attention-to-detail, some would say bossy, mode and left nothing to chance, even choosing Fab's and my dresses, which sent Fab into a hissy fit. She lightened up somewhat when the two put their heads together and Mother listened to her suggestions. I tuned the whole drama out. "Just let me know where to show up and sit."

Mother snapped, "You're not to suck one bit

of romance out of the day."

I mentally saluted and conveyed via a convincing smile that I'd behave.

* * *

Fab wanted the days after the meeting with Dilwen to be business as usual, but I didn't want to leave the house while the man was on the loose. The home and business compounds each had round-the-clock guards and would stay that way until Caspian was satisfied his daughter was safe. Neither Didier nor Caspian relented on the issue.

Three days after our encounter with Dilwen, Help called with an update, and Creole invited him to dinner. Then Creole called Didier and extended the same invitation to him and Fab, reminding him the information would be better firsthand.

We gathered around the table on the patio after the dishes had been cleared away, the guys having consumed a large amount of food and beer. I'd pushed mine around on my plate, having nursed a queasiness since the run-in with Dilwen.

Creole had banned any talk of the news until after we ate. Fab sighed in frustration, wanting the update as soon as Help walked in the door, but didn't say anything. Didier winked at her, which she responded to by snuggled into him.

"You're up, buddy," Creole said to Help.

"Got the warrant for Dilwen, went to arrest him, and he's nowhere to be found," Help said, his relaxed look gone, replaced with irritation. "We ran down every known address. We assume he got wind of his impending arrest and skipped town."

"He can't hide forever," Creole said with conviction. "He's too recognizable."

In the meantime… I was afraid to ask.

"What about the bodyguards?" Fab asked.

"Skipped along with their boss," Help said. "Whether they turn up alive or not depends on how much the men know. Dilwen wouldn't want them questioned. It's highly likely the District Attorney would offer them a deal."

"Great…more looking over our shoulders," Fab said.

"The beach house was a gold mine." Help nodded to Fab and me. "If Dilwen had gotten there ahead of us, he'd've had the place torched. He wouldn't have taken the chance that he didn't find everything."

"There was enough evidence to make your case?" Creole asked.

"Dilwen will be behind bars for a long time. There were lots of surprises, but the most surprising lead was the discovery of a boat that Dilwen owned in a dead man's name and used to transport drugs. Since it was parked a few spaces down from Spoon's, I used that connection." He winked at me. "Spoon allowed an undercover cop to camp out on the back of his boat and track the comings and goings."

"This is where you tell me that you did everything by the book, so every piece of evidence can be used against him," Creole prompted.

Help snorted. "Who do you think you're talking to?"

I watched in fascination as the two faced off and conversed in silent code. After a moment, both appeared to relax.

Didier rose and asked for a show of hands for who wanted refills, then went inside and came back with more beer. Fab and I had declined.

"Do you happen to know how Dr. A hooked up with Nicolette?" Fab asked.

"They met at a party up in Miami right after she'd had a blow-up with Dilwen," Help said. "I can see how the doc would be interested. Nicolette appeared to be the total package— brains, beauty. Except everything about her was fake, including her name, which was buried under several aliases. I bet not even Dilwen knew. It would've come as a shock for him to learn that his beautiful model girlfriend was a con artist."

"Nicolette and Dilwen break up," Didier mused, "and she stays in the drug business? Wouldn't that encroach on his territory?"

"If Nicolette hadn't overdosed, she was

headed to a showdown with her ex. He *had* found out, and it wouldn't have ended well for her or the doctor."

"Tell me you found something to get the charges against Dr. A dismissed," I said.

"Nicolette documented every thought she ever had, which I wouldn't recommend that anyone do, but it will end up helping your friend," Help said. "By the time of the split with Dilwen, she'd developed a *serious* habit, which Dilwen, to his credit, objected to. That was the catalyst for the breakup. It's my opinion that they would've gotten back together eventually, and that wouldn't have ended well for your doctor friend either."

"You can prove Nicolette was a dealer and using?" Creole asked.

"Yep," Help said in a tone that left no doubt. "Like I said, she documented everything, including her drug transactions — customer names, quantities, even drop-off preferences."

"There was no way this situation was going to end well," I said. "If she was developing a habit, she was headed for a downhill slide. I've seen it happen, and it's sad."

"Now we wait to hear of an arrest?" Didier tapped his fingers on the table.

"And hope Dilwen doesn't get bail," Creole said.

"You're quiet," I said, staring at Fab with a certain amount of suspicion.

"I'm in charge of planning the Spoon wedding reception, which keeps me out of trouble." Fab grinned at Didier.

Creole told Help about the re-wedding.

"My invite must've gotten lost." Help mock-frowned.

"Hmm..." I checked out Help. "Cute. Single. You're invited. We'll make sure you meet Mother. She's a one-woman dating service."

The guys laughed as Didier told Help about Mother's past fix-up schemes.

Chapter Forty-One

"Hurry up!" Fab nudged my arm. "We don't have all day."

Mother had chosen to have her nuptials at the same beachfront resort as before. She'd reserved rooms, splitting up the sexes — men in one suite and women in the other. Fab and I had wanted to stay at our own houses, but Mother had a hissy fit. As our wedding gift to her, she'd asked that we go along with her plans, extracting the same promise from the guys.

The clock was ticking, and soon, the three of us needed to be downstairs and on the beach for the late-morning wedding. Mother had assured us that it wouldn't be mind-numbingly hot because even the weather didn't cross her.

"Honey, what's going on?" Mother asked as she walked into the bedroom. "You're still getting dressed, dear?"

Mother had chosen all above-the-ankle dresses. Mine was white lace, with cap sleeves and a fitted bodice. The silk skirt had a slit that came up to mid-thigh, and the bodice was partially backless. As for Fab, her dress also white, a sexy twist on a silhouette and one-shouldered with a cut-out back. Mother wore her original wedding dress, an elegant, ankle-length, rose-colored A-line dress, low-cut with lace straps.

"We're almost ready," Fab said to Mother, a huge smile on her face, and kissed her cheek. "I'm very happy for you and Spoon."

"Me too." I blew her a kiss. "Where are the shoes?" I looked around for the boxes.

There was a knock at the door. Mother opened it and received a bag with a flower shop logo on the side. "The answer to your question just arrived." Reaching inside, she handed Fab and me each a small white box.

I opened the lid, and inside lay two fresh flower anklets made with plumeria wrapped around white satin ribbon. "These are beautiful," I said, hooking one on the end of my finger, holding it up, and inhaling the tropical scent.

"Since we're going to be out on the sand, I thought barefoot would be better and these would be perfect."

I sat on the couch next to Fab and slid the flowers over my toes and onto my ankle. Beside me, Fab did the same, and we both held our legs out.

"Come on, ladies, it's not good to be late for a wedding." Mother motioned for us to hustle out the door and into the waiting elevator.

Downstairs, we entered a private room with a

triple set of doors that opened onto the sand. The guests, all recognizable faces, appeared mildly bored and were three-deep at the open bar, drinks in their hands.

Mother's assurance that it would be only family was inaccurate by at least fifty people. Everyone we'd met since moving to the Cove was in attendance, and that included the poker group she'd established at Jake's. Apparently, either today wasn't a workday or everyone had called in sick, including my employees.

Kevin had also garnered an invitation, which surprised me but shouldn't have, as he was Liam's uncle. I hadn't seen the deputy since that day in his cottage. I'd heard via Mac that Kevin had confessed all to his superior, not relishing the idea that Rain might come back and blackmail him. He'd been on desk duty for a short time and was now back on the active roster.

The Cottages tenants were noticeably absent — maybe they'd been drunk when Mother went to deliver the invitations and she thought better of the idea. Whatever the reason, I was happy because their presence would have been a wild card.

All the guys, the groom included, were outfitted in white suit pants and dress shirts and standing outside at the head of a flower-bedecked aisle that ran down to the water. Spoon pointed out our arrival, and they came back inside. Creole tugged me to his side, brushing my cheek with his lips.

A waiter handed out glasses of champagne.

Caspian called for everyone's attention. "I'd like to offer the first toast to the beautiful bride." He tipped his glass at Mother, who smiled but appeared uncomfortable at suddenly being the center of attention.

Spoon gave her a crushing hug.

Mac approached Mother's side and waved frantically to me, a big grin on her face. Mother had asked her to be the wedding coordinator, seeing to all the last-minute details, and she'd been ecstatic. Leaving nothing to chance, Mother had also chosen her dress, and she looked as elegant as I'd ever seen her in a pearl pink A-line dress with fitted bodice.

Mac whispered in Mother's ear before producing a microphone. "Attention, everyone."

Everyone went silent, and all eyes turned to her.

"There are boats waiting onshore to take you out to a platform in the Gulf, where the ceremony will be held." Mac waved her hand in the direction of the beach. "Follow the flower-lined path. Shoes are optional."

Everyone laughed and headed out the door.

Hopefully, this platform wasn't too far out in the water, in case we needed to swim back for whatever reason. I kept the thought to myself. At a Spoon-Westin event, one had to plan for contingencies.

When I reached the shore, I spotted an extraordinarily large white platform rocking gently on the water. It had been built with wraparound bench seating and held enough chairs to accommodate all the guests. At the far end, a flower gazebo had been constructed for the bride and groom to stand under. The entire area was covered in white umbrellas, and each corner contained a planter filled with tropical flowers. Hibiscuses, a family favorite.

"It's so beautiful," I whispered to Mother. "You've outdone yourself."

"I knew you'd love it." She held my cheeks and kissed me.

"You did an amazing job." Fab smiled at Mother. "Isn't it time for a fight to break out?" she whispered to me.

I flashed her the "shush" face. Mother also heard and gave her a "behave" stare.

An older gentleman appeared at Mother's side. "It's a pleasure." He shook her hand. It took me a minute to recognize him as the preacher who performed Mother's first ceremony. "Are we ready?" He winked at me.

I nudged Mother, who hooked her arm through his and led him away. After a few words, he headed down the beach. She called Liam over, and they had a short conversation. Then Liam took charge, corralling the stragglers and herding them onto the boats.

It didn't take long to motor all the guests out

to the platform, leaving just the immediate family on the shore.

"Before we get the ceremony started, I have something to confess." Mother fidgeted and twisted her fingers, in direct contradiction to the sneaky smile on her face.

Bridal jitters?

"You're pregnant," joked Brad, who held Mila, wearing a pink ballerina dress, in his arms.

"You've decided not to get married...again," Fab said.

Didier was standing by her side, his arm slung over her shoulders. He smirked.

"That's not it," I said. "She wouldn't have sent the guests motoring across the water then."

"Don't be mad," Mother started again.

Brad groaned. "Do I want my daughter to hear this?"

Mila beamed at her dad, patting his cheeks. He smiled back at her laughing face.

Spoon stepped up next to his wife, putting his arm around her.

What already?

"Surprise." Mother threw her arms wide. "There's going to be a wedding all right, but it's Madison and Creole's."

You could hear a pin drop—it didn't matter that we were standing on the beach. I shook my head slightly, certain I hadn't heard right. Then Fab's look of shock registered.

Creole croaked, "What?"

"You can't blame me, really," Mother said. "The two of you forced me into doing something drastic. I couldn't bear the thought of the two of you sneaking off and eloping. I was beginning to have nightmares—was this the day I'd get the call?"

The Westins weren't easily stunned into silence. This was a first.

"I planned the perfect wedding for the two of you. Everything that I knew you'd love."

"Breathe," Fab whispered and shoved her hand into the middle of my back, rubbing gently.

"Mother, you didn't."

Was that me? No... Brad's shocked voice drifted through my haze.

"I got the idea from Madison," Mother said defensively. "She's always making things happen, and I thought I'd take a lesson from her." She paused and continued. "You're going to love it," she insisted again. "It's white. Beachy. Barefoot, even. Seashells. Everything that you would choose for yourself."

"Except that I didn't." My voice came back with a vengeance. "I never in my life staged a shotgun wedding." I gasped for breath. "What you've done is humiliate me. And what about Creole? He's a grown-ass man, who I'm certain would like to make one of the biggest decisions of his life for himself."

Creole put his arm around me and was in the process of pulling me to his side when I pushed away and ran down the beach.

My feet left the sand, my body whirling around. Creole set me down in front of him, his hands on either side of my face, holding me in place.

"I'm so sorry," I choked out, tears rolling down my cheeks.

"None of that," he said gruffly and brushed the tears away, kissing the corners of my eyes. He swept me into a hard hug and held me tightly until I stopped crying. "Madeline's one of a kind. If we'd thought about it, we should've known she'd come up with something like this—an ambush wedding."

"I'm..." My cheeks burned with mortification.

"Do you love me?" he asked.

"Of course, I love you." I smiled.

"And I love you, so that means we're in total agreement." He batted his eyelashes. "Finally, you laughed. As I see it, you've got two choices. We go on the run...now." He grabbed my hand. "Or we tie the knot right here. Your mother did do a pretty spectacular job."

"You must be caught in her spell." I held my hand to his forehead, which made him smile. "Are you taking into consideration that Madeline's going to be your mother-in-law and she's c-crazy? Meddling. And... I'll just lump the rest under 'other stuff,' as it escapes me at the moment. My apple might not fall far from the tree. As in, you'd be getting a crazy wife." I covered my face with my hands.

Creole peeled them away. "I've wanted you since the first time I caught you lurking in the dark, doing unsafe things because your kind heart was doing something nice for some weirdo." He kissed me. "It took me a while, but I cleared out the competition. Damn near had to die...a couple of times... You're it for me. Your wacky mother doesn't change my mind any." He dropped to one knee. "Will you marry me, Madison Westin?"

I dropped to my knees, nose to nose. "I will. Will you marry me, Lucas Baptiste?"

"You damn well bet I will." He grabbed me, falling back onto the sand, pulling me on top of him, and kissing me.

When we were done, he picked up my hand, sliding the engagement ring off my finger. "I'm going to need this."

"I don't have a ring for you." I pouted.

"What do you want to bet that Madeline's got that covered?"

"She's so nervy." I joined him in laughing.

"Let's do this." Creole helped me to my feet, and we walked back to where Fab, Didier, and Brad stood waiting.

I wondered where Mila, Mother, and Spoon had disappeared to but didn't ask, just happy that Mother wasn't standing there waiting for me to say something nice.

"You're holding hands. That's a good sign." Fab reached out and hugged me. "You okay?" she whispered. I nodded. "Do you love him?" I nodded again. "He's not a bad catch."

I hugged her again. "I'm so happy you're here."

"Well...is there going to be a wedding or not?" Didier asked.

"We're ready," Creole said.

Didier held out his palm to Brad, who reached into his pocket and slapped money into it.

"You bet against the nuptials?" I asked my brother in shock.

"I bet on elopement." Brad laughed.

"Listen up." Fab stepped up. "I'm in charge. I sent Mac to escort your mother and Spoon out to the platform with orders not to allow her to double back, and Mila went with them, excited about her part. I also told Mac that, if you were runners, she was to dump the job of explaining everything to the guests in your mother's lap."

Creole and Didier got in one boat, Madison, Brad, and me in the other.

"I think I may be able to take credit for making this actually happen." Fab beamed.

Once our boat pulled away from the shore, Brad asked, "You okay?" He hugged me.

"It was mortifying," I said, my cheeks burning. "Creole made it all better. I did point out about the DNA connection, and he didn't run off."

"Please… You're a great catch, even with a whack-job mother. Just remember, we do normal most of the time."

"You're next." Fab shook her finger at Brad.

"In the meantime, keep your girlfriend, or you'll be subject to Mother's dating whims," I said.

Our boat arrived just behind the guys'. Creole and Didier climbed the stairs and paused at the top, spoke to Liam, then continued down the aisle to the canopied area.

Liam waited at the top, one hand holding Mila's. She had a basket in her other hand.

"Mila is your shell girl," Brad said as we climbed the steps. "Think flower girl, only shells."

"Mother thought of everything." I would thank her later. Now that I'd calmed down, this was the perfect wedding. I bent and traded wet kisses with Mila, who was excited and ready to throw shells.

Liam walked Mila down the aisle.

Fab and I hugged, and she followed.

Brad turned to me, kissing my cheek. "You sure about this? It's not too late; we can steal a boat and go for a joyride…"

"We should do it anyway, just because we haven't had enough excitement for the day."

We both laughed.

"Creole gets my seal of approval. If not, he'd have been fish food a long time ago. You're not the only one in the family with connections." He hugged me.

"You're the best brother."

He held out his arm. "Let's get you married." He walked me down the aisle to where Creole waited, a huge grin on his face.

"May we begin?" the preacher asked.

Creole and I nodded.

"Dearly beloved, we are gathered here today…"

I barely had time to concentrate on the vows before the preacher asked Creole, "Do you promise to take Madison Westin as your lawfully wedded wife?"

"Yes, I do." Creole leaned forward and kissed me.

The preacher cleared his throat. "We usually save that sort of thing for the end of the ceremony."

Creole winked at me. "Sorry."

"Yes, I do," I said.

"You're supposed to wait for him to ask," Creole whispered against my lips.

I smiled at the preacher.

"Do you take Luc Baptiste as your lawfully wedded husband?"

"Yes and yes."

Creole kissed me again.

The guests gave a round of applause, showing their approval.

"*Now*, you may kiss the bride," the preacher said.

Creole scooped me into his arms and bent me back for a long kiss, to the continuing cheers of the guests. "You are beautiful." He bent his head and kissed me again soundly, his effort getting another round of applause and a few catcalls. "I love you."

The preacher cleared his throat. "Ladies and gentlemen, I'd like to introduce the married couple, Creole and Madison."

Chapter Forty-Two

"I should've known that something was up when your mother didn't bat an eye when I suggested having the wedding reception-slash-housewarming party at my house," Fab said in an amused tone. "She laughed at the audacity of it but patted my cheek and said, 'You plan it however you want, honey.' Since we want to keep our privacy, I didn't invite everyone from the wedding. Just family and a couple of friends."

Everyone had grabbed a seat around the dining room table, which could seat twice as many as were invited. A dressed-up version of Help sat across from me and Creole. I'd done a double take when he came through the door.

I gave him a thumbs up. "Almost didn't recognize you with your new look."

"Don't get used to it. I only clean up for special occasions."

Mac sat two seats down, eyeing the guests and guzzling her beer.

"Drink up," Fab invited. "My father has a car out front that will take anyone who gets sloshed home." She smiled at Caspian, who sat next to her.

"No one drives drunk," Caspian said adamantly. "Not even a little."

Mother stood and held up her wine glass, and all eyes turned to her. "Congratulations to the new couple," she toasted. "I'm hoping the two of you forgive my high-handedness."

"There's nothing to forgive." Creole tipped his glass back at her. "It was the perfect ceremony, and I know that my wife loved all your attention to detail." He leaned over and brushed my lips with his.

"You outdid yourself." Fab gave Mother a thumbs up.

I zeroed in on Spoon. "Did you know?"

"It took a while, but I squeezed it out of her," Spoon said. "I figured it was about time, and this way, you wouldn't break your mother's heart by eloping. I know that was in the wind, so don't deny it."

I wasn't the only one to stare at Mother when she giggled.

I blew her a kiss. "Thank you." I didn't like what she'd done but also didn't want to argue with her on my wedding day.

"Not another word until I get back." Brad pushed his chair back and stood, his sleeping daughter in his arms, and carried her over to one of the large sofas in the adjacent living room.

"You got an update on Dilwen?" Creole asked Help. "In custody, I hope."

Help shook his head. "A conversation for another time."

"One thing about Westin family dinners — there's always a certain amount of drama," I said. "How disappointing if we all acted like normal families and talked about..." I paused, unsure what to say, which brought a few chuckles.

"Your dinners are more fun than any others I've been to," Emerson said.

Brad smiled at her, kissing the top of her head as he sat back down.

"Show of hands." I held mine up. "Who wants to hear the latest update on a bad a-s-s criminal?"

Everyone's hands went up.

"I suppose I'm the last to know anything," Brad grumbled, but the nodding of a few heads showed that he wasn't the only one in the dark.

"Update on Dilwen?" Fab asked. "Might as well spill; that way, we don't have to repeat the story a dozen times."

"We should have this talk in private," Help insisted.

"Nice try," Fab said. "I suppose this means he's still eluding the law?"

Help sighed loudly. "Cops got a call about an intruder at Nicolette's beach house, and they made a grisly discovery."

I flinched. "He's dead? Or someone else?"

Creole pulled me to his side.

"DNA testing was done on the remains, and you won't have to worry about Dilwen bothering you again," Help said. "The cops have no suspects."

I could supply them with a list, but I won't.

"He must have been there a while." I squirmed. "Is that where he was hiding out the whole time?" No, come to think of it, he couldn't have been; not with the cops crawling all over the place, gathering Nicolette's collected evidence against him.

"How was Dilwen offed?" Fab asked. The woman liked details.

"The exact method is unknown," Help hedged. At Fab's exhale of disbelief, he added, "Dilwen was killed offsite, and his legs dumped in the living room. We believe the killer or killers contacted the cops, wanting them to know the man had been dispatched."

"Just the legs?" Didier asked, horrified.

"What about his bodyguards?" Fab asked.

"They vanished," Help said. "My guess is that they met the same end, but probably less grisly."

"Wonder who Dilwen crossed?" Creole mused. "Not your standard hit. Personal, perhaps?"

"Any of you got any clues who might have done this?" Help's attention wavered between me and Fab.

"The folks I know aren't homicidal," I said.

That was the truth, but some could be pushed in that direction.

"Case closed." Spoon brushed his hands together.

"This is the most interesting family dinner I've been to," Mac said. "If you need a seat-filler in the future, I'm in."

Relief flooded through me. The threat was over.

"Another interesting tidbit," Help said.

All eyes shot to him.

"Dilwen's lawyer — that Mark character — he skipped town and headed north. He reported receiving a threatening call saying that if didn't want to end up in the same condition as Dilwen, 'he'd git out of town.' He heeded the warning and left."

"That's interesting," I said. "I cut him off and blocked his number, knowing that he sicced Dilwen on us." I hadn't decided what to do about GC.

"Good riddance," Creole said.

"We need some happy news," Mother said.

"When are you going to tell the newlyweds?" Caspian asked Fab.

Creole stood and reached for my chair. "Let's get out of here while we can."

"Sit back down." Didier laughed. "It's good news that I approved."

I banged my head on Creole's shoulder and groaned. "They're all ganging up on us. We're never going to have a normal life."

"You're going to like it," Brad said.

I shook my head at the smiling faces. "Show of hands, how many of you know about this announcement?"

All the hands shot in the air, which I highly doubted — the rest just didn't want to be left out.

"So romantic," Mother gushed.

"They all look pleased with themselves, so we might as well hear them out," Creole said.

Fab poked Didier, who slapped his hands on the table in an attempt at a drum roll.

"Tomorrow morning," Fab said, "Caspian's driver will pick you up and drive you to the landing strip, where you'll be helicoptered out to his yacht."

She wasn't joking. I leaned into Creole.

"You'll have it all to yourself," Caspian said. "Except for the staff, who'll be there to make sure that you're well taken care of. I promise you won't even know they're there; that's how unobtrusive they are."

"That...uh...sounds like so much fun, but I can't go," I stammered.

"Why the heck not?" Fab demanded.

"That's generous of you," Creole said. "But I can't ditch the project with no notice."

"Got it all covered for you," Didier said. "Brad's going to get his hands dirty and do some honest work for once."

"There's no one to fill in for me," I said.

"I can do it," Mother said. "How hard can it be?"

Thank you. But not happening.

Fab's hand shot in the air. "I've got it handled."

Laughter went around the table until they realized Fab was serious and stared in disbelief.

"You know what you're getting with me," Mac boasted, a grin on her face.

I smiled back at her.

"I can be you," Fab said with confidence, which elicited more laughter.

"The cats? Jake's? What if a tenant gets arrested? Needs bail? Okay, you've got that part handled."

Emerson's hand shot in the air. "I'll play the lawyer. You're not forgetting that the charges against Joseph got dropped? I can't take credit because the complainant died. But I didn't ditch him as a client when he threatened to vomit in my car," she said, with sound effects.

"Just great," Brad moaned. "My daughter and my girlfriend, corrupted."

"Dude," Liam said, awed, "you just admitted to having a girlfriend."

Cheers moved swiftly around the table.

Brad leaned over and kissed Emerson, whose cheeks turned pink.

"I'm the one with the cat skills." Didier flexed his muscles. "I'll move the fierce twosome here after you leave. Fab can co-parent."

"You won't shoot any of her tenants, will you?" Creole asked.

"You're going to eat that smirk when you see what a good job I'll do." Fab glared at him.

I turned to Creole, who shrugged, then laughed. "We're outnumbered today."

"Before accepting your generous offer, I have a question," I said to Caspian. "Does your yacht happen to have one of those cool garages, with maybe a water toy or two in it?"

Caspian reached in his pocket, pulled out a hundred, and slapped it in Fab's open palm. "My daughter said you'd ask that. She didn't put you up to it to win the bet, did she?" He eyed me closely.

"I can't believe the money that's changed hands today," I said in faux shock.

"It's got a wide selection of water toys. There's also a pool table and arcade machines on the main level. You won't be bored," Caspian boasted.

"Not sure how we'll repay such extravagance," Creole said.

"Nonsense," Caspian assured him. "My daughter rarely asks for anything, and it is my absolute pleasure."

I had thanked Fab's father earlier for everything he'd done to ensure our safety. I knew his focus was his daughter but I appreciated that every measure he'd taken extended to me and Creole, too.

Creole waved his hand over his head.

I grinned up at him.

"I have a wedding gift for my lovely wife," Creole said. "Wife." He kissed me to accompanying cheers.

"I don't have anything for you." I pouted.

"You agreed to be my wife," he said, which was greeted by calls of 'awww.' "We'll be forming a company, MC Enterprises, sole owners and shareholders: you and me. And…" He drew an envelope out his pocket and handed it to me. "Our first project."

I opened and took out a sheet of paper, unfolding it and staring at the printed-out color picture. I burst out laughing and launched myself into his arms. "You bought us the Palace!"

"Got us an excellent deal, which I know will make you happy."

Mother gasped. "The adult motel?"

"That's the one—the run-down dump on the main highway," Spoon confirmed. "The one that's rumored to be haunted."

"It's a woman ghost," I said in awe. "Can't wait to meet her."

"Reassure us all that it's not going to be pay by the hour?" Brad asked.

"Pay by the night." I looked at Creole, and we nodded in agreement. I threw my arms around his neck. "I love that we're going to have a project." I nibbled on his ear.

* * *

Later that evening, Creole took my arm. "Sneaking out of here would've been my first choice, but I didn't want any more drama, so I got the okay." He raised his voice. "On behalf of my wife and myself, I want to thank everyone for coming today." He smiled down at me, hauling me to his side, and led me through the patio doors and out to the beach. The guests threw broken bits of shells, shouting, "Congratulations."

We walked down the beach, holding hands, leaving the wedding reception behind.

"We're married," Creole said. "We're lucky to have so many people in our lives that love us."

I snuggled against my husband. "We *are* lucky."

PARADISE SERIES NOVELS

Crazy in Paradise
Deception in Paradise
Trouble in Paradise
Murder in Paradise
Greed in Paradise
Revenge in Paradise
Kidnapped in Paradise
Swindled in Paradise
Executed in Paradise
Hurricane in Paradise
Lottery in Paradise
Ambushed in Paradise
Christmas in Paradise
Blownup in Paradise
Psycho in Paradise
Overdose in Paradise
Initiation in Paradise
Jealous in Paradise
Wronged in Paradise
Vanished in Paradise
Fraud in Paradise
Naive in Paradise

Deborah's books are available on Amazon
amazon.com/Deborah-Brown/e/B0059MAIKQ

About the Author

Deborah Brown is an Amazon bestselling author of the Paradise series. She lives on the Gulf of Mexico, with her ungrateful animals, where Mother Nature takes out her bad attitude in the form of hurricanes.

Sign up for my newsletter and get the latest on new book releases. Contests and special promotion information. And special offers that are only available to subscribers.

www.deborahbrownbooks.com

Follow on FaceBook:
facebook.com/DeborahBrownAuthor

You can contact her at Wildcurls@hotmail.com

Deborah's books are available on Amazon

amazon.com/Deborah-Brown/e/B0059MAIKQ